EXIGENT MATTERS

The Off The Grid Survivor Book 2

CONNOR MCCOY

CHAPTER ONE

THE LIGHT of the new morning shone down on the warehouse district of the city of Redmond. Ordinarily, the district was a hub of mechanized activity. Semi-trucks would rattle down the roads, carting large loads to their destinations. Upon arrival, forklifts would pull the cargo out and haul it inside the warehouses, for either long-term storage, or perhaps a short stay until they were transported to retail chains, or to fill online orders. In the modern age, consumers increasingly were ordering directly from the warehouses. So it was more common than ever to see parcel delivery trucks show up to transport the goods across the city.

Of course, such a scene would befit an ordinary world. But the world had stopped being ordinary just a few weeks ago.

One night, the sun that shone above had decided the world needed to be a little less ordinary. A massive solar storm lashed out and penetrated the Earth's atmosphere, sending out an EMP wave that shorted out all electronics. Power grids were taken out all across the world. Modern civilization effectively ceased to exist in the blink of an eye.

So today, things were very different. No cars, no trucks, no vehicles of any kind traversed the roads in Redmond's warehouse district. It was almost totally serene. The only activity today was purely human. At the moment, the largest warehouse in the district was being scouted by two men who couldn't be more different in lifestyle and temperament. The older man was driven by a determination to reunite his family. The younger man had been dragged into this situation by the first man, and although he was terrified of the danger to come, he was obligated to do this to right a great wrong.

Conrad Drake was the man motivated by family.

He wiped a bead of sweat from his face as he hurried down the sidewalk. Thanks to decades of physical labor, he was in great shape for a man six decades old. That wasn't to say he was free of ailments. His right hand was afflicted with working man's hand, and he had his moments of exhaustion. He had to admit he wasn't as swift on his feet as he had been in his thirties or forties. Still, it had been enough to carry him through a city that had degraded into utter lawlessness. He had fled from arsonists, psychopathic killers, and even the rain itself. It amazed him that he had come this far. He almost indulged in a certain amount of pride in his survival skills thus far.

But the truth was Conrad Drake still was scared down to his bones about this. Now that he was alone with his thoughts, separated from his partner in this mission, the old anxieties about what he was doing still shook him. Every now and then he looked above his head, still expecting to see somebody perhaps looking down on him from a great height. But in reality, he was too far from the other warehouses to be spied upon, and possibly shot at. Instead, he was hiking down a road that ran along a vast parking lot containing several parked vehicles, all immobilized by the solar event. With their microchips and electronics fried, they never would move again. The good news was that the stalled vehicles provided great cover for Conrad and his companion not far away. It was a bit of relief for him, allowing Conrad to calm his fears and do the job he swore he would carry out.

Even though the warehouse loomed large, it still was just fifty yards away. Thanks to its immense size, Conrad could gather valuable intelligence while not having to walk right up to it. The peculiarities of the post-EMP world also helped. Upon entering Redmond, Conrad found the daytime was mostly quiet, with the only glaring exception thus far being a run-in with arsonists in the city's business district. But the warehouse district had turned out to be a different story. So far, Conrad had not spotted a soul walking the streets, or even the parking lot that buttressed the warehouse.

Just then, the small two-way radio on Conrad's belt buzzed. That must be Conrad's companion. He pulled the radio off and turned on the transmitter. "Tom. What's up?"

"Found a couple of men taking a walk outside near the east end. You see them?"

Conrad stopped and took cover behind a green four door car. "No, not yet. Give me a minute." He took out his binoculars and checked. "No, wait I see them. Looks like a couple of little dots on the horizon. Good for you for spotting them."

"Thanks," Tom replied, sounding a bit grateful for the compliment.

Conrad could understand why. During this trip, the pair hardly had shown great admiration for one another. This journey had been strained to say the least, but the stakes were too high. As Conrad had put it, Conrad was the man Sarah had loved and Tom was the man Sarah did love. The two of them had to free Sarah from her captivity.

Sarah. Conrad's face tightened. She was somewhere inside that structure. Thus far, they hadn't found a clue exactly as to where she might be. And worse yet, she wasn't the only captive. If Tom was right, multiple women had been abducted and brought here for insidious purposes. The warehouse was run by Marcellus Maggiano, a restaurateur-turned-warlord who extended an iron grip on this small city, luring in able-bodied men with promises of food, drink, and power in exchange for doing his bidding. The solar event had done more than destroy modern technology. It had loosed evil men to do as they wished.

But Conrad was determined to get Sarah out of there, so he brought Tom, Sarah's boyfriend, along to assist. The pair recently had camped out in a warehouse loft some distance away, but now were scouting Maggiano's warehouse. Tom and Conrad couldn't just break in there and fight their way to her. Their rescue would take careful planning and some definite cunning on their part.

So, their mission was clear. They had to find a place on the warehouse property to stage a diversion. It would draw out as many men as possible while Conrad and Tom moved in to find Sarah. It was simple and could be effective, provided they could find the perfect place to stage a ruckus. So far, the two of them were relaying information about the warehouse and its guards. Still, Conrad hadn't hit upon that vital piece of info that could lock this plan into place.

Conrad moved in closer to the warehouse, on the eastern side. In a strange way, he also felt obligated to keep Tom alive. It was an awkward pairing, fueled in part because Sarah was once Conrad's wife. But she had left him thirty years ago, and today Tom was her lover. Conrad knew Tom had kept Sarah happy for a long time. If he reached

Sarah but lost Tom, it would seem like a failure on his part.

Conrad scratched his hand. He still wasn't getting anywhere. He had to move in closer. Fortunately, several cars and a few old, rusting barrels lay between him and the building. They would provide adequate cover to move in closer.

Once he had closed the gap, Conrad resumed checking out the warehouse exterior. Unfortunately, this part of the facility wasn't all that remarkable, with its closed overhead doors, reclining ramps, and stairwells to small doors to the inside.

He was about to turn and head back in the other direction when a familiar scent caught his nostrils. He inhaled more deeply to be sure his mind wasn't playing tricks on him. It was fresh smoke, mixed with the odor of cooking fish. It reminded Conrad of summer afternoons near the lake when he cooked outdoors. Yes, now he remembered. It was after he had made some fine catches in the lake. He'd then slap the fish over a cooking grill. The present scent was uncannily similar.

Conrad crept in the direction of the smell, still sticking to the cover available on the parking lot. Stopping behind a set of barrels, he gazed into his binoculars in the warehouse's direction. Two men with their shirts off surrounded a pan on top of a small burner, which in turn topped a small propane tank. One of the men was stirring a set of fish on the pan.

Is that propane? Conrad focused the lens a little better. The tank was unmarked, but it could have been filled with propane, perhaps before the solar event occurred.

Just then, a third individual stormed his way into view. He was dressed in nice looking brown slacks and a white tank top. Whoever this guy was, he was mightily pissed at the two men. He shouted at them, but from this distance Conrad couldn't hear more than just loud ramblings, although a four-letter word or two still was easily audible from here.

One of the men held up his hands in defense while the other shouted back. The well-dressed man pointed back in the warehouse's direction, to somewhere past Conrad.

He's worked up over something. Conrad swung his binoculars in the direction the man had pointed. It was beyond the eastern corner of the warehouse. A set of large tanks were located there, near a closed overhead door. The flammable logo and warning decals practically shouted to the world that there was gas in there.

I get it. Those two must have filled up from over there, Conrad thought.

Conrad returned his gaze to the shouting match. The man in the tank top was jabbing his finger in the face of one of the men. Then, he turned and pointed to the open doorway. Someone else was emerging, an overweight older gentleman with a big hat that protected his head from the sun. He also was dressed in neat, fancy looking pants, and wore a buttoned shirt that was open up top but buttoned down at the stomach, where it fought a battle to contain the man's girth.

The moment the older man stepped outside, the two men suddenly stopped talking. In fact, they stopped doing anything. They just stood there as if Death himself had approached. The man in the tank top spoke calmly to the older man. One of the two "chefs" tried to explain himself, but quickly silenced himself when the older man looked at him. Then, the newcomer simply walked up to the pan, jabbed the fork in one of the fish, blew on it a little, and then finally took a bite out of it.

The two "chefs" looked more petrified than ever.

I wonder if that's Maggiano? Conrad thought. It had to be. He fit Tom's description of the man, plus he commanded fear the likes of which Conrad never had seen outside of thugs or crime bosses in movies or on television.

Maggiano—if that was him—took a few more bites out of the fish. Then he motioned to the man who had tried to explain himself earlier. Maggiano wiggled his finger in a "come closer" gesture. The man obeyed.

Maggiano then jammed the fork into the man's arm.

The man leaped backward while screaming loudly and horribly. Conrad winced. Then Maggiano barked something to the other "chef" while gesturing to the gas tanks. He waved to the front door. Both of the "chefs" hurried to the door, with the wounded man cradling his jabbed arm. Maggiano barked a few instructions to the first well-dressed man, then turned and left.

Why do I get the feeling that poor bastard got off easy? Conrad only could guess, but it seemed as though these two men had decided to have a little outdoor cookout, only they had siphoned off some propane because they were probably too lazy to build a camp-fire. The older man in the hat, probably Maggiano, was pissed that they were wasting valuable fuel, and only refrained from killing them because he liked their cooked fish.

But as Conrad watched the well-dressed man drag the gas tank inside, he pondered what would happen beyond those closed doors. What brutal means of enforcement did Maggiano exercise over those who stayed under that roof?

———

TOM RICHARDS WONDERED, for the umpteenth time, what he was doing here.

For one thing, he was scouting out a large build-ing, checking on its sentries and trying to find areas of vulnerability that he and his partner Conrad could exploit. But that was a job for soldiers, a SWAT team, even policemen. But a former technical consultant? It was ludicrous even thinking about it.

Chill, Tom thought. *Hey, you've seen plenty of Bruce Willis movies. Maybe you can find one of those air ducts to shimmy through and sneak over the bad guys.* Another part of him, the more sober and cynical part, warned him that in real life air ducts typically were not big enough for human beings. It was not going to be that easy to penetrate that building.

At the moment, Tom was on the western side of the warehouse, about forty yards away from the facility itself. The binoculars that Conrad had given him did a good job of zeroing in on the place. So far, the only things of interest were the few guards he spotted outside, and the air conditioning and heating system on the building's northern end.

After nursing some disappointment, Tom retreated toward the edge of the western end. He put his binoculars back up and studied the furthermost window. It was a first story window, so it wasn't difficult to see inside. He saw movement.

Hey now, who's this? Tom focused the lens as much as possible. No doubt about it, there was a female figure on the other side of the warehouse glass. She was just standing there, her back to the outside world. She was nodding as if someone was speaking to her.

Her hair was blond. *So, that's not Sarah*, Tom thought. Sarah had dark hair. Even so, Sarah might still be hard to spot from a distance.

Tom kept a close eye for a while, until the woman retreated from view. Tom was about to turn away and search elsewhere, but then a second lady appeared in the warehouse window. Again, she wasn't Sarah. But two women showing up in a row piqued Tom's interest. He had to investigate this further.

Gently, he panned to the left side, to the next window over. Being further away, it was difficult to make out anyone, but there was definitely a feminine figure behind that glass. Now he was more certain than ever he had hit the jackpot.

Okay, Tom, you may have just found the women! he said to himself. *They must be being kept in that quarter of the building.*

He took down the binoculars. But then he saw a bald man in a white T-shirt and dirty jeans patrolling the parking lot, quite close to Tom, just a few yards. More ominously, he was brandishing a rifle in his arms.

"Shit!" Tom said in a loud whisper. How the hell did he not spot that man?

He turned around, looking for instant cover. An old car lay a few feet away. Keeping his head down, he dashed for it, then rolled around back.

Damn. I hope he didn't see me.

Tom looked under the car. The patroller's feet marched past, unnervingly close, but he wasn't heading directly for Tom. He was instead making a loop out from the warehouse and then back toward it. He only stopped to spit on the cement.

Even so, Tom didn't move. He was paralyzed with fear. This was just another reminder of how dangerous this mission was, and how likely it'd be that he could get killed. He waited another few minutes before looking back under the car. He spotted no sign of the sentry. He hesitated another several minutes before looking around the car. To his relief, he spotted no one in immediate sight.

Just then the radio on his belt buzzed. Tom yelped. Then he let out a curse before snatching the radio.

"Tom?" Conrad's voice filtered through the speaker. "Hey, you there?"

"Yeah!" Tom coughed. His throat was dry. "Yeah, I copy."

"It's been thirty minutes. I've gone over this side of the building with a fine-tooth comb. I think I found us a good place to throw a party for our friends in this building."

"You did?" Relief claimed Tom's insides. At least Conrad had done the heavy lifting for both of them. "Perfect. Let's fall back to HQ."

"You find anything out there?" Conrad asked.

"No. I mean, yeah. I think I found where they're hiding the girls. They're on the north side, near the western corner. I saw some girls through the windows."

"Great. Enough chatter. Let's get going," Conrad said.

"Okay." Tom switched off the radio. He let out a long breath. At least now he'd be retreating from Maggiano's property. He'd be sure to live at least through the day, until the sun went down. Then, their plan, whatever it would turn out to be, would go into action.

Tom stood up and cast a last look at the building. He wondered what was going in there. He had had a taste of the brutality of Marco Valentino and two of his men when he was slammed in the head with a rifle and left unconscious in the street. All three of them were working for Marcellus Maggiano. He rubbed the back of his head. The bump still was there. It would be a long time before it healed properly.

As Tom retreated from the parking lot, he pondered what Maggiano could be doing with Sarah at that very moment.

CHAPTER TWO

JACK WATCHED as Maggiano raised the glass, three-quarters full of wine. "Cheers," the old man said in a vague Italian accent.

The woman sitting across the table raised an identical glass. "Cheers," she said, softly.

The two clinked their glasses, then drank. Jack eyed the wine bottle on the table with some envy, yet he knew not to touch it. If Marcellus Maggiano wanted Jack to join in, he would say so. The elder restaurateur shifted slightly in his seat, struggling a bit against his own girth. Jack fought the urge to smile at Maggiano's slight difficulty with his weight, as Jack never had had weight issues, even when he indulged himself in lavish, fancy meals.

Maggiano let out a sigh. "Better enjoy this while you can."

He sat back, letting the sunshine wash over him through the office windows. While Maggiano stuffed his female captives and his henchmen in the barracks in the main part of the warehouse, Marco held court in the main offices near the eastern end of the warehouse. "It's a bitch trying to keep this stuff cool without refrigeration. Fortunately, Marco has found cool places around here to store my drinks."

Jack's ears bristled at the praise for Marco, but let it pass. He knew Maggiano found Marco Valentino, a fellow restaurateur, quite useful to his burgeoning empire. Unfortunately, Jack held a much dimmer view of Marco, not only due to the man's slights against Jack's manliness and courage, but for his rape of one of the women under Maggiano's roof. As far as Jack Sorenson was concerned, these women were his sanctum, and Marco had trod on forbidden territory.

But for now, he put the anger aside and focused on the woman sipping wine with Maggiano. What was her full name? Jack scratched his head. Oh, of course. It was Sarah Sandoval. He always took great joy at thinking of her name, perhaps because he particularly enjoyed women with Latin heritage. As always, he did his part to make Sarah look appealing. Even though she was in her mid-fifties, she had aged well, and the spandex sports bra and biker pants Jack had provided had accentuated her body to its fullest.

"It must be hard to do anything," Sarah said, "The way things are now."

"The way things are now, there's nobody left to look over my shoulder," Maggiano said gruffly. "There's no detectives snooping on my affairs.

There's nobody to show up at my door and serve me an arrest warrant. There's no police to put cuffs on me. No judge to throw me in jail." Maggiano drank the rest of his glass. "I think it's perfect the ways things turned out. How many men get to be kings in their own time?"

"I guess not many," Sarah replied.

"Exactly." Maggiano poured Sarah more wine. "Jack, did your boys bring the books in from the library?"

"They brought in the first load last night," Jack replied. "I made sure to haul in the classics."

Maggiano grinned, slightly, but to see a smile from him at all was enough to ease Jack's nerves. "I'd like my ladies to have some brains between their ears. I've heard from some of my clients that they want their companions to talk at some length." Then he downed a large swig of wine. "They want learned women who can discuss poetry and literature. Not vapid stuff such as clothing or..." He snickered. "I suppose discussing reality shows now is rather pointless."

Jack reached into his pocket and pulled out a faded brown book, *Crime and Punishment* by Dostoyevsky. He chuckled, then set it on the table. "Besides, I'm sure without television or the Internet at your fingertips, it does get boring in the barracks."

Sarah swallowed. "Boring? It didn't seem boring last night."

"What do you mean?" Jack asked quickly.

Sarah looked down at the table. "I heard...scream-ing. A girl near my room. It didn't last long. Then I heard loud footsteps. Somebody walked away." She shivered. "I looked in later. She was sitting in her bed, quaking and crying. She wouldn't tell me what was wrong."

Jack looked to Maggiano and said, "Interesting."

Maggiano raised an eyebrow. "Is that all?"

"Yes," Sarah said softly.

"I'm sure it's just an emotional outburst from captivity." Jack spread his arms. "It's to be expected. We've seen it before."

"Then who left her room?" Sarah looked up at Jack. "Someone was there. I heard him."

"Who? The men are ordered to stay out of the women's quarters. And, of course, I make sure the doors are locked at night." Jack cleared his throat. "Of course, I'm not the only one around here with access to the women's barracks."

Maggiano looked at his glass, frowning. "This is actually the second time I've heard this little tale, and you know what it means when two different people start telling the same story."

"But the only person I saw near the barracks last night was Marco," Jack said, "And he knows the price for mistreating your..." He glanced at Sarah. "...property."

"You know who this girl is?" Maggiano asked, "Bring her to me by noon. I want to talk with her."

Jack nodded. "Of course, of course."

————

JACK HELD Sarah's arm as he led her from Maggiano's office into the women's barracks. They were a hastily constructed yet secure enclosure of wooden rooms accessible by this main hallway. An barred iron door secured it from the rest of the warehouse.

"Magnificent performance," Jack muttered. "You had him convinced. That's no small feat, but I suspect he's taken a liking to you."

"But that wasn't a lie," Sarah said.

"Of course not," Jack replied, "Marco is guilty as sin. But sadly, there were no witnesses. So, why not create a few instead? It's not much, a few 'vague' recollections, nothing too specific, but in the end the signs point unmistakably to one Marco Valentino."

Jack stopped at the room where Sarah had been assigned. He flashed her a smile. "And you see how that works?"

"You really have it out for him," Sarah said.

"Half the ladies in this building have it out for him. You would, too, in time. But Marco is ruthless. He has to be taken out in the right way. I don't think Maggiano would appreciate Marco being eliminated without a good reason."

"What happens when he's gone?" Sarah asked.

"Life goes on as normal." Jack lifted Sarah's hand. "Maggiano rules the town, and I take care of business in here. A nice arrangement, don't you think?" Then he kissed Sarah's knuckles.

"No freedom, I guess," Sarah muttered.

Jack chuckled. "Freedom? Well that's an elusive concept. We're all prisoners of something." Jack then pointed his finger in the middle of Sarah's bra. She recoiled, but Jack took hold of her and kept her steady. "I'm a prisoner to my passions. Actually, I think we all are."

Sarah trembled a little. Jack didn't move his finger.

"You've definitely captured Maggiano's interest," Jack said coyly. "He will expect great things of you in the near future. My advice? Try pleasing whoever Maggiano decides to send your way."

He was about to walk off, but then he stopped. "Oh." He fished out *Crime and Punishment* from his pants pocket. "Almost forgot." He put it in her hands. "A little homework. Try reading a lot of it each day. You never know when Maggiano will call upon you."

Then he walked off, leaving Sarah standing in her doorway. Once he got farther away, he chuckled. Sarah seriously was hoping she'd earn her freedom by helping him, wasn't she?

Cute, he thought as he reached the end of the barracks. *Real cute*.

After leaving the women's barracks and heading off into the warehouse's storage area, he found himself with a less inviting sight. Marco Valentino was seated at a table near scaffolding that held some of Maggiano's bigger crates. Five other men sat with Marco. The smell of cigarette smoke hung in the air.

The men were playing cards while drinking beer or smoking cigarettes.

One of the men held up his arm. It was bandaged with a gray tourniquet, a reminder of his transgression against using the propane without permission. He got lucky. It turned out Maggiano liked his cooking and planned to ask him to cook for Maggiano again—every week until the day he dies. The alternative for refusing would be far less pleasant.

"Hey!" Marco shouted loudly. "Jack! How about you pull up a chair and join the game?"

Some of the men shouted "Yeah!" through their cigarettes.

"Tempting," Jack said while trying to hide his disgust at the thought of socializing with these human chimneys. "But Maggiano has other plans for me today. I'll have to take a rain check."

"Figures." Marco sat back in his chair, putting down his drink to wipe sweat out of his short dark hair. "We're playing for this week's supply of meat rations, but I guess Jack doesn't want to lose his precious piece of meat for this week, huh?"

The men sitting with Marco laughed and chortled. Jack frowned, but then he put on his best smile possible and responded, "I'm guilty as charged. Contentment is a gift."

"You call it what you want, I call it being a scaredy cat." Marco glanced at his cards. "Four of a kind! Who beats that?"

"Aw, shit!" One of the players slapped down his cards.

"Too rich for my blood!" another bellowed.

"Looks like Marco eats well this week!" chimed a third.

Marco sat back, eyes narrowed at Jack. "See Jack? That's what you get when you take a risk." He chuckled. "You get it all."

Jack twitched. "How delightful for you. Fortunately, I have everything I could want. Now, if you'll excuse me."

Gritting his teeth, Jack marched toward the end of the warehouse. He had had enough of Marco's slights, from the veiled to the open ones. Marco had no idea that Jack was playing his own game, and before it was over, Jack would indeed end up with the winning hand.

———

TOM FLUNG open the door of the small office building they had picked as their rallying point. This small office lay in the shadow of two big warehouses out back. Its proximity to Maggiano's warehouse, plus its low profile, made it a good place to operate out of while they scouted. Plus, if anything went wrong, they could retreat here.

"The guys I saw outside looked bored as hell," Tom said. "I don't think they really expect anything to happen. They just go outside to shoot the shit or whatever."

"Or in the case of those two men I saw, enjoy a cookout," Conrad said as he walked through the door.

"That had to be Maggiano you saw out there," Tom said with a loud huff. "The guy kicking their ass for using the fuel. I never met him, but I used to hear stories about his temper. You never rip off Maggiano's stuff and get away with it."

"So, I guess it's shitville for those two men?" Conrad said.

Tom laughed. "You said he ate their fish right off the plate. Odds are it's just pissville, then. That means he might spare them, but don't be surprised if they walk funny from now on." He shook his head. "Or maybe end up missing a finger or two."

The pair dumped their backpacks in the small back office. Tom picked up a roll of paper towels he found in the bathroom and tore off a piece. "So, you found us a place we can stage that diversion?" He wiped the sweat off his face.

"I think so." Conrad opened his pack. "Let's eat first, get our bearings."

Tom walked toward the bathroom. "Suits me. I got to use the john."

"Remember that toilet doesn't flush," Conrad spoke up.

Tom swung open the door. "Does it matter? I'm only going to use it once. I'll just shut the door when

I leave. It's not as though this place is going to be used by anybody anytime soon."

He then slammed the door shut. For the moment, Conrad was alone again.

Alone. That word suddenly filled him with melancholy. For a long time, he had been fine being alone. Well, he had been alone for long stretches at his homestead. And sometimes he had his company. What he didn't have for the thirty years after his divorce from Sarah was family.

And then one day, out of the blue, family came knocking on his door.

Liam, Conrad thought. *I wish you were here. We needed more time together*. He had sent him away, back to his home. But he had a good reason. Once Tom had filled him in on who took Sarah, Conrad knew he could not throw Liam into that kind of danger.

That, and Liam had a lover who was carrying his child. Liam's child, and Conrad's grandchild. Conrad made it clear that Liam had to protect his family. Liam and Carla's child could be part of a new future for this country, and perhaps the world itself.

Conrad started fishing supplies out of his pack. "Liam," he whispered, "I'm sure you made it back safe and sound. I'll do my damnedest to come back soon with your mom."

Fortunately, he had packed away something that might just help him free Liam's mom. He assembled the materials on the ground and quickly began working.

CHAPTER THREE

As he marched toward the homestead in front of him, Liam Drake's mind raced with possible scenarios to get out of this fix. It wasn't every day that he was being threatened by a woman aiming a shotgun at his back. But then again, life had ceased to be anything resembling normal since the solar storm occurred. He and Carla had come here expecting to settle down after a long trip, only to be accosted by a mysterious woman with bleached blond hair, dark eyebrows, big brown eyes—and a shotgun aimed at them. Liam and Carla's efforts to flee were quickly aborted by this woman's weapon. If they didn't march back to the house, they'd likely be killed.

Of course, anything Liam planned to rescue themselves from this woman had to take Carla's well-being into account. The young athletic lady next to him was not only his love, she was carrying their child. To Liam, this beautiful lady with short brown hair and her baby were his prized treasure, so he couldn't do anything foolish or they also would pay the price.

Damn, he thought, *How did this happen? We were just coming back to Dad's home. There wasn't supposed to be any trouble.* He thought back to when they had left. His father had locked up the homestead tight and secured the fences and gates. Even if someone had gotten onto his dad's land, how would they break into the house without heavy tools? Was this woman the only intruder, or were there more invaders waiting for them inside?

Liam and Carla kept on going until they reached the front steps of the porch. Their mystery lady then walked faster to pass around them until she reached the front door. "Alright, hold it there," she said, "I'm not stupid enough to let two strangers inside. Let's talk about what you two were planning. I see a couple of bikes and backpacks down there." She gestured to the bicycles and packs lying on the ground near the driveway. "So, you two have come a ways, haven't you? You say you didn't come to steal Conrad's food. So, why are you here?"

She said Dad's name again, Liam thought. *Does she know him?*

"Let me guess." The woman smiled. "You two were looking for a love nest! Didn't want to get it on out in the woods. I get that. There are things out here that'll bite your balls off or leave you with one hell of a rash! You figure there's a nice warm bed inside to know each other biblically, if you understand my point." She rolled her eyes. "It probably looked like the safest place in the world for ya, I bet."

Liam's face burned, not just at the woman's insinuation, but at her loud voice. It seemed she lived her life expressing herself this way, as she had yet to lower her tone just once. Also, her voice betrayed a Northeastern accent. Liam could almost picture this woman shouting over the car horns of a busy New York street.

Their captor finally had paused her rambling, allowing Liam an opening to talk. "We're not here to cause any trouble, but I have to ask, you said 'Conrad.' Do you mean—"

But the woman suddenly stormed right up to him, cutting him off. Liam nearly jolted backward. Did this woman consider talking to be a provocation?

She was staring at him. Something had caught her attention, and it shocked her, for her eyes widened quickly.

"My God," she said in a quiet voice, the first time she hadn't yelled. Then, she dropped her shotgun. She stepped backward, clasping her hands on her mouth. "You're his. Conrad. His boy. You got hair as dark as his when he was younger and those cheeks! Damn, there's really no mistaking it. You're Conrad's son!"

Liam couldn't take it any longer. "Okay, how the hell do you know my dad? We came here a few days ago, left with him, and now we come back and find you! Just who are you?"

The mystery lady backed up against the porch's banister. "Conrad," she said, "Why isn't he with you? Where is he?"

"Why don't you answer my question first?" Liam asked.

"Tell me, please!" The woman practically shook as she shouted.

Liam was confused. She obviously was pleading. Could he tell her everything, about their journey to Redmond to find Liam's mother and Conrad's ex? Yet, this woman seemed a little off her rocker. Or maybe she was just an excitable person. It was hard to tell.

"He's a little over a day away, in Redmond," Liam said. "He was fine when we left him. He sent us here so he could take care of important business there." He then took a step closer, feeling a tad braver to be more assertive with this woman. "Now, what's the deal? Are you a friend of his?"

The woman grasped a hold of the banister. "So, he ran off somewhere with his son. Makes a lot of sense. Just my luck, I come back after five months, and he's not here." She laughed, but Liam could detect the worry bubbling up in her throat. "Of course, it didn't help that the damn power went out, but hey, it wasn't any big surprise." Then she looked at Liam. "Your father's like a vault of survival knowledge. He knew everything I asked him."

Liam studied this woman's eyes carefully. She clearly was talking emotionally about his dad. He was starting to think she was more than an acquaintance...much more. In fact, given how his dad had lived for the past thirty years, she fit Liam's image of who Dad's possible new companion could be.

But why didn't Dad mention her? Liam frowned. Perhaps this woman and his dad had been too out of contact for him to think she'd stop by so suddenly.

She straightened up. "My name's Camilla. Camilla Pitzo."

Then she pointed to Liam. "And you're Liam. I remembered that." She grinned. "Your dad told me. And who's your friend?"

"Carla!" Carla replied.

"Carla, huh? That's a sweet name. I have a cousin named Carla." Then she locked eyes with Liam. "So, Conrad up and went to Redmond. Important business, right? Mind telling me what it is?"

Liam still didn't feel ready to lay out the tale, but maybe he could delay it a little until he felt comfortable around Camilla. "Carla and I have been on one hell of a long trip. Let us go inside and get our bearings. We'll then tell you the whole story."

Camilla nodded. That seemed to agree with her. "Alright." She then leaned over and retrieved her shotgun. "Get your bikes into the garage and your packs inside."

Once Camilla stepped inside the house, Carla quickly turned to Liam. "Okay, what do you think?

You want to grab the bikes and get the hell out of here?"

Liam kept his gaze on the now closed front door. Carla's suggestion was tempting—very tempting. Why take a chance that this woman didn't really know his dad? What if she just broke into the homestead and discovered his dad's identity? She might even have found out that Conrad had a son as well.

He frowned. Something in that didn't seem right. His dad didn't have a picture of him as an adult, so Camilla couldn't have recognized him. And even if she had found some pictures of his dad, would she have made the leap to know he was Conrad's son? She detected the familial similarities in their faces. Wouldn't that be too much for a casual scam artist?

On the other hand, retreating would be the safest option, plus it would take Carla out of possible danger.

Damn, Liam thought, *this isn't as easy as I thought*.

Finally, he walked up to his bike and stood it back up. "I think we should take a chance that Camilla really does know Dad." He started rolling his ride toward the house, but stopped next to Carla. "But have your gun ready, just in case."

———

AFTER STOWING their bikes in the garage, Liam and Carla walked through the front door. Each step felt uneasy. In the short time he and Carla had stayed here, it had felt like home. Now he felt like he was walking into a stranger's house.

Still, as he looked around the living room, it didn't seem like it should be that way. The house was exactly the way he and Carla had left it. Nothing was out of place.

There was one crucial difference. A backpack much like the ones Liam and Carla had been carrying lay on the sofa. It was unzipped and flipped open, revealing clothes, small zippered bags of hygiene and medical supplies, and a couple of canteens.

Liam glanced in the direction of the kitchen. Through the door, Liam could see Camilla, with her back turned to them.

"Carla, stand in front of me," Liam whispered, then bowed his head to Camilla's pack.

Carla let out a silent "Oh," and did as she was asked. With Carla in front of him, Camilla wouldn't notice Liam leaning a little closer into her pack. It seemed a little strange, but Liam wanted to take a measure of this mysterious woman, and her belongings seemed to be the best witness for or against her.

The inside of her bag was marked with a bumper sticker that read: "America: Love It or Leave It!" A few American flag stickers dotted the inner pouches. A few paperbacks were stuffed inside one of the compartments. Liam slipped a couple of them out. The pages were yellow and worn. The titles all talked about survival and world politics.

I think Dad has one of these books, Liam thought.

When he was little, his dad took him to library sales. His father had a great interest in history, politics, and the outdoors. Frequently, he'd buy up old or used books on the subjects. It started to annoy his mom after a while.

He winced. He put the books back and tried to think of Camilla again.

Liam then noticed a couple of photographs peaking out from one of the folds in the bag. His father and Camilla, wearing big smiles, posed in each of them. In each of them, his father looked younger. In one of them, his hair was mostly dark with silver specks, and in the other photo, his beard was shorter, trimmer, and fewer wrinkles lined his face.

"She definitely wasn't lying about knowing Dad," Liam said quietly.

"No kidding. Looks like they've been hanging around each other for years," Carla looked over her shoulder. "They sure do look happy."

These were pretty old-fashioned photos, too, taken with a camera, and not a phone. Sadly, photos taken with smart phones and not printed out would be lost for all time. The fact that he could see pictures of Dad at all during his thirty-year exile was a miracle.

Liam looked back into the kitchen. Camilla worked in there as if she knew the place from the top down to the bottom. It was almost as if this place was as much home to her as it was to Dad.

As Liam continued to look over the bag, he

spotted a handgun nestled inside one of its compartments. He poked his finger into the fold next to it
and found a spare clip. Between that shotgun and this
gun, this was a woman who was packing.

"Almost ready!" Camilla called from the kitchen.

Liam quickly stepped back. Carla followed him.
He didn't want to be seen anywhere near her belongings. He and Carla exchanged a few more whispers.
They seemed satisfied that Camilla might not be
dangerous, and that they should hear her out before
making a final judgment.

Camilla then stuck her head out of the kitchen.
"I'm sorry for not asking this, but are you too okay
from your trip? I should have seen if you needed any
medical attention. Scrapes, cuts, bug bites, snake
poison?"

"No," Liam said.

Carla shook her head. "We're good."

Camilla nodded. "Well if you got here in one
piece, be glad. You never know what's lurking out on
the roads nowadays."

———

For the eighth or ninth time in the past few
minutes, Lance Wilkins rapped on the glass sliding
window of the old store. He knew Rod was in there,
and Lance was sure as hell not going to leave unless
he got something from him. Lance's stomach was so
empty he was sure it would devour his own organs in

a mad attempt to consume anything. At this rate, he would smash through the window just to quiet the growling of his stomach.

Then, just as he raised his fist again, the window slid open, revealing a slightly annoyed middle-aged face. "Lance, do you have anything between those ears? I told you I got nothing for you. Nothing!"

"But you must have something! Old apples, fruit, anything you munched on!" Lance clung to the window sill as if he had to for dear life. "C'mon Rod, I don't care. Anything I can shove in my mouth! I'll even eat crumbs."

Rod shook his head. "You never listen. I told you our farm was filled to capacity. I told you there's barely enough here to feed the refugees, and you come barging in every day begging for food. You're a sturdy man. Use those muscles. Go. Work for your supper like everyone else has to do."

"But where can I go? This town's my home," Lance said.

"Now it's nothing but a refugee camp." Rod's expression grew sad. "Times were good when you could work a chickenshit job and chow down a greasy cheeseburger at night. You got to think differently now." Rod then reached behind him and pulled up two crackers wrapped up in plastic. "These things are probably stale. You understand that, right?"

"I don't care. I'll take them." Lance snatched them up. "Thank you."

"Don't thank me yet. If you're serious about

finding food, if you really want somebody who'll feed you, I got word over the ham radio that somebody's looking for men that got strong arms. That's pretty much it. It's not too complicated, so even a knuckle-head like you should be able to handle it."

"Really? Where?"

"Hold up." Rod started scribbling something down on a piece of paper. "Here." He shoved it into Lance's hands. "It's thirty miles down State Road 22, south of here. There's a turnoff. You can't miss it."

Lance nodded. "Thanks."

"You want to thank me. Go there and stay there. Because until we expand the fields in town, this place doesn't need any more mouths to feed, and certainly not able-bodied youngsters like yourself. You under-stand me?"

Lance shook his head. "Right, right!"

"Good. And be grateful you got this information. This job is still in this state. Anything else, and you'd have to head north into South Dakota or Minnesota. That's be one hell of a trip, wouldn't it? Now get going." Rod then shut the window and locked it, loudly.

Lance almost crumbled the crackers in his hands, but his ever-present hunger stopped him in time. Instead, he stuffed them in his jeans pocket and ran off.

As he dashed from the shop toward the first round of refugee tents, fresh anger welled up inside him. How could this town treat him like this? How could he, someone who's lived here all his life, be refused food? Wasn't he in the same boat as everyone else?

The problem was, Lance Wilkins wasn't a rancher or a farmer. He had been a cashier for a parts store. It didn't require more than punching a few buttons on a cash register or using a computer to handle inventory. It paid him enough for a good life in his cramped apartment. He still rang up a thousand dollars in debt on his credit card, but hey, who didn't have that problem?

Then the power went out, and Lance found himself with no job and no worthwhile skills. Not that it mattered, since money now was worthless as well. The only way to get food was to grow it. That didn't sound like too big a problem, until the town accepted a whole bunch of refugees from up north. The sheer number of people overwhelmed the local farms. Then the survivors had to make choices. Some people were asked to leave, to find other farms nearby and help expand them. That would take off some of the pressure down here. Indeed, a few of the residents decided to pull up stakes and head out for greener pastures.

Lance had not. He fumed. He effectively had been squeezed out. He didn't know how to farm and struggled with it, but now it didn't matter as the refugees, including those who were sick, had to be fed first. Lance had no assurance of any food beyond the bare minimum to survive. So, for the past few days, Lance had resorted to begging. Soon, he even began stealing. It would be an apple here, or a pear or a squash there, when someone had their back turned.

He looked at the paper in his hands. Thirty miles? That would be one hell of a long walk. But it'd be better than journeying to Minnesota, that's for damn sure.

As he passed by the latest round of tents, he spotted a bicycle leaning against a wooden light post. The owner absentmindedly had left it there instead of securing it. Perhaps the owner did not think anyone would take it.

Whoever he was, he would be dead wrong.

That morning Lance pedaled away from the refugee camp and out onto State Road 22. He vowed he wouldn't stop by this place ever again. He would find his own way in the world, and wouldn't be hungry again.

CHAPTER FOUR

JACK PACED AROUND the young lady. Molly was the victim of Marco's little "hissy fit" last night. She stood perfectly still, having calmed down a lot since her ordeal. She was a pretty young lady in her twenties. Jack had taking a liking to her recently, having put her in one of his clothing store's fine dresses. Marco had stopped by during one of the fittings, and it was plain he wanted to help himself to Jack's conquest.

The door to her quarters was closed. Jack wanted to be sure no one could hear what would come next. For added security, he had a woman outside keeping watch, one who hated Marco and agreed to help out Jack. Should Marco come around, she would knock on the wall in a specific manner.

"The seeds of doubt are planted in Maggiano's mind." Jack flicked his fingers, imitating someone dropping seeds into the ground. "Now, we're ready for the final step."

"I don't understand," the girl said.

"We need a little bit of visual evidence." Jack patted Molly's shoulder. "Maggiano isn't going to care if you don't look a little battered for your trouble. He cares about your physical appearance, your looks. He can always work with that. But if Marco had caused some obvious harm, well, that's different."

"But he didn't...I mean, I'm not..."

"I know. That's why we have to make you look the part," Jack said, "Take off your clothes. All of them."

Molly trembled. "I-I don't know. I don't want to."

"What are you talking about?" A tinge of anger rocked Jack's voice, but then he stopped and suddenly raised an eyebrow. "Of course. What a fool I am. You're still traumatized. I supposed exposing yourself to another man must be difficult."

Molly nodded.

"But this is different. Your body is now a weapon, a tool of revenge." Jack fished his hands under her jaw and chin, and braced her face so she looked at him. "It will help you make the man who hurt you suffer a thousand times over for what he did to you. I swear it. But I need you to help me."

"Okay," she said softly. She obeyed, and took off all of her clothes.

Jack smiled at the sight before him. He already had fitted one of his red dresses to another of the ladies this morning, but nothing compared to Molly. This girl, with her magnificent form, was definitely his favorite. "You are a goddess."

The woman smiled, perhaps for the first time in a while. Her smile made it even harder for Jack to do what he had to. "A shame I must do this." Then he drew a small knife.

Molly's eyes widened. "What are you doing?"

Jack suddenly grabbed her and cupped her mouth. "Relax. I'm creating the evidence." She struggled, but Jack pinned her to the wall. "Don't worry, these will not be life threatening and will heal in time, I promise." He whispered, "Sadly, some sacrifices must be made."

He held her tight, muffling her screams as he made the first cut on her thigh.

———

TOM RECLINED against the warehouse's outer wall. "Jack Sorenson," he said, "That's probably the guy you saw before Maggiano showed up. I spotted him once coming in to see Marco about a deal."

"So, all the big boys are staying in that warehouse." Conrad rubbed his hands together. "If we took them all out, this city might be freed."

"Save that for an army, if it ever comes around. We're here to rescue Sarah," Tom said, "I, for one, don't want to be within twenty miles of those people ever again."

"Right." Conrad let out a loud breath. "I hate the idea of leaving Redmond in the hands of those thugs, but between the two of us, rescuing Sarah is perhaps the most we can do."

Tom glanced at Conrad's gun. It lay in its holster on the floor. Conrad had taken it off earlier. "So, do you mind if I ask you something?"

"It's your dime. Shoot," Conrad replied.

Tom cleared his throat. "I try not to judge people. I like to think I don't care what other people do. I'm just a little puzzled why you decided to, you know, prep. Go off the grid, grow your own food, that kind of thing." Indeed, with his gray hair and thick beard, Conrad looked the part of a grizzled loner, a big contrast to Tom's clean-shaven face and upscale clothing, which had been dirtied and torn by the recent days' events.

"Don't get me wrong, it's worked out great for you. You can handle the apocalypse a hell of a lot better than I can." Tom chuckled. "But what drove you to do it?"

Conrad leaned back against the wall. "Did Sarah talk a lot about my 'crazy' behavior?"

Tom shook his head. "Bits and pieces."

Conrad looked up at the ceiling, trying to mentally put together how he'd tell this tale. "You know, the funny thing is, if you had met me, say, thirty-two years ago, you would have met a man in a suit and tie and..." Conrad stroked his beard. "...a young face with no whiskers. I used to work for an advertising firm. I was one of their top salesmen."

Tom smiled. "Really? Wow, that really is surprising. What changed? Did the divorce really drive you away from the city?"

"I think being on my own, being a rancher, was always in my blood from the start," Conrad said. "The Drake family was a rough-and-tumble sort. We loved to fight, and I don't mean the good kind of fighting. We had our ranch down south, near the border with Kansas. It was a place where drinks flowed and tempers flew." He scratched his chin. "I grew up scared. I never knew when someone's temper could lead to someone getting punched real bad, or if someone finally would grab a gun and end an argument in the worst possible way."

Tom raised an eyebrow. "Shit. I'm sorry to hear that."

"Since I couldn't count on my dad or my brothers for a stable home life, I learned to fend for myself. I trusted only what I could make with my hands. I thought, once I got older, that I could join the rat race in the city. I married Sarah, had Liam, and things were normal, or so I thought." He shook his head. "I guess I kept hungering for a different life. Maybe Sarah picked up on that. Maybe I didn't know what I was doing until it was too late."

Tom leaned his right arm against the office wall. "Sarah's a woman who loves stability." He gently punched the wall. "It's hard to imagine her in your world of guns and ham radios and whatever else you got."

Conrad glanced at the sunlight pouring through

the door. "Well, it's a world that's got all of us whether we like it or not. We probably should start putting together our plan."

"Right." Tom spread his arms. "So, it's a night raid. Guess we should start talking about our plan of attack."

Conrad frowned. Suddenly, he wasn't so sure about his original plan to attack the warehouse. "We probably should hold off on that for a moment," he said. "Let's think about this. Say we free Sarah. This city comes alive with all sorts of strange people at night. Actually, nighttime here is almost like daytime normally. We wait until evening, we might escape Maggiano's men only to run into who knows what that's lurking out there."

"So, what?" Tom shrugged. "We'll just come back here and hide until it all blows over."

"And if they see us duck in here, they'll shower the place with bullets. Actually, scratch that. We could barricade ourselves in, and then they turn around and torch the place."

"Well, I'm sure storming a warehouse full of men with guns is going to be dangerous." Tom chuckled. "You're not going to tell me you thought this would be easy."

"Of course not." Conrad paced back and forth alongside an office desk. "But like anything in life, you need a plan. A way in, and a way out. We can't get out of there and find ourselves without a way to escape." He stopped, then reached for his backpack.

"That place looked pretty sleepy to me. I bet those bastards won't see us coming if we hit them now."

"What?" Tom straightened up. "You want us to go in there now, in broad daylight?"

"You heard right. I think this is our best chance."

Tom shook his head. "Yeah, our best chance to get picked off. They just have to see us coming and we're lying dead on the concrete in about five seconds with blood gushing out of our chests."

"We've gotten close to the warehouse already. We can make it inside before they see us. Besides, most of those men are inside and asleep. We go in fast and we can reach Sarah while they're stirring from their beds."

"And what about our escape? We won't have the cover of night to help us."

"But we'll have a sleepy city and fewer hooligans to try stopping us," Conrad replied. "If we can make tracks out of the warehouse district, we'll have a lot more places to hide, maybe throw them off our trail."

Fresh sweat trickled down Tom's face. "We don't have a working car. We don't even have bikes. There's no transportation at all. We're all on foot. What if Sarah's in no condition to run? What if she's hurt, or drugged?"

Conrad scowled. "Look, we do this now or never. If we delay, sooner or later someone will spot us and rat us out to Maggiano and his boys. Besides, our supplies are finite. Our food and water's going to run out soon, and two hungry and thirsty men aren't going to be more likely to pull Sarah's hide out of the fire. No, this is it. We free her and then hightail it back to my place. There's no other choice."

Tom clenched his jaw. "Fine. But what about the distraction you want to set off? How are you going to do it?"

Conrad showed Tom his special project. "I made sure to pack some surprises. I just finished assembling them." Then he laid his special creations on the floor. They were six small plastic tubes with small wiring looping out of them. Conrad turned one of them over, exposing a tiny box on the other side.

Tom frowned. "What the hell are those?"

"Plastic explosives. Not very big ones. I imagined I'd only need to blow out doors or maybe a wall, something to get you out of a tight spot. But if I attach these to those gas tanks, the stuff inside them will make a blast much bigger than what these babies can produce on their own." Then he pointed to the box. "This here's a timer. Cheap stuff, but it's effective."

Tom's mouth stayed open for a while. "I don't know why the hell I'd be surprised. So, building bombs is another one of your big survival skills?"

"Not exactly something you'd do in the suburbs, right?"

"Not unless you want Homeland Security beating down your door," Tom replied.

"Well, nowadays we got nobody to rely on but ourselves." Conrad put down the explosive, then pulled out a belt. "A little Velcro and a little tape, and these should stay put until I reach the tanks. Now, hopefully, we'll intersect somewhere in the building. But first, you must keep an eye out and make sure you have a clear path inside. But Maggiano's men may end up coming out of the warehouse on your end. So, you'll stay and keep an eye out for how many show up. I'll radio you and tell you where to go if there's too many henchmen around for you to make an approach."

Tom grimaced. "You sure these things won't explode, you know, bigger than you think?"

"It's just an educated guess, Tom. We're playing this whole thing by ear. Besides, you said the women are probably on the northern side near the west. The propane will explode on the east."

Tom nodded. "Yeah." Conrad might know what he was doing, but Tom hated the thought that this might go wrong.

Conrad began fitting the explosives to the belt. "Look, um, you may want to get yourself together. Take a drink. Try and relax yourself. We're heading out soon."

———

ABOUT HALF AN HOUR LATER, Conrad checked himself in the office mirror. His gun, taser and radio all were attached to his belt for easy use. He also had his extra clip on him just in case. His plastic explosives rested in a small belt slung over his shoulder.

His pack rested inside an office closet. Having his provisions on him just would weigh him down. He would go in with just what he needed to carry out this rescue. If their plan worked, they'd retreat back here, grab their stuff, and flee from the warehouse district.

If we're lucky, we can make some distance before the sun goes down, Conrad thought. Otherwise, they'd escape from Maggiano and his men only to end up with the city's crazed inhabitants going after them at night.

Beside him, Tom was looking at his gun on his belt's holster. That seemed to be all he could do. He had no other armaments, and unfortunately, had nothing to protect his chest beyond a flimsy shirt and pants. This man clearly didn't look ready for the ordeal to come.

But I guess that's what makes a man brave, Conrad thought. He knew he had to say something to encourage him. Hell, it might help to encourage Conrad himself.

"Guess there's nothing to do but to do it," Conrad said.

"Yeah. Guess so," Tom replied.

Conrad looked at him. "I know I didn't give you any choice in this. Hell, I wouldn't blame you if you were pissed at me. But I want you to know that you should be proud of what you're doing, putting your neck on the line like this."

Tom loudly exhaled. "Well, like you said, I owe her one."

"Yeah, you do. But you're still going into this fight, and that matters." Conrad sighed. "Look, I said we should go all out for Sarah, and I meant that. I just don't want you to think this should be a kamikaze run. If you're in a bind, and retreat's your only option, then you take it."

Tom looked a little confused. "What about you?"

"Let's just say I won't be so quick to make a run for it if I know I can free Sarah, regardless of the outcome."

Tom twitched. Conrad sounded like he was alluding to a suicide run. "But your son. You're going to have a grandchild. Don't you want to see them again?"

"Yeah, I do." Conrad bit his lower lip. "Right now, more than anything. It's just that on the list of priorities, I think Liam seeing his mom again ought to come first."

Tom nodded. "So, this really is just for your kid. Not for Sarah. I mean, you don't owe her anything. She didn't tell me much about your divorce, but from what I gathered in all this, you two had a hell of a falling out."

"Yeah. Yeah, we did." Conrad straightened up. "Maybe it wasn't anything I did. Maybe it was. But I figure if I do this, it'll prove to her in some way that I did once love her and I would put my ass on the line if she was in trouble. Other than that, and helping out Liam, I don't expect anything from her."

"If I was in your shoes I don't think I could do it. I don't know if I'd have it in me."

Conrad actually smiled a little. "You know what? I don't think anybody knows if they got it in them until the situation calls for it. God knows what you'll be capable of in the next couple of hours."

Tom looked back at his gun, and pondered what he might be using it for.

"Well, I think we've yammered long enough. You ready?" Conrad asked.

Tom looked to the door. "There's no way I can be more ready. Lead the way, Conrad."

CHAPTER FIVE

JACK KNOCKED LIGHTLY on the office door. "Come in," Maggiano barked.

The door easily pushed open. Maggiano waited in his chair. Jack stepped inside, then gestured to the open doorway. "I brought her in as requested. She is, understandably, very upset. Please indulge her."

"Just bring her in, Jack," Maggiano said scowling, with a hand under the table, grasping a gun on his belt's holster. "This had better be worth my time."

Jack reached through the door and pulled in Molly. She was wearing a long light yellow skirt, and a buttoned-up beige shirt. Her footsteps were very slight. Jack had to keep dragging her by her arm. She was in such shock that she didn't seem to be walking under her own power.

"Alright." Maggiano's eyes focused on her. "I've heard a couple of the women talking bullshit about you screaming last night. I want to hear it from your lips, and if you lie to me, I'll shoot your pretty head off. Now, did someone rape you?"

Molly said nothing, just nodding once.

"Who the hell was it?" Maggiano asked.

"Actually, I think you should see the evidence first." Jack stepped up to the woman's side. "Before any accusations are made."

Maggiano curled in his fingers. "Show me."

Jack then grabbed the back of Molly's skirt and yanked it off, uncovering her pink underwear and several white bandages wrapped around her legs. Some of the bandages were stained red.

Maggiano's eyes widened. "What the hell is this? Who did this?"

Jack clasped his hands around the woman's shoulders. "She was eager to protect her virtue, but it seems her assailant had other plans."

"Name." Maggiano shook with fury. "Give me the goddamn name, now."

Molly swallowed. "Mar...co. Marco."

Jack's eyes widened. "Well, that does change things, doesn't it? You can't deny what you see."

"He did this?" Maggiano's face tensed up. "That arrogant little punk. He thinks he can do this to my property?"

"It may be premature to declare him guilty." Jack released the woman and approached Maggiano. "I say we give Marco one last chance. He's invaluable to your empire, isn't he? Why not set up a test to prove his innocence? After all, there are other men here who are more than capable of..." Jack rolled his eyes. "...a bad night."

"A test?" Maggiano stood up. "What the hell do you mean?"

Jack smiled. "She can describe her attacker in great detail, if you understand my meaning."

"Really? Maggiano turned to the woman. "Well, get on with it." The crime boss stood tall enough that his gun was in plain sight. "And be quick about it."

———

CONRAD'S TARGET was in sight.

Apprehension gripped Conrad's stomach. He was about to approach closer to Maggiano's warehouse than he ever had been before. The fact that there were palettes and barrels to help cover his approach made the mission feel a little easier.

No guards, Conrad thought. *At least none so far*.

The only trouble spot was the warehouse's main office, a short distance from the propane tanks. There was a glass window that allowed anyone inside to look out into the parking lot. Conrad made sure to stick to cover whenever he was sure he was in view of the office.

At the same time, Conrad couldn't resist stopping and looking into the office with his binoculars. But most of the time he saw nothing except shapes that vaguely shifted around. They could be anything from human beings to a blowing curtain.

I'm hoping Maggiano and his top boys are in there, Conrad thought. The propane was pretty close to the office. If the gas went off, the explosion might take them out, too.

The thought of that much killing did stir up Conrad's insides, but he fought his discomfort. No, he would have no qualms about taking out Maggiano or any of his men. He took care of his distaste for killing on the journey through Redmond. The stakes were too high for him to freeze up now. Besides, Maggiano and his henchmen committed great crimes. And with no police, army or judge to lay down justice, it was up to men such as Conrad to preserve order.

By now, Conrad had moved out of the office's line of sight. From this spot behind a stack of palettes, it'd be a straight shot to the propane tanks.

A short jog later and he arrived at his target. Conrad sat behind the propane tanks. These tanks likely were used to power the forklifts that picked up palettes and took them into the warehouse for storage. If the warehouse's forklifts didn't have any microchips or electronics, they might not have suffered damage from the EMP, but Conrad saw no evidence these tanks were in any kind of regular use. Odds were the forklifts might have been fairly new, and probably were fried when the solar event hit.

Conrad eyed the gray tank before him. The gas inside was highly flammable. It wouldn't be much of an effort to ignite it and make a big explosion. It would do all the damage needed to draw the men out of the warehouse.

He removed his plastic explosives and attached each one onto a propane tank. No gauges were available, so Conrad couldn't tell which ones were full and which ones were empty. However, judging from the reaction of the men outside earlier playing chef with that fish, there was likely a great deal of propane still in here.

He was about to attach the last explosive to a tank when he heard soft crunching on the cement. "Shit!" Conrad whispered. Someone was coming.

Conrad took the explosive and scooted backward into the warehouse's dark shadow. This couldn't be a worse time for company to arrive, as it was impossible to see much from behind the propane tanks. A guard could be almost on top of Conrad before becoming visible, and then it might be too late.

His gun. He was almost certain to have to use it. He could take out the guard, drag him into the building's shadow, then finish setting the explosives. Provided his gunshot didn't attract attention, he still could pull off this plan.

A shadow then crossed into Conrad's line of sight. It was likely a man. But then the shadow stopped. Conrad's throat caught. Did the guard see the explosives on the tanks?

Dammit, step closer. At this moment, it would be so much easier if the guard actually did spot him. Conrad was ready. One shot and it would be over.

The shadow didn't budge. He was just standing there, turning his head from left to right.

Move! Conrad thought.

Then his radio buzzed. *Shit!* Conrad quickly switched off the radio's sound. Did the guard hear that?

Conrad waited. And waited. And then the shadow just turned his head before leaving.

Conrad decided he had to risk crawling out to get a look, any kind of look out there. He crept out to the side of the tank and got a glimpse of the parking lot on the building's north side. There was a tall, muscular man with a rifle, actually much farther away than Conrad had feared, walking away from Conrad's position. The sentry seemed unalarmed. Evidently, he did not notice Conrad or his handiwork on the tanks.

"Thank God," Conrad said softly.

He hurried back to the tank and attached the last explosive. Then he turned on each timer. He had prepped the timers so they were linked together. Their countdown would synchronize once they all were activated, ensuring that each explosive would go off along with the others. In two minutes, this whole collection of tanks would blow sky high.

His work complete, Conrad took one quick look for sentries before dashing back onto the parking lot. From there, he made his way back to his vantage spot behind a barrel. He was close, but not so close that he'd get caught up in the explosion. Conrad wanted to be in easy range of the doors on the right side of the propane tanks. He could dash inside during the ensuing commotion.

He picked up his radio and called in. "Tom," he whispered, "You read me?"

"Yeah," spoke Tom, "I, uh, I read you. Copy. What happened? I tried calling you, but I didn't get an answer."

"Had to lay low. Guard got too close." Conrad looked at his watch. "Timers are set. Give it a minute and then the fireworks will go off."

"Okay," Tom said.

"When I penetrate the inside, I'll see if I can find Sarah. If not, she may come out to you. Good luck out there," Conrad said.

"Same to you, Conrad," Tom said.

Conrad put the radio back on his belt. "Keep it together, Tom," he whispered. "Odds are you may be the one to find Sarah." He sat back and waited. There should be just thirty more seconds to go.

———

TOM TOOK up a position facing the west side of the warehouse. Goosebumps formed on his arms and neck even as the sun shone brightly overhead. His fears weren't helped by the long delay in Conrad responding. Tom wasn't sure if Conrad had bought it early, and if he would have to abort and flee. Now his body tensed up waiting for the big boom Conrad was about to create. Then there would be no turning back.

I can't believe this. Any moment now I'm about to go into an actual shooting fight, or worse. He wasn't so stupid to think he wouldn't make it through this without having to shoot his gun at another human being, which was something he never had done before. Tom never had given serious thought about having to take another person's life. It made him sick to his stomach. Even worse was the realization he was sure to be outnumbered. He could take out one shooter only to be cut down by three, four, or who knows how many.

This could be my last day alive, he thought. The very thought crawled through him like spiders creeping through his bowels. What was the only thing keeping him from ditching Conrad and running off into the city? Why had he stuck with this crazy old man for so long?

Sarah.

His hand gripped harder around his radio. He had let her down. Worse, he had betrayed her. When Marco and two of his boys showed up to stop Tom and Sarah from fleeing town, they were ready to put a bullet in Tom's head. But instead of putting up a fight, Tom offered Sarah up to them. They rewarded his cooperation with a rifle butt to his head.

Since then, Tom had tried to push the guilt out of his head, but guilt was a tough bitch to deal with. Perhaps he finally had recognized there was little left in this world to live for, and that those things he did have, he should hold onto tightly, with no hesitation. Sarah was one of those things.

I saved my own skin, but for what? Tom winced. Without her, what did he have? A ruined city. A professional career destroyed with the ravages of the solar event's EMP. A house filled with electronics that, thanks to fried microchips and a destroyed power grid, were no better than junk. Now he didn't even know where he'd get his next meal from.

Conrad said he couldn't trust anything but what he made. Damn. I know what he means now.

He looked at his weapon. The west side of the warehouse remained quiet. Maybe all the action would occur on Conrad's side. If so, he could sneak around behind them and take out any armed resistance. He might, as Conrad had suggested could happen, be the one to free Sarah.

Conrad. Damn you. If I never went to the monument center downtown, I wouldn't have met you, and I wouldn't be in this mess.

At the same time, Tom had to admit Conrad had given him a lot to think about. Part of Tom even felt a little grateful that he had met Conrad. Sure, Conrad may be crazy as shit, but damned if he wasn't right about how the world could came crashing down around them. Tom had to admit Conrad was more prepared for this horror than Tom ever could have been. Hell, Tom had no inkling that such a disaster *would* happen. This was the kind of stuff for fringe radio shows and conspiracy websites.

I guess if my life had been as rough as his, I'd have turned out like him, Tom thought. He never had imagined he could put himself into this kind of peril for anyone. Perhaps Conrad was right that nobody knew what they were capable of until the moment arose. Tom got the feeling if he got out of this ordeal alive, he wouldn't be the same man he used to be.

Any second now, he thought.

CHAPTER SIX

LIAM AND CARLA sat at the table while Camilla poured each of them a tall glass of sweetened tea. After sliding a glass each toward them, Camilla picked up her own and raised it.

"A toast," she said, "to the Midwest."

Liam and Carla clinked their glasses against Camilla's. Their host chuckled. "Always wanted to say that." She took a sip from her glass.

Carla twirled her right forefinger in the air. "You're not from around here, are you?"

"Nope," Camilla replied, "I'm from Queens, and we don't have stuff like this there."

"I thought you might be from the East Coast," Liam said.

Carla sipped before commenting, "It's called New Jersey."

"Oh Lord." Camilla coughed, "my family called Jersey the bastard cousin of the New York City area."

She smiled deeply. "No, I'm from the city." She took another sip, then sighed. "We have bagels, lox, and great pizza but none of this." She looked into Carla's eyes. "So, what about you, Carla? Where do you hail from?"

"Here. This state. Midwestern by birth," Carla said. "Never been to New York. Been to Minnesota a couple of times. That's the furthest north I've ever gone."

As Liam drank more tea, he kept an eye on Camilla's facial expressions as she spoke. It was clear she was making conversation and seemed to enjoy their company. Still, Camilla was dancing around the elephant in the room—where was Liam's dad?

And I've been dancing around it for too long, Liam thought. He had hesitated for too long. This era was too dangerous and life was too precious and short to bother with covering up his father's current where-abouts and situation. He'd have to deal with Camilla's reaction when it came.

"So," Liam said, "you want to know where my dad is?"

Carla's eyes widened. She probably didn't expect him to launch into it. Camilla, on the other hand, seemed calm and serene.

"If you could give me the whole lowdown." Camilla folded her arms. "You haven't wanted to, have you?"

Liam tilted his head away from her. "I'm sorry," he said, feeling more than a little guilty, "But I hope you can understand that meeting you was a hell of a shock. Dad didn't mention you."

"It's alright." Camilla smiled, but it was a little pained. "I didn't exactly greet you with open arms when you popped onto the driveway."

Carla laughed softly. "The shotgun on the porch was a little much."

"Yeah, yeah, you're right about that." Camilla blew a lock of her hair out of her face. "Go ahead. I'm ready to hear it all."

Liam straightened up. "I came here with Carla because my mom's trapped in Redmond. I'm sure you know about Sarah, my dad's ex-wife?"

Camilla nodded. "Yep. I know the whole story." Her voice then turned cynical and sarcastic. "Did she decide to beg on her hands and knees for Conrad's forgiveness?"

"No, no, it's not like that," Liam said, "You know she had custody of me, so I lived with her for most of my life after the divorce. I actually had my own place when everything went to hell. Anyway, I was cut off from her when the power went out. With all the chaos, there was just no way I could get through the city and find her." Liam curled his fingers into fists. "But I knew there was a chance my father could. I always believed he was one of the toughest men out there. I remembered my mom saying he was a prepper. I figured he'd know how to help us."

Liam then spelled out the whole tale about how he and Carla journeyed to the homestead and enlisted

Conrad's help, and about their trip to Wynwood, and later Redmond, where they ran into Tom, and finally, their splitting up.

"That's...that's how it all ended up," Liam said. "My dad's probably reached Maggiano's hideout by now. Maybe, maybe he's already found my mom."

There was no more to say. Camilla had sat there, not commenting, not questioning, doing nothing but just sitting there and taking in the whole tale with a crooked look on her face. Liam wasn't sure what to say next. He glanced at Carla, who seemed just as unsure.

There still was a bit of tea in Camilla's glass. She drank it. Liam and Carla continued to wait. About a minute passed. She frowned for a while. It was plain that she was registering all the pain and turmoil that he had experienced when he had parted from his dad.

Or was she angry that Liam had plucked his dad out of the homestead in the first place? Perhaps the thought of Conrad being reunited with Sarah at all upset her, even though Liam had made sure to mention that Sarah had a boyfriend and expressed no interest in returning to Conrad.

Finally, she spoke up. "Damn him."

A chill ran down Liam's back.

Folding her arms, Camilla looked away. "Damn him for going on a vacation without me."

Liam and Carla exchanged puzzled looks.

"I told him if he went out on an outdoor adventure, he was going to haul me along with him." Then she laughed. "I am going to make him pay so much when he gets home." A tear then welled up. "If he does."

The high tension escaped Liam's body. Camilla hadn't lashed out in anger. However, it was clear she was hurt, even alarmed, by the news.

Camilla wiped her face. "So, he sent you two back? Damn. We shouldn't be waiting around here for him to come home. We ought to be out there helping him."

Liam nodded. "We wanted to, but he was adamant we come back here."

"Fine. Then you can help me help him. He's crazy to think he can survive out there by himself," Camilla said.

"Well, he's not quite by himself...." Liam began.

"Yeah, but that Tom fellow didn't sound like a big he-man from what you told me," Camilla replied. "Conrad's a good man, a strong man, but he's never fought for his life like you're talking about." She looked at the table. "Did he ever shoot anybody?"

"He was shot *at*," Carla said, "but we never took anyone out."

Camilla shook her head. "Conrad's not a killer. He's a much gentler man than he might appear." She slowly raised her head. "I don't doubt he'd do anything to save his family, but this world turned a lot meaner in one day. I just don't want him to die alone out there."

Liam sat back. "We want to do all we can to help

Dad get back here safely. But, I'm not sure Carla and I can play a direct role in it. We didn't explain exactly *why* he sent us back."

Camilla raised an eyebrow. "Really? Well, I definitely want to hear this."

———

MARCO STORMED through the wooden hallway that ran through the men's barracks with one of the men, Barry, at his side. "So, what does Maggiano want with me?" Barry didn't say what it was when he met up with Marco to bring him in. That was weird. Maggiano always made his wishes clear in advance.

"You'll find out." Barry kept his gaze at the exit door as they approached it.

"I'll find out?" Marco scowled. "What is this, a surprise birthday party or something?"

Barry rolled his eyes. "Look, I was told to bring you to Maggiano, okay? I don't ask questions."

"And who told you not to do that?" Marco asked as Barry reached the iron door of the barracks.

Barry turned around and looked Marco in the eye. "You did." Then he flung the door wide open, permitting them both into the warehouse's main storage area.

As Barry closed the door, Marco's skin started itching. He had a bad feeling about this. He thought of the gun on his belt, under his jacket. He brought his right hand close to it.

Barry led the way again. The front office loomed just ahead. The tiny window in the door made it impossible to see exactly who was inside, though Marco was sure Maggiano was in there.

This better be damned important, Marco thought. If Maggiano was just calling him in to do something menial when one of these brutes could do it, he might finally do the old coot in once and for all. Again, he thought of the gun under his jacket.

But once Barry opened the office door, Marco was stunned to find not just Maggiano, but four armed men standing in a semicircle. Jack was also there, arms folded, reclining against the back wall.

"Maggiano," Marco said as pleasantly as possible. "What's going on?"

Maggiano sat behind the steel table, his elbows propped on its surface, the man eyeing Marco with a frown that chilled him to his bones. "We're having a little trial here, Marco. Nothing too fancy."

A fresh bead of sweat dropped down Marco's face. "What trial?"

Barry then shut the door—hard, and turned the door's lock.

"The charge is defrauding the Maggiano Empire," Maggiano replied. "The penalty is death. Seems you've damaged one of my girls."

"What are you talking about?" Marco asked, "I haven't done anything to any of the women."

Maggiano snapped his fingers. One of the men

brought forward Molly, her legs exposed, showing off the bandages.

"Now, where'd that come from?" Maggiano asked.

"I don't know!" Marco retorted. "What the hell are you talking about?"

"She says you did this," one of the men said.

"That's a lie!" Marco's blood boiled. This girl was setting him up! "I never did that to her! She cut herself to screw me over!"

"With what?" Jack asked mildly, "You think we're dumb enough to give the girls knives? They don't have anything sharp to cut themselves with."

"Shut up!" Marco shouted. "I didn't cut her, and you can't prove it worth a damn!"

Jack pointed to Molly. "But you do admit you assaulted this woman?"

"I don't admit to shit." Marco turned to Maggiano. "What did she tell you? She cried rape just to get sympathy? To have you kill me? C'mon, these bitches lie. They'll do anything to get free, or have us turn on each other. Who are you going to believe, me or some tramp I grabbed off the street?"

Maggiano sat back. "Well, we do have a problem, don't we? You're right, Marco. We have worked together very closely, and loyalty counts for at least a damn in my book. I'd hate to punish you by mistake." Then he leaned forward. "But fortunately, we do have a way to clear your name."

The four men plus Barry closed in on Marco. "What are you talking about?" Marco asked.

"This girl has given us a detailed description of her attacker." Then he glared at Marco. "So, it's very simple. You show us what you got, and we'll see if she's telling the truth."

The four men quickly closed in. "What are you talking about? Show you what?" Marco asked.

Barry pointed at Marco's abdomen. "Drop 'em."

Marco's eyes widened when he realized what Barry was telling him to do. "Shit! Have you lost your minds? You think I'm going to expose myself? Forget it!"

"Stop wasting time, Marco. Do it," Maggiano said.

"Like hell!" Marco shouted.

Marco's hand flew for his gun, and might have reached it had one of Maggiano's men not grabbed his arm and pulled it away. Barry and the other three quickly seized Marco and wrestled him to the ground. Marco erupted with a long string of expletives that drowned out the sound of ripping clothing.

"Get off me!" Marco screamed, "You're dead! You're all goddamn dead!"

In the back corner, Jack folded his arms and smiled at Marco's humiliation. Seeing this spectacle alone had made his plans worthwhile.

Looks like I got the royal flush, Jack thought.

CHAPTER SEVEN

CONRAD LOOKED AT HIS WATCH. "Five seconds," he whispered.

This was it. He lay down low and covered his head with both hands while pinning his ears. Then...

The tanks blasted open in a loud explosion that quaked the ground under Conrad's belly. Even with Conrad covering his ears, the bang was so loud he yelped.

Fire lashed the side of the warehouse. The heat was incredible, even from this distance. It was enough to sting any part of Conrad's skin that was exposed. Suddenly, he heard a loud pelting sound all around him. Conrad feared he was being shot at.

Then, a smoldering metallic fragment bounced off the concrete next to him. It was flying shrapnel from the tanks. Conrad cursed himself. Of course the explosion would tear off debris and fling it all around. Shouldn't he have thought of that?

He continued to lie down as flat as possible. A piece of flaming metal soared past. The hairs on the back of Conrad's neck stood up. That was close, too close.

While still on his belly, he glanced upward. Fire covered the side of the building. The sound of pelting metal had ceased, along with the explosions. Only roaring flames remained, unless there were pockets of gas the fire had not ignited yet. If so, Conrad had to move, and quickly.

As Conrad rose to his feet, he took note of the rising column of smoke. The thick smoke was climbing ever higher, enough that it could be seen from great distances. This was no small fire.

Forget the people inside the warehouse, he thought. *This will be noticeable for miles.* Conrad had hoped he could flee with Sarah and Tom while the city slept, but if the bang of the explosion didn't rouse some of the city's inhabitants from their slumber, the continuous smoke certainly would. This ruckus could draw in gangs, arsonists, looters, or just desperate people.

I'd have been better off fleeing under the cover of night, Conrad thought. At least then the smoke, in a city with no working street lights or lampposts, would have been obscured. Had he made a fatal blunder by setting off this blast in broad daylight?

"Shut the hell up, Conrad," he said to himself, "It's time to do what you came here to do."

And that time had arrived, for Conrad could hear

voices coming from the building. Conrad held tight to his gun. They were coming.

———

JACK FOUGHT the urge to laugh. Things couldn't have gone better.

In the center of the floor, Marco lay on his knees, stripped of everything except his shoes and his boxers, which he was tugging back over his privates frantically. His shirt and pants lay on the floor next to him, while Barry had collected Marco's gun.

Marco wiped his face with the back of his hand. Blood dripped down his bottom lip. A bruise marred his cheek from where he was slammed to the floor. Barry and the other men all had guns drawn on him. Disarmed and almost naked, Marco didn't dare make a move.

Maggiano cracked his knuckles. "So, she was telling the truth." He flashed a look at Molly. "You were pretty damn accurate, kid."

She swallowed, while trying to blink back tears. On the ground, quaking, Marco turned to his victim. "You...bitch..." Then he coughed.

"Unfortunately, I have little use for damaged goods." Maggiano then pulled out his pistol and aimed it at Molly's face. She only had time to widen her eyes in fright before Maggiano pulled the trigger.

Bang.

Molly dropped to the floor. Two of the men

looked at each other, communicating unspoken shock between them. Even Jack was startled. He figured Maggiano wouldn't bother with such an extreme action as offing Molly, as Jack took care to leave the woman's face unharmed. Jack also emphasized that the cuts would heal soon. But Jack forgot Maggiano was not a man who liked to lose. When things didn't go his way, no one would be spared Maggiano's wrath.

"Now then." Maggiano turned his gun onto Marco. "You've really pissed me off, Marco."

Marco's breathing grew louder. "I didn't cut her. That's a setup!" he cried, "Fine. I had my way with her. I needed to blow off some steam. You're going to tell me you don't enjoy one of these bitches every now and then?"

"If I do, it's my call, not yours," Maggiano replied.

Marco now was hyperventilating. "But this is all a trick! Somebody else slashed her up. You kill me, you don't find out who's been playing you! And then it'll happen again!"

Marco then turned around, and caught Jack in his vision. "You." Jack turned around. "You did this. You set this up, didn't you? You knew I raped her. You had her fix me up!"

Jack shook his head. "Marco, why don't you just face the fact that you screwed up? You've always had a short fuse and now you broke one of Maggiano's girls. Your..." He grinned. "Your manhood confirmed it."

"You're a dead man, Jack," Marco muttered coldly.

"The only person who decides who dies is me." Maggiano rose from his seat and leveled his gun.

But whatever action Maggiano was about to take was cut off when a loud bang suddenly rocked the office. A chunk of the wall high above abruptly tore off and fell down, impacting right on top of Maggiano. The impact and rising dust and smoke instantly made it impossible to see.

The explosion slammed Jack into the back wall. He shouted in pain. His ears rang badly, and his vision blurred. He felt along the wall. His limbs quaked so badly it was almost impossible to get up. "Damn!" he cried out, "What the hell!"

Finally, he managed to climb onto his feet and prop himself up, but just barely. The office floor was impaled by a pile of smoking metal, with a small fire burning on top. Barry was flat on his back, his eyes wide open, blood trickling from his mouth. Shrapnel had impaled his chest. Another of Maggiano's men was buried under wreckage. He did not move. Maggiano himself was not visible at all, but Jack recalled he was directly under the debris when it fell. He was likely struck and killed on impact. There was no sign of the other three men, but they could be buried under the wreckage as well.

Jack then looked up. A hole had been blasted in the wall up above, with smoke gushing out. Small orange flames poked from the orifice, and they were growing bigger and hotter by the second.

Jack braced his head. He feared he had been seriously injured, but he was in no sharp pain, only feeling battered. He looked down at his body. No blood trickled through his clothes.

"Hey!" Marco's voice cried out.

Jack's vision finally stabilized. He spotted Marco on the other side of the room, against the wall. A small piece of debris pinned his leg, but otherwise he had escaped the crash of the wreckage.

"Hey!" Marco shouted, "Get me out of here!"

Jack glanced up at the growing flames in the wall.

"Hey, asshole!" Marco yelled, "I'm talking to you!"

Jack spread his arms. "Hey, what's the problem? You're a big man. You can climb up and over that shit."

Marco pushed on the metal pinning his leg. It moved, but not by much. "Dammit, this hurts like hell! Give me a hand! Maggiano's gone. This empire ain't his anymore. You want to divide it up? Get me out of here and we'll talk!"

"Thought you said I was a dead man." Jack laughed. "Looks like you're the one who's dying today, Marco, just not in the way I thought! And why should I save your ass when I can rescue the pretty ladies under this roof?"

"You did set me up! This was your goddamned plan!" Marco shouted, spit shooting from his mouth.

"Yeah." Jack pointed to the smoking hole. "Well, I didn't plan that. Still, it looks like I'll be running this operation from here on out. I guess I just played my winning hand!" He turned, but then stopped and looked at Marco. "Oh, by the way, the ladies will be throwing themselves at me when I'm done. I'm not so impotent I had to force myself on a woman."

Marco's face quaked. "You bastard! I'm going to gut you like a goddamn fish! You hear me?" His string of threats was cut off as he choked on the growing smoke.

Jack coughed himself. He beat it out the door, leaving Marco to his fate.

———

As soon as Jack approached the iron door to the women's barracks, one of Maggiano's men, tall with a shock of tall dark hair, dashed up to him. "What the hell happened?"

Jack unlocked the door. "Something outside exploded. Took out Maggiano. Marco's gone, too. I'm in charge."

The man looked back in the direction of the main offices. The rising smoke made it hard to see back there. "Damn. What blew up? A gas line?"

"Got me." Jack flung the door open. "Get the men and check around the building."

Three more men approached. "You!" Jack called to them. "Arm up! Get some rifles, now! We're going to clear the women out until we can find out what's going on outside!"

As the men hurried off, Jack hurried inside. In all likelihood, there had been some kind of accident.

The propane tanks were just outside. However, Jack couldn't discount the possibility that somebody might be attacking the facility. Maggiano did have his enemies. Or maybe the authorities finally had got their act together and were taking the cities back.

One of the men approached with a rifle. Jack grabbed him by the shirt and whispered, "Keep it quiet about Maggiano. We don't want the women to know. They may try something."

The man nodded. "Good." Jack released him. "Follow me."

The first room he hit was Sarah's. "Hey," Jack said, "Up and at 'em. We're going outside for a little suntan."

She rose. "What was that bang?"

"Nothing you need to worry about. Now get going." Jack stood back, letting Sarah out of the room. She had changed out of those spandex clothes. Too bad. Now that Jack was king, he'd make some permanent changes to these ladies' attire.

He hurried toward the end of the barracks, shouting orders. *It's good to be the king*, he thought.

———

TOM'S HEART raced as he climbed back to his feet. Conrad's little "distraction" proved to be a mighty one, as the bang rang through the air and shook the ground hard, enough that Tom had to cling to the car he was taking cover behind. He braced himself to keep from falling over.

Once his initial shock had passed, he looked from one exit to the other on the west side of the building. They should be streaming out of the building like rats fleeing a sinking ship. His hope, perhaps in vain, was that the blast took out a lot of Maggiano's men and enabled the women to escape. But the cynical part of Tom jibed that he never could be so lucky.

They'll come out with the women, Tom thought. The only question was how many.

Three windows were within easy viewing range. From where he stood, Tom easily could spot moving shadows through the glass. Unfortunately, he could not make out actual people. He couldn't tell whether women or men were rushing by, if prisoners of Maggiano were dashing by, or if they armed henchmen.

Then, they started to emerge. It was sporadic. A man dashed out of a side entrance and ran off around back. Another sprang from a second-story door, near a loading door. The warehouse escapees were just a man here, a man there. *Where the hell were the women?*

The warehouse's back door sprang open. Tom tensed up.

Three men poured out of the back entrance. So, that's where they were coming out. Tom leaned a little closer. Those three brutes were carrying high-powered machine guns. It wouldn't be a shocker if

Maggiano had those babies squirreled away before the power went out.

Another man rushed out, nearly bumping into the armed man. Tom instantly recognized him. Jack Sorenson. So, one of the bigwigs was coming out. He looked a little disheveled, with unkempt hair and a brown tint on his clothing that could be dust. Perhaps he had been too close to the blast and had been roughed up by it.

Then, a woman followed. She was dressed in pretty ordinary clothing—blue jeans, a white shirt and a pink buttoned shirt that was fully open. Her hair was limp, clearly unwashed and untreated.

Another woman followed. She was dressed quite differently, in a tight fitting red dress and even heels. Tom couldn't believe it. Why the hell would she go through the trouble of dolling herself up like that? And where'd she get the dress from? Was it hers? Then Tom spotted Jack walking a little closer to her as she approached.

Yeah, that makes sense. I bet Sorenson dressed her up.

More women filed out, but none looking as ravishing as the lady in red. They were mostly disheveled, with open shirts revealing smaller under-shirts underneath, likely to cool themselves off in a building that had no air conditioning. They varied in age from women who looked uncomfortably young— Tom thought a teenager or two could be in that procession—to women in their thirties, forties, or maybe middle age. They looked reasonably healthy, with none of them appearing emaciated, malnourished, or injured. None of them hobbled or limped.

Makes sense if Maggiano wanted them in prime condition for his brothel, Tom thought. *Speaking of which, where the hell is Maggiano? He ought to be coming out of there, unless he's leaving on Conrad's side. Damn, there's no way Conrad will see this.*

Sweat poured down his face. He wanted to save Sarah. But what about these other women? Could he save all them, too? How many were down there? Eight? Nine?

No, there were ten now. Tom's heat sank when he watched the tenth woman emerge into the open sun.

"Sarah," he whispered.

No mistaking it. Her gray hair, her trim frame, it all gave her away. Her clothes were different from when she was abducted, but they were plain, beige khaki pants and a gray shirt. She didn't seem injured, but from this distance it was hard to tell. The particulars of her condition would have to wait. She was alive. That's all that mattered.

I must get her out of there. But there's too many men down there with guns. If he picked off just one of them, the rest would return fire. They may even gun down the women out of revenge.

Dammit, Conrad, why couldn't you be here instead of me?

CHAPTER EIGHT

CONRAD DIDN'T HESITATE for another second. *Now*! he thought. He raced toward the door and flung it open. He waited just a second to peek inside. No shouts. Nobody noticed the door opening. Nobody rushed to stop him.

Then he ducked inside. A din of smoke hung over the warehouse interior. Thanks to a few boxes on the ground, Conrad found some easy cover. The building rose several stories, with the wall to the right lined with scaffolding that held a few boxes. Some of the boxes were open, allowing Conrad to spot packed food and guns inside. Not all of the spaces were occupied. Some of them lay empty.

The center and left side of the warehouse, however, were taken up by a wooden structure about a story high. It looked like a large wooden rectangle in the middle of the warehouse, and judging by how new the lumber looked, it seemed to have been built recently. The structure was far too small to house anything big. These must be the barracks Tom had told him about.

Looking up, Conrad got a look at the damage from the propane explosion. The blast had blown a hole in the wall above and rained down debris on the back end of the barracks. There was enough metal to completely crumple two of the rooms. Conrad winced. He was sure there had to have been men inside, likely crushed to death before they knew what had hit them. Smoke and dust also covered up the view of the offices, but judging by how close they were to the gas tanks, they must have sustained heavy damage.

The iron door to the barracks was wide open. Conrad hurried toward the wall to his right. This wall wouldn't be next to the explosion site and thus wouldn't be hot from the burning fire. At the same time, he dug into his pocket and pulled out a hand-kerchief, then covered his mouth and nose with it. This would help block out the smoke that poured from the open wound in the wall.

It'll be hell trying to stay quiet if I start hacking, he thought.

A man then ran out of the barracks. He was pant-ing, his eyes wide with fright. He headed to the open door Conrad had come out of. He had a holster on his belt with a handgun inside. He wasn't scrambling to man the outside. He was running scared.

Maybe if some of them panic and flee, that'll cut down on men guarding Sarah, Conrad thought.

As he crept alongside the wall, he spotted the second set of barracks just a few feet away, possibly the area where the women were kept. A corridor ran right between the men's barracks and the women's barracks. No one was coming from that direction. Conrad hurried into the hall.

No sounds were coming from the women's quarters. Slowing his pace, Conrad strode close to the wall to listen for anything: cries, shouts, talking, or even the movement of feet.

Finally, Conrad dared to knock on the wooden wall. Nothing. He knocked again. Still nothing.

They must have moved out the women already. Damn.

Conrad sped up until he reached the other side of the hall. He had emerged on the other side of the two barracks and was back out in the open area of the warehouse. This sector of the building was much quieter. There were lines of freezers, likely used for preserving food for the Maggiano line of restaurants, scaffolding for the hosting of crates and boxes, and a forklift sitting near a closed overhead door.

Conrad almost started off into the open storage area when he decided to look back at the barracks. Each had an entrance into this part of the warehouse that was wide open. Conrad quickly ran to the door of the women's barracks and peered inside.

There was nothing but a small hall and open

doors. *Still as a tomb*, Conrad thought. Still, he ran in and did a quick check of the rooms, just to be sure.

Satisfied that the barracks were empty, he dashed back out to the open storage area. Then the radio on his belt buzzed.

"Tom!" Conrad said as he pulled the radio off. "Damn, I hope he spotted Sarah." He switched it on. "Tom, do you read?"

"Conrad!" The voice coming over was a harsh, frantic whisper. "Conrad, you there?"

"Calm down! Just talk to me," Conrad called back.

"I see her! I see her!" Tom repeated over and over again.

"Sarah?" Conrad spoke.

"Yeah, it's her. Dammit, it's her. There's nine more women out here. But there's three men with rifles. I-I can't get a clear shot, and if I shoot they might turn on me..."

"Calm yourself! It's enough you got eyes on her. Look, we're in a position of power here. I think the explosion took some of their boys out, and they're a little disorganized. Have they started searching for us?"

"I don't see anything but what I just told you," Tom replied.

"Alright. Sit tight. I'm coming your way. I'll check in in a couple of minutes."

"Right. Um, ten-four," Tom replied.

Conrad put his radio back on his belt. At last! Sarah was within reach.

———

MAGGIANO MOANED. He tried to draw in breath, but horrible pressure gripped his lungs like a vice. He tried to move his legs, but felt nothing but a huge weight on them, along with intense pain. He knew his legs had been crushed, and that debris had pinned them down. He blinked his eyes, seeing nothing but a light blur and smoke. He heard nothing. The explosion had shattered his eardrums.

"He...help!" It was sheer agony trying to speak. He tried again, only to cough loud and hard. Blood then dribbled down his chin. Blood and fluid was gathering in his lungs.

He was dying.

Dammit! This can't be how it ends! Somebody get your ass down here and help me! Maggiano's mind screamed a strain of vile curses that never would escape the confines of his own mind.

Just then, a shadow passed over him. The shape was indistinct, but Maggiano was certain a man just had passed by him, perhaps climbing over the debris that pinned him down to the floor.

Maggiano spoke quickly, fearing his chance for rescue was fading fast. "Hel...help..." But the shadow didn't stop. Maggiano was being left for dead. None of his men would show up to deliver him from his fate.

He coughed again. Now his throat was being

stopped up by fluids and blood. It was a struggle for him to breathe at all.

It was unthinkable that he would die this way. Who did it? Who was the son of a bitch who bombed his warehouse? Did the state's National Guard come in and retake the city? Perhaps the army had shown up to impose martial law.

His right arm twitched. He raised it. Yes, he still had feeling in it. He reached out, trying to grab something, anything, to pull it away to free himself.

I'm king, Maggiano thought. *I'm king...*

And then his arm fell limp. Marcellus Maggiano had breathed his last.

———

TOM PUT his radio back on his belt. Now all he could do was wait for Conrad to tell him what to do.

It was hard to tell from this distance exactly what was going on. The women were just standing around, but Tom couldn't tell their mental and physical states from here. Were they active? Lethargic? Maybe drugged? If they were alert, maybe they could make a run for it if the armed men around them were taken out?

I won't know unless I get closer, Tom thought.

Several vehicles, chain-link fences, and light posts lay between him and the warehouse. He plausibly could close in and take cover without being noticed. None of the men were looking his way. Besides,

Conrad might want him to take action, so Tom should be closer to the warehouse.

Tom crept out from his spot. He hurried past a chain-link fence, trying to keep his footsteps as soft as possible, even if it seemed ludicrous that the men could hear him from this distance. Besides, he still didn't know if someone was lurking closer by. Better not to take chances.

Now he reached a large semi-truck. Tom slid along the driver's side until he could look around the truck's hood. He could see the faces of the women much more easily. Looking at them tied a knot in his stomach. They seemed lost, confused, and docile. They didn't turn their heads or look around for an opportunity to escape. Their clothing ranged from dirty to relatively clean, but plain, except for that woman in the red dress.

Tom crept out a little more into the open. Jack Sorenson was next to the woman in red. In fact, he never had left her side, as far as Tom could remember. He held the woman's arm while speaking to her. Tom still couldn't hear him clearly, but Jack's mannerisms and smile reminded Tom of how Jack had flirted with the ladies at a party he attended last year. Jack could practically glide about a room and charm any woman who was remotely available. Of course, Tom also had read online some disquieting rumors about Jack's activities with women. Jack was the kind of guy who looked pleasant on the outside, but was a snake on the inside.

Some things don't change, even when the world ends, Tom thought. But the woman in red wasn't who he wanted to check on. Sarah. Where the hell was she?

He inched out a little farther. He had lost track of Sarah since he had closed in on the warehouse. His legs shook the more he stepped away from his cover. He had to find her, no matter the risk.

Then, a woman with short gray hair turned around. Sarah finally stepped into Tom's line of sight.

Sarah was a woman who could jump out of bed at the break of dawn. Not here. She looked tired, her gaze down to the concrete. Her arms were clasped around her chest. Her lips were slightly open. She wasn't doing anything but waiting, as if she had no expectation she would be delivered from her fate. Most of the women, Tom could see, had similar looks on their faces.

Tom's skin started to burn. He was the man who put Sarah in this horrid position. God knows what these men had done to her. He wanted to rush out there right now and save her.

Control yourself, Tom thought. *You'll be picked off in a cold minute.*

He returned to the side of the truck and crouched down. "C'mon Conrad," he whispered, "You got to take charge of this damn thing." *If not, I might do something real stupid.*

———

SOME OF THE freezer doors gaped open as Conrad jogged past. *This whole place is a monument to a lost era*, he thought. These freezers and refrigerators would cold-store food bound for groceries and restaurants. Cold food was one of the great breakthroughs of the modern age. It made food so convenient in modern societies that unless you were completely destitute, you didn't have to fear going hungry. Sadly, that no longer would be the case. This warehouse never would be put back to its original use without a massive rebuilding of society, and God only knew when that would be.

Conrad approached the back wall of the warehouse. *But then they had to go and turn this place into a prison camp*, he added to himself. The sight of more weapons inside some of the crates reinforced that brutal reality. The anger over that injustice helped quell his fears. Coming here had been initially terrifying, but he took comfort in the fact that at least he could fight back. The women being held here had no chance of fighting back on their own.

I'm surprised this place isn't more stocked with guns, Conrad thought. Then he glanced behind him and noted the barracks ended almost in the middle of this vast facility. *Maybe he figures on expanding his lineup of prisoners. Save some space for more captives.*

His right hand burned a little. Conrad thought his working man's hand was acting up again, but as he turned around he found he was in the path of sunlight from an open doorway.

Quickly, Conrad ducked into the shadows of the scaffolding. That was the door Tom had eyes on. The women must have been filed out through there. He couldn't afford to be exposed to the outside until he got a good look at who was standing outside, and what he could expect if he charged through the exit.

Just then, he heard the creaking of a door. Conrad ducked into the shadow of an overhang. Then he turned back in the direction from which he had come.

Somebody had pushed the door to the men's barracks all the way open. A lone male just had come out. In the shadows of the scaffolds it was hard to see what he looked like.

Conrad pulled out his gun, then remained still. He had done his share of reading up on how to move with stealth, how to find places to hide and blend in as much as possible. At first it seemed like magic to him, stuff that you would see in ninja movies. But now that he was in such a situation, he appreciated learning about those tactics. He feared that someday he'd have to ward off thieves and bandits when society broke down. He didn't imagine he'd need those skills on a rescue mission.

The newcomer shuffled out into the open space of the warehouse. He approached Conrad's position, but not too quickly. He seemed hurt.

As he got closer to the open doorway, the pouring sunlight illuminated his features. He was bare-chested and wearing a fancy pair of pants that now was covered in dust. It brought back memories of Conrad's time in the city. He'd see executives wearing fine dress pants such as those, although they were naturally part of a business suit. He wondered if this man was one of the big shots who allied with Maggiano. He sure wasn't the man who Conrad spotted with the two men cooking the fish earlier.

Marco Valentino. I think that's one of the other men Tom described, Conrad thought. The idea that this man might be Marco filled Conrad with both anger and dread. This could be the man who kidnapped Sarah!

CHAPTER NINE

CAMILLA BROUGHT IN FRESH DRINKS, lemon-based carbonated soda that she had preserved since the EMP. It was stuff from cans she had stored away. She said she would save that stuff for a special occasion, and meeting Conrad's son and his lover certainly fit that bill.

She looked at Carla and Liam. The pair just recently had returned to their seats. "I apologize if I took your room," she said with a chuckle. "It's alright. If you prefer it, Conrad's got other rooms in this house."

Liam slid his seat farther under the table. "It's fine. Carla and I just had to get our stuff unpacked."

"God, I need a bath." Carla rubbed her face. "Sorry, I'm still not used to the outdoors. I loved playing outside when I was a kid, but that was a while ago." She chuckled.

"Well, I won't keep you long. I'm sure you two

want to seriously settle in. But..." Camilla slid two glasses of soda in their direction. "A little something special."

"I wasn't sure I'd ever have this again!" Carla guzzled down the drink greedily.

"Yeah, we certainly appreciate everything we have now," Camilla said with a smile. "So, what's the story with Conrad sending you back here? You still need to tell me that before you take your bath."

Liam and Carla filled in Camilla on why Conrad had sent them back. Camilla's expression brightened up when she heard the truth.

"Really? So, Conrad's going to be a granddad!" She threw her head back and laughed. "Lord, I can't wait to get on him about that."

"Yeah. He was pretty adamant that we had to come back here," Liam said.

"Well, that explains everything," Camilla said. "I figured his boy would hook up with some pretty lady. You've inherited his looks."

Liam coughed while Carla giggled. "Guess so," he said.

By now it was clear to Liam that Camilla truly possessed feelings for his dad. Before he showed up here with Carla a few days ago, he feared his father was a complete loner, shut up in a house off the side of the road with nobody to care for him, not a lover or even a friend. But as it turned out, his dad had met someone who cared for him. Knowing that fact lifted his spirits.

"We gotta keep a close eye on you two." Camilla looked at Carla and raised her eyebrows, "You're making the next generation of survivors, probably even the people who will run this country."

Carla laughed. "Yeah, looks like it."

"First one for you two?" Camilla asked.

"Yeah." Carla replied.

"Then your baby will be the smart one." Camilla chuckled. "First child's always got the best head on its shoulders. I'm the third one in my family, so I guess that explains me." She laughed. "Yeah, it's all up to you. I think my oven's burned out." She patted her thighs.

"Do you have any kids?" Carla asked.

Camilla shook her head. "No. Sorry, but I didn't bring any little ones into this world." Then she looked at Liam. "None with your father, either. Hey, you could have opened that door and found yourself with a little half-brother or half-sister." Then she laughed loudly.

Liam coughed. *How the hell did Dad hook up with her? She might share his interests, but damn, she's a million times more expressive. I think she's talked more than I heard my dad talk during my whole life.*

Liam decided to change the subject from his dad's love life. "So, we're safe here?" Liam asked, "You were wondering if we had a safe trip over here. It's been pretty wild out there. I'm hoping Dad's home can be a safe place to raise our family."

"Well, thanks to your dad's hard work with the

crops and animals, we can live off the land until you two are old and gray." Camilla's head bowed slightly toward her cup. "But the truth is, no one is really safe anymore, not even here."

"What do you mean?" Carla asked.

Camilla curled up one of her fingers. "Your dad's butted heads with a few people over the years. Some of them think he's a crazy coot. Nothing really bad went down with them. But one man's different. He's like your dad's evil twin. His name's Derrick Wellinger. Guess your dad didn't mention him, right?"

Liam shook his head. "We really didn't have a lot of time to catch up on the past thirty years."

"Well, it's too bad we can't bury Derrick in the past, but the truth is he's become very dangerous recently." Camilla sipped again. "Derrick and Conrad met maybe twenty years ago. The two of them got along well in the beginning. Derrick was another prepper. He had his own homestead off State Road 22. He bragged he was going to turn that place into his own little country if the U.S. ever got nuked or shut down." She formed air quotes with her fingers. "The Republic of Wellinger."

Carla smirked. "This guy sounds like a real piece of work."

"You have no idea." Camilla suddenly hiccupped. "Excuse me. At first, they seemed to share similar interests. But things went sour pretty quick. Conrad had good instincts. I knew he was successful in the city before he went off the grid. He didn't leap for the cheapest land he could find. Derrick did."

"Sounds as though he really stepped in it," Liam said.

"Oh Lord, yes, yes, a thousand times yes." Camilla laughed.

"The land was far worse than Derrick thought. He didn't bother to check the water table. He didn't get more than a slight history of the land, so he didn't know if it was a good crop producer. He didn't even check the soil. It just had some good-looking trees and he figured he was up Easy Street for the price. Then during the first spring he found he couldn't grow a damn thing." Camilla's eyes widened. "Then your dad offered to help."

"Didn't turn out well?" Liam asked.

"Derrick said no. Then he still couldn't make the land fertile. Then he realized he'd have to empty out half his savings to re-till the land or accept Conrad's help." Camilla bit her lower lip. "He took some supplies, some fertilizer, and some seeds from him, then made it clear Conrad had to stay away from his property after that. Conrad didn't care. Derrick never forgave your father for giving him charity."

"Sounds like this guy has ego issues," Carla said.

"It only got worse after that," Camilla said. "Derrick's rage just built. He knew he wasn't in your dad's league. He saw what Conrad had turned this property into, and it just bit him in the ass every time. Then the sun did its damage to our world. Now

Derrick's out to prove he's not a failure. When I saw you two lovebirds show up, I was afraid Derrick sent you." She sighed. "Thank God I didn't do anything stupid, especially now that I know that Carla's carrying."

"That's why you came here," Liam said, "You wanted to warn him."

"Warn him, sure. Actually, I was planning to stay and help defend the house. Two guns are better than one." Camilla patted her hip. "Of course, I always said he shot better than me."

Carla turned to Liam and rolled her eyes. Liam wondered if Camilla still was talking about guns. "So, you expect Derrick to send somebody here?"

Camilla's expression turned a little grimmer. "I heard from a little birdie when I was bartering for seeds a few miles north. Derrick had put out the word that he was offering good land and crops if you had a good aim to offer him. Now, I know Derrick's not talking about his land. I put two and two together and figured he might be looking to take some land for himself, by force."

Carla chewed on one of her fingernails. "Think he might come here?"

Liam let out a sigh. "Son of a bitch." He just knew things wouldn't go this well for them.

Camilla nodded. "Could be. Look, you two might want to consider bailing out of here. Maybe Derrick's not that crazy, but if he is, you may have jumped out of a frying pan and into a blazing oven."

Liam leaned back in his chair. "Maybe. But where would we go? Any town we'd go to would be a wreck."

"Camp out in the woods, maybe?" Camilla asked.

Liam shook his head. The thought of having to leave again terrified him, and this time out into the unknown. At least when he had left Dad, he was heading to a comfortable and supposedly secure house.

"Look, we don't know for sure that this Derrick is coming here to start trouble. Maybe we should wait a little while. Besides, Dad might show up. If Carla and I leave, he won't know where to find us."

Camilla smiled. "Truth is, I'd like to have some company under this roof." Looking up at the ceiling, she sighed. "It's damn lonely without Conrad." Then she looked at them. "Hey, why should I be spooking you with stories like that?" Camilla then rose from her chair. "Let me gather all this up. You two must be tuckered out."

Camilla took the glasses to the kitchen. Carla then scooted her seat close to Liam. "What do you think?"

Liam sat back in his chair. "About what? Pick your topic, I think there's a bunch of them."

Carla chuckled. "About Derrick, and that our butts may not be safe."

Liam gave it a little thought. "I don't know." He glanced at Carla. "But God knows I'd rather stick around here than try finding somewhere out in a city or town filled with psychos who may want to blow our brains out." He sighed. "Maybe I'm tired of running around. I want someplace normal for us. And this is probably the best it'll ever get."

Carla scooted a little closer. "I think this place is great." She wrapped her arms around Liam. "And I don't want to run any more either."

Liam bowed his head, leaning it in Carla's direction. "I wish Dad was here. And Mom. I want them both back."

Carla leaned in a little closer and kissed his cheek. "I'm sure your dad will be back soon." Then she chuckled. "Oh my God, this is going to be awkward."

Liam looked up. "Why?"

Carla chuckled. "Think about it. Your dad, his ex, his ex's boyfriend, and your dad's girlfriend, under one roof. What do you think that's going to be like?"

Liam sucked in his lower lip. "Maybe we should just build a log cabin in the woods and live there."

Carla laughed.

———

LANCE PEDALED AS FAST as he could, but so far State Road 22 had nothing to offer him but more fields on either side. Where was this turnoff he was supposed to find?

Damn, I hope I didn't miss it! Lance's arms quaked with rage at the thought. The monotony of this journey could have dulled his senses so much that he might not have noticed the turnoff as he passed by.

He was reduced to daydreaming about his old life as if he was watching reruns of a reality TV show. He thought of his last birthday, his twenty-second, and how he had guzzled cake, potato chips, and beer.

His mouth started to water. Those were three things he knew he'd never get to taste ever again. Lance swore loudly. Why'd he have to be born now, in this time, if this kind of hard life was all he had to look forward to?

He shook his head, flinging sweat off his brow. No, he hadn't reached the turnoff yet. The journey was thirty miles. He hadn't pedaled that far yet. He knew what pedaling a long way felt like. He had tried reaching another town once, about forty miles west, only to turn back when he heard barking dogs in the distance. A refugee at one of the camps told horror stories about survivors being attacked by feral animals, and Lance sure as hell didn't want to risk that.

Lance's stomach started rumbling, no longer satisfied with the crackers he had eaten a while ago. Food. Dammit, he needed to eat. No, he had to keep going. If he stopped, he feared he wouldn't be able to climb back on and start again. Besides, he was out of food. He had no choice but to press on.

So, he pushed onward for another agonizing hour. His vision started to blur. His deprived body protested loudly.

Grass, he thought. *Maybe I'll just munch on some grass. That should shut my stomach up.*

Then, just when he was seriously going to stop to look for some grass to eat, he discovered the turnoff. He laughed loudly. This trip wouldn't be for nothing after all.

He made the turn. Hope gave him that extra burst of energy to speed up, even though the road's incline made going fast slightly dangerous.

As he crossed onto a flat, wide-open field, he discovered a fence stretched out before him. A tall, pudgy man stood in front of it, holding up a hand. Lance got the message and slowed down. Then he stopped, but was so weak he actually tumbled off and spilled onto the grass.

Lance panted wildly. The agony of the journey finally had caught up with him. It was almost impossible to roll onto his side, yet he managed it. The man at the fence simply stared at him.

Why isn't he helping me? Lance thought as he pushed himself onto his palms. From there he finally sat up before climbing to his feet. His legs quivered. He had to spread his legs a little to keep from falling over.

"So, what's your story?" the man asked without a hint of concern.

Lance wiped loose grass off his jeans. "I-I've come a long way."

"Yeah, I get that. What are you here for?"

Lance straightened up. "To find work. I was told that Wellinger needed a strong hand. I could have food, water, and a place to stay."

"You heard right." The tall man finally approached him. "You bring a piece with you?"

"A piece of what?"

"You know, a piece. A gun."

Lance shook his head. "I don't have anything except a few clothes."

The man suddenly drew a pistol from behind his back. Lance froze. "Hey! What the hell is this? You're not actually going to shoot me?"

The man didn't react for a whole minute. Fresh sweat poured down Lance's face. Then, the man laughed as he turned the pistol around, the handle facing Lance.

"A little joke. The gun's not loaded. But you're prepared to use it, right?"

Lance nodded. "If I have to."

"That's what I want to hear." He offered it to him. "Name's George. Friends call me Big G."

"I'm Lance Wilkins." He took the gun. "Thanks."

"Don't mention it. I was beginning to wonder if anyone else would answer Mister Wellinger's call. We did our best to put the word out." George popped the gate open. "You'll find there's a few more of us here. Mister Wellinger will be by very soon, and he'll let you know what you need that gun for."

Lance followed George a short way until George came to a stop. Lance looked around, finding five more men all standing, sitting on crates, or leaning on the fence. A red-bricked homestead lay a short walk away.

"Here we are." George grinned. "Stick around. Relax. This is where Mister Wellinger wants us to meet."

Putting his weapon under his belt, Lance frowned. With the short grass and bare spots of just dirt, this land didn't look fertile at all. It didn't look like anything that could grow a lot of food, and it certainly didn't compare to the farms back in Lance's hometown. So, where was the food for the workers going to come from? Did Wellinger have a supply line from better farms?

Lance also took noticed that every man here was armed. Some had handguns on their belts, while others carried rifles. That probably wasn't unusual given how violent the outside world had become, but George seemed particularly interested in whether Lance was armed. Clearly, guns were part of Wellinger's upcoming task for them.

"Oh, one more thing." George then turned around and whistled. One of the men sitting on a crate reached beside it and picked up a plate wrapped in a plastic covering. Then he handed it to George, who handed it to Lance.

Lance couldn't believe it. Under that wrapping was a plate of dirty rice, meat, corn and potatoes! He almost wept with joy.

George grinned. "Mister Wellinger is like our own personal Messiah." George spread his arms. "He's going to lead us to the Promised Land."

Lance looked around. Two of the men had heard George and nodded in agreement.

"Dig in." George slapped Lance's arm. "You'll need your strength. Mister Wellinger will be by with our mission."

Lance began unwrapping the plastic, but then stopped. "Mission?"

"That's what I said. It's going to be exciting." George then winked before walking off.

Lance eyed the weapon he was just given. He couldn't imagine what he would be asked to do with it, but after the hell he had endured the last few days, he flat out didn't care what would be asked of him.

CHAPTER TEN

CONRAD KEPT CLOSE to the wall as Marco walked by.
Conrad feared any moment now that Marco would
turn and spot him. But Marco didn't look in Conrad's
direction or behaved as if he had no regard for
anything around him except the straight path ahead
to the open doorway.

Marco, yeah, it's got to be him, Conrad thought. Tom
had described Marco a little during their journey to
the warehouse district, and it seemed to make perfect
sense. Looking at him, he looked every bit the thug
Conrad had imagined him to be.

In fact, Marco looked even worse now. Judging
from the man's appearance, he had been through hell.
He walked with a limp in his right leg and his right
pant leg was torn near the thigh. The look on Marco's
face was particularly horrifying. The skin under his
right eye was dark, perhaps from an injury. A bruise

marred his left cheek. His eyes were locked ahead of him, and they seemed almost demonic.

By now Marco had passed Conrad. Thanks to Marco's slow walk, he wouldn't be at the front door in less than a couple of minutes.

This fellow looks like bad news, Conrad thought. He thought of the gun in his right hand. Marco's back was turned to Conrad. Conrad easily could take him out. If he was the one who stole Sarah away, then Conrad sure as hell ought to plug him for what he had done.

Maybe. But the sound of a gunshot also could draw in the men from the outside. They could flood into the warehouse, and Conrad could end up with a firefight on his hands.

Marco now was much closer to the door. Conrad decided to risk approaching him. He stepped out from his hiding spot and hurried to the next bit of scaffolding. Then he slipped inside. Marco didn't turn around.

Conrad was close enough to get a good view outside the door. He spotted some of the women, along with the three men with guns, plus Jack Sorenson on the far end.

Only three? Maybe the explosion took a lot of them out, or they're scattered around the grounds looking for me and Tom. In any case, the odds didn't seem quite so bad.

Suddenly, his radio buzzed. Conrad quickly grabbed it. He didn't need Marco to hear that. He turned and held the radio close to his ear.

"Conrad! Conrad, do you read?" Tom whispered.

"Yeah. What's changed?" Conrad asked.

"I spotted a couple of men on the other side going back inside. Looks as though they may be easing back into the building. The smoke from your bombs looks like it's dying down."

"Damn," Conrad muttered. Maggiano's men may be deciding that the fire isn't a real threat to the building, and they can start herding the captives back inside. He couldn't put this off any longer.

"Tom, I want you to close in and shoot one of the gunmen. Maybe the girls will run free." Conrad stood up and faced the open door. Marco just was stepping over the threshold into the open air.

"You want me to open fire?" Tom asked with evident apprehension.

"If the women don't flee, I'll at least have just a few to deal with," Conrad said.

"Conrad, are you sure?"

"Do it now!" Conrad shouted, and then slapped the radio back on his belt as he quickened his pace toward the door.

———

A RAGING inferno of anger burned between Marco's ears. It fueled his battered body with the energy it needed to push that debris off his body, walk past the flaming wreckage, and leave the room before he succumbed to the smoke. He didn't care to check in any of the rooms in the barracks, even the ones that had been damaged in the blast. If he heard any cries for help from the men's barracks, they didn't register. His ears still were ringing slightly, even after he had climbed his way out of that room. He might have suffered some hearing loss because of the explosion.

If he had, it'd just be another reason to blow Jack's brains out.

The fact that Maggiano was killed in the cave-in was a bonus. Now Marco didn't have to worry about being under the crime boss's thumb any longer. That indignity was removed, plus Marco got to enjoy a taste of revenge for Maggiano having his boys strip him naked in that office to verify Molly's "description" of her attacker. In one fell swoop, everyone who had wronged him was dead. All but one.

And once Marco splattered Jack's brains across the concrete, he'd take over Maggiano's empire. He'd possess all the women, the armed men, the weapons, and the food. And last, but not least, the city of Redmond.

But first thing's first. Jack was going to die.

Marco emerged out the door. The women all had evacuated out into the open. Jack was on the end of the procession, chatting with a woman in a red dress. Marco couldn't make out what Jack was saying, but the nodding of the man's head, the smile on Jack's face, told him that Jack once again was working his magic on the women. It just enraged Marco even more.

Looks like I'm about to play my winning hand, Marco thought. Jack obviously figured these ladies would be his reward once this ordeal was over. Marco would show him otherwise. *If you wanted me dead, you should have shot me with a gun. I always said you weren't a tough guy. Yeah, you played me good, but there's no substitute for a bullet in your chest.*

He raised his gun, though his arm quaked. He was so messed up that a good aim was very difficult. He'd have to do this quickly. One errant shot, and he'd likely be dead before he got another chance.

———

TOM'S FEET MOVED. God help him, it was almost a miracle that he was heading right for the fray, but doubt, fear and anxiety were taking a back seat to the very real chance he could save Sarah. He jogged down the concrete lot to about fifty yards from the women and their armed captors. Then he stopped behind a parked service truck, feeling he could not approach any closer without being easily seen.

Then he took a careful look at the men with guns. One of them, a burly man in a dirty white T-shirt, was too close to three women. Tom's shot easily could hit any of the girls by accident. Tom's experience with firearms was scant. He was no marksman. A second armed man was likewise standing near two women. Again, Tom's bullet might either hit him or strike one of the ladies.

A third man was much farther away, about ten yards from the group. He was gazing around, perhaps taking a look for possible intruders onto the warehouse property. He was Tom's best bet to take out one of them without hitting any of the women.

He aimed his gun in the man's direction. *I'm really going to do this*, he thought. The anxiety threatened to return. He knew once he pulled the trigger, everything would go down in a hurry.

Then Tom spotted someone new entering the scene, a man who changed his mood in a big hurry.

Marco just had stepped out of the open doorway. He looked badly hurt, walking with a limp. Oddly, he had no shirt on, just beaten-up pants. He also was clutching a gun and moved like a man ready to kill. Conrad was nowhere in sight, so Marco wasn't targeting him. Instead, Marco was marching up to the crowd of women.

But it didn't matter to Tom who Marco was gunning for. The fact was, Marco was here in the open, and he didn't know Tom was looking at him from a distance.

Marco! You stole Sarah from me! You humiliated me! You made me look like a coward!

Tom's arms tensed up with newly flowing anger. Of all the human beings on this Earth who could compel him to pull the trigger of a gun and end a life, Marco Valentino was the one.

Tom squeezed the trigger.

———

By now, Marco was outside and closing in on the crowd of ladies. Although the women were haggard and beaten down, seeing Marco closing in roused some of them to step away, giving him space. It was all the better for Marco, since it also opened up space between him and Jack.

Marco's gun now was aimed at Jack's upper chest. Two more women gasped and retreated a few steps toward the warehouse. Jack's attention still was squarely on the woman in red, who by now had noticed Marco's approach and gasped loudly. Finally, Jack turned to face Marco, just as a shot rang out.

A shout followed, ringing out in the daytime air—Marco's.

Marco Valentino stumbled backward, drops of blood shooting out of a gaping wound in his upper chest. Then he slammed back-first into the concrete. Around him, most of the women shouted or screamed in fright.

"Marco?" Jack spun around. "Who did that? Who shot him?" The armed men weren't pointed at all in Marco's direction. Instead, they were turning toward Tom. Jack turned and spotted Tom by the service truck some distance away.

Tom had two options—shoot or take cover. He chose the latter, ducking behind the truck to evade the gunfire that was sure to come.

But almost simultaneously, Conrad charged out the door. He tased one of the shooters, causing the man's shot to miss Tom by a good several yards. Conrad then aimed his gun at a second man, who only now was turning around in Conrad's direction.

The shooter didn't turn quickly enough. Conrad squeezed the trigger, and in seconds the henchman fell to the hard ground.

The third armed man, however, did have enough time to turn around and spot Conrad by the warehouse.

Conrad tried to turn around and aim, but his shot only whizzed past the shooter's arm. The last shooter's rifle now was pointed squarely at Conrad's chest. Conrad was wide open.

But before the last shooter could take out Conrad, a loud pop rang out. Conrad's would-be killer lurched forward, then fell to his knees. Blood poured from his mouth. Some distance away, Tom had gotten to his feet and taken the shot, saving Conrad's life.

Meanwhile, Jack had turned and run toward the warehouse, shouting and screaming. "Hey! Hey! Get some damn men here, someone's shooting at us!"

Forget him, Conrad thought. This commotion would be drawing out more henchmen anyway, if any bothered to stick around. No sense in bothering with somebody who wasn't joining in the fight.

As he turned in Tom's direction, he locked eyes with the woman he once declared to be the love of his life. When she turned and saw him, a tremor ran through her body.

"Sarah," he whispered.

CHAPTER ELEVEN

LANCE ADJUSTED THE HAT AGAIN. It still was too big, but it would do to shield his head from the sun. After being deprived of so much for so long, he was grateful for whatever anything people would give him. And so far, the men at this ranch had been generous. He was given water in a canteen, food on a plate, a hat and, certainly not least of all, his gun. For the first time in a long while, his stomach was full.

But after a while, Lance's gratitude and euphoria turned to boredom. Standing still for even a few minutes quickly would eat at him. He had been standing in this fenced area with the other men for a while. He didn't see anybody his age. Lance had graduated from high school just last year. All these men seemed like they could have logged in a few years at college at least.

So, he turned his back and leaned against the wooden fence to stare out at the land beyond. Rows of crops stretched from left to right. Closer by was a homestead, perhaps where Derrick Wellinger lived. He itched to take a look around there. No one seemed to pay attention to him. So, he grabbed onto one of the wooden posts and began climbing. The fence was just slightly taller than he was. Climbing over it would be no problem.

"Hey."

That voice made Lance stop his leg from swinging over the fence's top. He turned to his right. A tall man with a greasy black mustache and severe blue eyes gazed at him. "We do have a gate, kid."

"Oh." Lance blushed. "Right. I just thought this would be more fun." Then he scowled. More fun? That was his excuse? "I mean, it's okay to take a walk around here, isn't it?"

"Knock yourself out. Just don't take any of the crops. This is all Derrick Wellinger's land. We've already taken a look around. Nothing special. So, what's your name?"

"Lance Wilkins."

"I'm Cal." Then he leaned back against the fence. "Can't blame ya for wanting to stretch your legs. I want to get started with this." He cracked his knuckles. "I heard over the ham radio that there'd be some excitement in this job."

Lance didn't doubt it. Cal radiated such tension that it looked like he would turn and tear one of the wooden posts out of the ground with his bare hands.

He decided to get over the fence quickly and begin his personal tour of Derrick Wellinger's land.

A few minutes later, Lance's footsteps had taken him to the edge of the crops. Thanks to his full belly, he wasn't tempted to take so much as a leaf from the cabbages. It helped that the rows of cabbages, corn, and squash looked healthy enough. But as Lance approached the edge of the crops near the home-stead, he frowned. Tomato vines hung near the house, but the vines look wilted. Some of the wooden poles that held the vines were cracked and worn.

And as he studied the homestead, the signs of disrepair loomed even larger. The house's siding was frayed and cracked in places. Additionally, the roof was missing a few shingles. Lance was no expert at farming or ranch maintenance, but he still had picked up a few tips on how to properly maintain up a farm property. And so far, the Wellinger farm was mostly good, but not great by any means.

But does it really matter? Lance took a step back-ward. *This place still is growing crops. I could live here if I had to.*

"Hey, man!" George called from behind him. Lance turned around. The jovial George was tromping up to Lance. "Taking a look at Mister Wellinger's land? Pretty good, right?"

Lance turned around. "Yeah," he said.

"Well, time to head back to the pen." George pointed to the fenced infield behind them. "Kendall just came in. Derrick's a couple of minutes away."

Lance turned around. "And then we get our jobs?"

"You bet." George playfully slapped Lance on the back of his shoulders. Lance winced. George was friendly, but he could make someone's skin burn from his friendly slaps.

George led Lance back to the other men, now numbering seven in all, including Lance and George. A moment later, someone new approached from the path leading from the road. Everyone cut their chatter short. Lance leaned out a little further to take a look at the newcomer.

With his short blond hair, smooth skin, and easy-going walk, he betrayed no signs of middle age. His build was stocky, and as he got closer, Lance could see he had blue eyes. He wore a white cowboy hat, buttoned-up blue shirt and jeans. His clothing had some dust on it, but didn't look too dirty.

George pulled open the gate, allowing Derrick Wellinger into the field. Once inside the fence's boundaries, Derrick slowed his pace while taking a good look at everyone. His gaze sent a slight charge down Lance's spine. The way Derrick looked at everyone felt like a mix of pride and entitlement, as if a king had come to inspect his subjects, being pleased to see them, while expecting their obeisance.

Even so, Derrick looked like a guy who would command admiration. He had that square-jawed look that resembled the visage of Western cowboys or soldiers from old movies. He wasn't very rugged, though. Almost all of the men here sported some kind of facial hair. No surprise, as priorities such as finding food overtook things such as shaving. Derrick's face, however, was smooth.

"Well, look at all of you. Some of you probably came from just down at the corner. I bet a few more of you had to hike all the way here from one end of the state or the other. If you're here, it means you don't have a chance anywhere else." He crossed close to Lance.

"Maybe some of you were shut out. They wouldn't spare a crumb or two for you guys. There are other mouths to feed, and you, well, I guess you can last a little longer without a meal. I bet that's what they told you." Derrick stopped and turned to pan over all the men. "Well, gentlemen, your time finally has come."

Then he walked to a spot in the middle where he could be seen easily by all of them. The sun shone over his white hat, making it partially glow near the top. "This world only will offer what we can take, and there's one hell of a prize waiting for us. There's a homestead..." Derrick pointed over their shoulders, toward the road. "...a short distance that way. We won't need bikes to get there. It's got crops and animals that can feed you all until you're old and pissing in your diapers. The rows are dug, the plants are growing, and we can keep harvesting seeds to keep the crops going year after year. And it's going to belong to all of us!"

A few of them smiled. Some nodded. Derrick paused to let it sink in.

"But first we must serve an eviction notice on the current owner. You heard right. There's only one person living there. His name is Conrad Drake. I know him well. He's an old man with no family. He's a know-it-all. A loner. He's got nobody. And in this new world, it's not like he's going to get a call from old friends or a cousin or whoever cares even to remember him. Naah, he won't be missed."

Lance swallowed. Was Derrick talking about killing this Conrad guy? Sure, Lance was desperate, but he didn't picture killing another human being. And yet, another part of him actually seemed quite okay with that idea. After all, there were six other men here. Odds are one of them would off Conrad before Lance even got to the front door.

"It's going to be easy. Shooting fish in a barrel. He's just one man. And if any of you are a little concerned about putting your ass on the line anyway, I'll make sure I'm the first thing he sees." Derrick smiled. "I've got a few things I want to drill into old Conrad's head before I drill a bullet into it."

That last comment drew laughter and chuckles.

"So, what do you all say?" Then he raised a fist. "This is us! This is our moment! The world may have burned down around us, but we're going to live like kings until the day we die!"

The men began cheering loudly. Then Derrick pulled out his gun and fired a few rounds into the air.

"Yeah, that's what I want to hear!" he shouted, "So today, we saddle up. We'll go in and take it for ourselves! It's our land now!"

Lance's heart quickened. At last! Not only would he eat, he never would have to worry about food again. His only regret was that Rod and all those who had doubted Lance wouldn't be here to see him enjoy his great success.

CHAPTER TWELVE

IN THE MOMENT when Conrad laid eyes on Sarah, it seemed time had snapped backward three decades. No, it spiraled backward even longer than that. For a moment, Conrad saw a vision of a young Sarah Sandoval in her twenties flashing before his eyes, and it wasn't hard to see why. While the woman standing before him showed her age, with her graying hair and deepening skin under her eyes, her cheeks remained smooth and her body was fit. Conrad even forgot that they weren't married any longer. The divorce somehow had disappeared in the limbo of pleasant memory.

Sarah seemed just as awed by his presence. Conrad didn't doubt she never expected to see him again. Was she astonished that, despite their acrimonious parting, that he had come to save her? Perhaps she was amazed to see his face again at all.

Conrad remembered words from their past. *"So,*

what do you think, Sarah? A nice house out in the country-side, a place to open the front doors and let the breeze in without sucking in car fumes?"

Sarah would laugh in response. *"Sounds like the hill-billy in you is coming out again. Sounds great for a week, Conrad, but I wouldn't want to live out there."*

"Hillbilly." It was Sarah's nickname for Conrad, due to his background. At first, Conrad took it with good humor. After all, Conrad couldn't deny his home was rustic, and that his family was rambunctious, even uncivilized. However, in time, it started grating on him. Perhaps it was one of the early signs that things were going south for the two of them.

Still, in the thirty years after they split, Conrad sometimes had wished to hear Sarah's hillbilly jibes again.

"Conrad!" Tom shouted. "Sarah! C'mon, get your asses in gear! Why are you standing around?"

Sarah shook, as if Tom's voice had pulled her out of a deep mental limbo. "Tom?" She turned around, finally getting a good view of Tom. "Tom!"

Tom nodded while letting out a laugh. "C'mon, Sarah! We're getting you all out of here!"

Tom's call also had caught the attention of the other nine women. By now, Conrad himself had returned to reality. He waved toward Tom while shouting, "Run, ladies! Run to that man over there! Go!"

Some of the captives already were rushing toward Tom. Conrad's call provided the needed motivation for the rest to hurry. Conrad, however, wasn't ready to bail just yet. He reached down and snatched a rifle from one of the men he had taken out with a taser.

Sarah remained. "Conrad?"

"We'll need some firepower." Conrad stood up with the rifle. "God knows how many men will be on our tail." Then he pushed the weapon into her hands. "Take it. Go, now!" Sarah nodded as Conrad hurried to the henchman Tom had taken out with his weapon.

"Alright," she said. She turned and fled toward Tom's position.

Conrad's instincts told him to flee, but there was one more downed man to relieve of his gun, the one he had shot. They'd need all the firepower they could gather just to make it out of Redmond.

As he slung the two rifles over his shoulder, he heard a man shouting, "Hey! Where the hell are you going?" Conrad turned and found Jack gesturing to the women headed toward Tom. "Get your asses back here!"

A guttural moan drew Conrad's attention down to the concrete by his boot. Marco laid nearby. He fought to speak amid erratic breathing. "Damn... Jack...cares...only...women..."

Conrad had no time to digest what Marco could be talking about. For a moment, he contemplated finishing off Marco and sparing him further suffering. *No*, he thought. *Get Sarah out of here. Forget about them.* Besides, he didn't want to make himself too comfortable with killing. This bastard probably didn't have long to live in any case.

"Dammit! I need men over here!" Jack turned back to the warehouse. In the distance, a pair of men dashed around the far corner. Conrad picked up speed toward the crowd of women who just had reached Tom's position. Gunfire would be headed their way, and soon.

In a half-minute, he had reached Tom. Sarah was there, staring at a relieved Tom.

"Sarah," he said, "baby, you're here."

Sarah reached out and hugged him, but not too deeply. She pulled back a little. Clearly, she was happy, but the reality of Tom surrendering her must have eaten at her the whole time she was in captivity. Indeed, she parted from him quickly, more so than Tom expected, for he seemed disappointed that her embrace didn't last.

Conrad didn't have time to ponder it further. A loud gunshot smacked into one of the nearby barrels. He fished one of the rifles off his shoulder. Three men near the warehouse were aiming their rifles at them, with Jack shaking his arm in the direction of Conrad and the women.

"Shoot the men! Stop those bastards!" Jack screamed. "I want the women back, now!"

Conrad turned his rifle and fired a few rounds back in their direction. By now the women had gathered behind Tom and Sarah. "C'mon, make tracks!" Conrad shouted. As he approached Tom, he slammed a rifle against his arm. "Good shooting. Now let's see how you do with this."

Tom quickly handed Sarah his gun. "Here." She took it, not expressing any outward happiness at seeing him, instead just nodding.

Conrad hurried to the front of the pack. "Alright, ladies, stay close behind us! Any one of you get too far out by yourself, it's your hide!" He picked up the pace as the end of the warehouse property was in sight.

But then two more men approached from the edge of the lot, one with a shotgun, another with an assault rifle. The women suddenly stopped. Conrad, thinking fast, turned and emptied several rounds into the man with the assault rifle. However, the man with the shotgun was too far away, and able to spin around and turn his sights on Conrad. He might have nailed Conrad, too, if another shot hadn't felled him in time.

Conrad turned and looked over his shoulder. Sarah was holding the rifle, her fingers around the trigger. Then she began shaking, as if she just realized what she had done. Tom, next to her, reached out and took her shoulder.

"Easy, Baby. Take her down," he said.

Sarah lowered her gun. Conrad couldn't help but feel guilty. Taking a life was the one thing he had dreaded for a long time. Sarah probably didn't even have a moment to think about what she'd do until she did it.

Thank God, Conrad thought. *She saved my life. But she'll be shook up. Hell, she'll be shook up from a lot of things.*

"Come on." Conrad started off at the head of the pack. "We got to keep going."

————

"HEY!" Jack waved to Ira. He had caught his attention as he emerged from the west side of the warehouse. "Get over here!" Jack already had gathered four other men and had begun pursuing the women when he spotted Ira. He wanted all the men he could find to hunt down the women and drag them back.

"Jack! What's the deal?" yelled a skinny man in a dirty green T-shirt. Ira held onto his weapon as he jogged down the parking lot, sweat flying off in all directions.

"We've been hit," replied Jacob, a bald man with a glare that could melt iron. "They came in and stole the women."

Ira then turned back in the warehouse's direction, toward the west entrance, where Marco lay. "Hey. They iced Marco?" Marco's leg then slid a few inches. "He's alive!"

Jack grabbed Ira by the shoulder. "Forget him!" Jack's hold dragged Ira almost a foot. "He's as good as dead. We're going to recover the women. Now let's go!"

Jack speed-walked toward the end of the lot. He was mad. Madder than he had been in a long time.

Who the hell was that old man who just came out of the warehouse? Who was his friend who shot at them?

This was my moment, he fumed to himself. Maggiano's dead. He had left Marco to die in that burning room, only for him to survive, but then to take a bullet, so he was nothing to worry about. Jack should be at the top of the Maggiano empire. Instead, his grand prize was abruptly ripped out of his hands. But who the hell would come rescue these women? Jack would have expected the U.S. Army, or perhaps a resurgent National Guard or even a new police force. But how many did he spot? Just two?

"Binoculars," he called. "One of you has to have them. Look down the street!"

One of the men, Laird, pulled off a pair from his belt and looked through them. "Down there!" he pointed. "Yeah, they're headed toward the Riard Buildings!"

"Good." Jack quickened his pace. "Let's go!"

———

CONRAD DIDN'T BOTHER with niceties in opening the office door. A couple of rounds from Conrad's gun blasted the lock free of the doorframe. Then he kicked the door fully open. Conrad, Tom, Sarah and the other nine women had retreated to this small office, as Conrad and Tom had planned. Now it was time to grab their supplies and get out of the warehouse district.

"Alright, ladies, I hate to ask for this, but I need a couple of pack mules." Conrad pointed inside with the muzzle of his gun. "I got a backpack in there, it's the heaviest. I need someone to grab it and carry it. Tom's got one, too. It's lighter. Hurry!"

Two women quickly dashed past Conrad—one Caucasian and red-haired, another African American and short-haired—and took up the packs. "Alright, Tom and I are going to keep the fire off us!" Rifle raised, Conrad hurried to the rear of the party. They had outdistanced the gunfire, but stopping like this would let their pursuers close the gap, and quickly.

The two women hurried out of the office with the packs. At the same time, a gun round struck the building high up near the roof. A few of the women shrieked. Conrad squinted. "Where are you bastards?" he whispered.

A few shapes approached, difficult to see from this distance. There were three, no, make that four of them, all clutching rifles like the ones Conrad had recovered. Conrad aimed and fired off a few rounds in their direction. They quickly slowed and ran toward the nearest cover.

By now the party now was in full retreat from the office building, down the street that would lead to the end of the warehouse district. Conrad turned and hurried after them.

"Conrad!" Sarah shouted from the middle of the pack.

"Keep going!" Conrad called, "I'm your cover! And don't scatter!"

Conrad kept a rear-guard action as they passed warehouse after warehouse. When he thought their pursuers were getting too close, he opened fire again.

I can keep them jumping, but I can't keep this up forever, Conrad thought. *I'm not a spring chicken, and these ladies aren't exactly in tip-top shape. I've got to lose them.*

He was so lost in his thoughts that he nearly smacked into a barrel. A familiar odor grabbed his nostrils. He found a small round cap and turned it, then pulled it off. Red liquid splashed inside. Diesel fuel!

He looked up and found they were on the grounds of another warehouse, half the size of Maggiano's, but that had some of the same trappings, with a forklift, a red service truck, and a few barrels. He quickly shoved one of them. Empty. He kicked a second one. Again, empty. Perhaps this lot had been raided and this barrel got overlooked.

Probably some lazy son of a bitch didn't care to check these too carefully. Conrad pushed the barrel over, letting the fuel pour out onto the concrete. *Lucky for us.*

Tom stopped. The rest of the women slowed their pace. "Conrad, what are you doing?" Tom shouted.

"Making us some cover. Keep moving!" As the

fuel flowed, Conrad dug into his jacket. He kept some matches handy so he could see in darkness.

He pulled one out, then struck it hard against the side of the barrel. Finally, he flicked the burning match into the fuel.

The small flame quickly grew tall and wide. Conrad ran as fast as he could. The flame raced down the slick of fuel, creating a small wall of fire behind them. As Conrad approached the group of liberated captives, the fire, along with the accompanying smoke, now was tall enough to cover their escape

———

"WHAT THE HELL?" Jacob called out as he and the rest of Jack's force spotted the flames up ahead. The group quickly slowed their pace. With the wall of flames ahead, it now was impossible to catch any sight of the fleeing captives.

Ira coughed. "Damn," he said.

"Where the hell did that come from?" Laird covered his mouth with his arm.

Jack stopped. "They went this way. We got to keep moving!"

"We're going to have cut around, get to Sam's Boulevard on the other side," Jacob said. By now the fire had cut fully across the street. "There's no way we can make it through that blaze."

"Damn!" Jack let loose a string of epithets into

the sky. This would delay them, badly. That old codger probably set this fire somehow to block them.

Jack turned toward a set of office buildings. The alley through the two structures would lead to Sam's Boulevard "I am not letting them go. Those women are mine," he repeated over and over again.

CHAPTER THIRTEEN

CARLA PUSHED OPEN the outside door to the kitchen, permitting Liam and Camilla through. The trio's clothes were dirty and reeked. "Now that is how you milk a goat," Camilla said while clutching a small metal pail full of milk. She set it down next to Conrad's wood burning stove. "See? You're a newbie at farming, aren't you? Well, you learn something new every day."

Liam wiped fresh sweat off his face. "Well, that was definitely an experience. I had no idea goats had to be pregnant before you could milk them."

"I wonder if Conrad knows Lacey's expecting?" Camilla patted Carla on the shoulder. "It's a regular baby boom on this ranch, isn't it? People, goats. Hell, I wonder if any of the sheep are expecting."

Carla stretched her arms. "Maybe we can ask them tomorrow." She leaned against the back wall. "I am absolutely beat."

"I am, too, but I'm sure there's more to do around here before the sun goes down," Liam said.

Camilla smiled. "Look, I think I've put you two through enough today. How about you two lovebirds hit the showers and get some sleep?" Then she sniffed loudly. "Besides, you really do need to change out of those clothes."

"Sure, I...Damn, I forgot the plumbing doesn't work anymore," Liam said. "Dad said he has his own well. Carla, I'll go find some buckets to fill up the tub."

"Why?" Camilla asked, "You don't need to draw the water yourself. Conrad installed his own pump and pipe systems."

Carla's eyes widened. "Wait, we have running water?"

"I guess you two didn't receive the grand tour when you showed up here," Camilla said with a grin.

"We were pretty much in a hurry," Liam replied.

"Today's full of surprises for you two, isn't it? But anyway, yeah, Conrad put in a pump in his well, plus he has his own cistern tank outside to collect rainwater. You can turn the faucet and fill up the tub. Just don't go hog wild with it. It's not like you can fill her up and take a bubble bath." Camilla laughed. "You'll be fine. Plus, you can drain out the dirty water when you're done."

Liam shook his head. "Amazing."

Carla sighed. "A shower. Oh God, I didn't even think I'd get one ever again. Liam, can I go first?"

"Hey, the tub's big enough for both of you, am I right?" Camilla then playfully swatted Liam on his arm.

Liam, in turn, smiled. "I think we both want to take it easy for a while. Sure, Carla, go in first."

———

CAMILLA LOOKED in the direction of the room Liam and Carla stayed in. The thought of what those two might be up to put a smile on her face. It even made her feel young again.

Then she strolled up to her bag, still lying on the sofa. She felt compelled to dig out one of her old photos tucked away in a small compartment. After fishing the photograph out, she gazed at it with fresh eyes. Camilla Pitzo, age thirty-four, stared back at her. Her face was free of age lines, her cheeks seemed to glisten in the sun, with a little help from makeup. Her blonde hair was lighter, frizzier, and flowed longer down her shoulders. But the most striking difference was young Camilla's clothing. She wore a long brown business skirt and jacket over a white blouse. Behind her lay the skyscrapers of the Queens borough of New York City. This Camilla worked in bank offices and later, a prestigious trading company.

"You sure have come a long way," she whispered to the image in her hand. It was true. For a time, Camilla was part of the city lifestyle. She had worn enough nylon stockings and skirts to last a lifetime.

Not unlike Conrad, she thought. *Well, minus the nylon and skirts*.

Camilla had seen the pictures of Conrad in his days in the city. Sometimes she thought their histories were a sign that they were meant to meet each other. Both shared common backgrounds, with Camilla and Conrad spending their young adult years in urban settings before heading out to the countryside to begin new lives. Camilla, though, had lived in the city longer than Conrad had, which was probably why she never truly put down roots after that. She spent her late thirties and beyond bouncing between five states. Basically, she had become a nomad.

Camilla put the photo away. The past had to tend to itself for now. The concerns of the present and the future beckoned to her. She had more reason to push Liam and Carla off to a shower and bed. She wanted time to herself, to prepare. She had been nursing fears about what could hit this homestead for too long. Tonight, she would prepare.

Her boots made loud thumps on the wooden floorboards as she marched down the hall, all the way to the end, until she hit a closed door. This door possessed two locks. Conrad had good reason to keep the basement secure. Camilla pulled out her set of keys and turned each lock.

Damn, I hoped it wouldn't get this bad, she thought.

She grasped the door and pulled on it. The door was hard to budge. Without a working air conditioner, the heat caused the wood to expand. Or maybe Conrad wanted the door to be hard to open.

Once she yanked the door fully open, Camilla proceeded down a set of stairs into the yawning darkness of the basement. She set her lantern down on a small table, the light of the lamp showing off a collection of weapons on the walls. Conrad had turned his basement into an armory.

Camilla thought back to when she first saw this basement. It was only half as loaded as it was now, but the sight had surprised her. Conrad explained that if society should break down, there'd be nobody coming in to save his hide if things got desperate. Anything could happen. Factions of the country could go to war with each other. Enemy countries might seize the opportunity to invade the United States. Or desperate folks would band together to take over properties that were growing food.

I guess nothing will surprise me now, she thought as she started counting the guns. As she got up to ten weapons, she chuckled. *Damn, you couldn't have expected to use all these yourself.* Obviously, he couldn't expect to buy new guns at a gun store if a catastrophe struck, but Camilla wondered if Conrad expected to take in wards. Conrad acted as if he expected to be alone, but Camilla pondered if that was truly the case.

"Maybe you hoped someone would come along. Someone young. Someone to carry on after you've gone," she muttered to herself.

She pictured an ancient Conrad, his gray hair lying against his shoulders, age spots covering his arms and face, his robust face now sunken in. He would just be sitting in the easy chair in the living room with no strength left to fend for himself. Instead, he'd just sit there and die. The house would remain locked up unless someone discovered it and broke it open, finding Conrad's decayed body.

Camilla picked up a magazine. "What a horrible way to go," she whispered as she clutched the magazine. Compared to a lonely, aged death, dying on one's feet with a gun in hand seemed much better.

Of course, Camilla didn't necessarily want that, either. And with Liam and Carla under this roof, she vowed that wouldn't happen.

She chose that moment to look off to the rear wall of the basement. A giant steel door stood there, with a security access panel. This was Conrad's worst case scenario, his absolute last resort. When the chips were down, if he couldn't defend the homestead any longer, or if the environment had grown too hazardous, he would retreat here, open this door, and duck inside the shelter beyond. The access panel included both a PIN number and biometrics. There was ample food and water in there, enough for months.

Camilla chewed her lip. Being trapped in that shelter didn't appeal to her, either. She feared being cooped up in a tight space, not able to escape, just living there until all the supplies ran out or her body just gave up and died. In the years since she fled New York, she had grown to love the wide-open outdoors and couldn't stomach the thought of being enclosed for so long. No, she had to win the battle she feared would come.

She returned to counting the weapons and ammunition.

———

GEORGE SLAMMED the box down on the ground hard near Derrick's feet. "Here's your gear. I see you've already got your guns." George and Kendall then opened up the box, revealing several small backpacks.

"This will be about two-day journey," Derrick said as George and Kendall pulled out the packs. "We'll have to pitch camp at least once. Don't worry about provisions. We'll have more than enough to make it to Conrad's ranch."

George and Kendall passed the packs around to the men. Lance eagerly unzipped his, finding a water canteen, a few extra magazines, and a piece of dark wool cloth. He pulled it out and unfolded it. There were a few holes in it. He stuck his finger through one of them. The holes were oval shaped.

He then turned and noticed Cal slipping the cloth over his head. Lance got it. These were ski masks. Actually, they looked like masks armed thugs on television or in movies would wear.

Cal then turned in Lance's direction. "Pretty sweet, huh?" he asked.

Looking at it from the outside, Lance wasn't sure. "Yeah," he answered anyway.

"A little psychological warfare," Derrick said with a smile. "Covering your face, you don't look all that human." He made a fist and held it to his heart. "Instills a little fear, especially in superstitious old men. Of course, it's your choice if you want to put them on."

Ethan, one of the youngest men besides Lance, slipped on his mask and laughed. "Check this out," he said with a laugh. Then he coiled his fingers as if he was holding a gun and made shooting sounds.

As Lance let his mask drop into his bag, Sandy passed by. "Shouldn't be so damn eager to get into a gunfight," he said quietly, "They don't know what it's like to shoot somebody. Bet most of these men only shot anything playing their computer games."

Lance looked up at him. "You don't sound like you want to get into a gun battle yourself. Why are you coming along?"

Sandy looked to the road stretching forth into the horizon. "'Cause I don't have a choice, kid. Not a man on this team does. You think I'd rip a man's property out of his fingers if I had any hope of feeding myself?" He looked at Derrick, who now was several yards away, talking with George and Kendall. "He's all we got. Personally, I just won't care what we got to do next. So, if you got a conscience, son, you better bail while you can."

Sandy then plodded in Derrick's direction. The other men started to take up their backpacks. Lance gazed at the mask one more time. Was he sure he wanted to do this?

His stomach then growled. Quickly, Lance found a small set of crackers wrapped in plastic and pulled them free.

Don't be stupid, he thought as he opened up the crackers and chomped on them. Of course he would.

CHAPTER FOURTEEN

MARCO'S KNEES wobbled as his weakened legs struggled to support his weight. Not a soul was around. He had been lying there on the concrete while the women fled and Jack rounded up the remaining men to go hunt them down. None of the guys, not a single one, had gone back to check on him. They all had left him for dead.

He clutched his upper right shoulder. The bullet must have penetrated clear through. He rubbed his fingers. Blood, but not a lot. He peered down on the ground. A few splatters of blood. Nothing major.

Suddenly, he gasped for air. God knows what that bullet did to him. Without a working hospital to x-ray the wound and provide treatment, he might be dying for all he knew.

He staggered forward. No, the warehouse. He had to get in there. Break open some of the medical supplies they had stowed away in there. If he just could plug this damn hole in his shoulder, maybe shoot some antibiotics, he'd be able to heal.

And then when Jack comes back, I'll bury a bullet in him so deep he won't recover, he thought.

Still, each step was laborious. It seemed as though it'd take forever to reach the warehouse's west entrance.

Then, a low growl stopped him in his tracks. He turned. A trio of dogs was approaching slowly from the left side of the lot.

"Dogs?" he whispered, "Why the hell now?" Then he remembered. The sentries usually would frighten away strays with gunshots. But now there was no one around guarding the warehouse. The lot was still.

As the dogs closed in, Marco could make out the drool on their lips. *Holy shit! This is a feral bunch. My gun. Where's my gun?*

He raised his hands. They were empty. He must have dropped his gun somewhere. He looked around. The concrete was bare. Did one of the guys take his gun, assuming he was as good as dead?

"Son of a bitch," he said.

Now he had no choice but to run for the warehouse. But he didn't progress more than an anguished few steps before the dogs raced toward him, barking loudly. Marco's hand was a few steps too far from the door handle when the first dog jumped on top of him.

If Marco had not been wounded, he might have had a chance. Instead, he instantly was pinned to the concrete. A dog's teeth sank deeply into his neck, severing his jugular vein.

It would not be until more than a day later when another human being would approach the warehouse to discover the savaged corpse on the ground once known as Marco Valentino.

———

CONRAD GLANCED over his shoulder again. No, still no pursuers, although with all the building corners, fences, stalled vehicles and wooden utility poles, it wasn't hard to imagine that stalkers could be on their trail. Maggiano may well have ordered his men to track them and keep at a safe distance until Conrad's party decided to take a rest. Maggiano's goon squad would then move in.

"Hey," the young lady beside him said, "You need me to keep watch for you?"

Conrad turned to her. "If you wouldn't mind helping out an old man. What's your name?"

"Rachel." The woman seemed to be in her early thirties. She was dressed in a white shirt and red shorts. "I just don't want to, you know, keep my back turned. I don't feel safe."

Conrad nodded. God only knew what these women had been through, and some of their behavior had unnerved him. Some of them were withdrawn, twitching, even muttering to themselves occasionally. "I understand that," he said. "If you see anything, holler. I'll see if I can steer us to someplace where you all can take shelter."

Rachel turned so her head was looking more to the side. "I will. And, thanks for saving us."

"No problem," Conrad replied.

Conrad hiked up to the head of the pack, where Tom was leading. It amused Conrad that, for once, Tom was the man in charge, after Conrad had spent this whole endeavor coaxing Tom along. But for the moment, it made sense. Conrad wanted Tom to lead them out of Redmond's warehouse district back to the business district, where Conrad, Tom, Liam and Carla had found the stores raided by Maggiano's men, and Tom knew this city well. Those stores had been gathering places for refugees until they were attacked and the women kidnapped. Although Conrad had recovered Sarah, he could not leave these ladies alone in this ruined wasteland that had once been a thriving city.

If I have to, I will lead all these women back home, he thought, but it was a grim proposition to make the journey home with this many survivors. A group this size would make for a slower trek, plus they would be more easily spotted by bandits, looters, or simply the desperate. From what little he had got out of the ladies thus far, many, if not all, of them were Redmond residents. One of them even voiced a desire to go back home and see if any of her relatives had gone there looking for her.

He slowed his pace as he approached Tom and

Sarah. Sarah walked a step or two behind Tom. Conrad kept quiet as he studied them. At first, Sarah had expressed joy at being rescued, but as time passed her euphoria had melted away into a bit of a scowl. There was unfinished business here between these two. Hell, there was unfinished business between her and Conrad, but Conrad had no desire to pick that old scab.

Conrad tilted his head so he wouldn't be looking at Sarah. *I've been on the receiving end of that look*, Conrad thought. He pitied Tom, although Tom had surrendered Sarah to Marco, so at least he deserved it. But since the pair weren't saying anything, Conrad felt free to speak up.

"So, what do you think, Tom? Got any place in mind? The sun's headed down and we don't have a lot of time left."

They were approaching a city intersection. Tom slowed a bit. "The only place I can think of that Maggiano didn't hit is Tao's Laundromat. They were definitely taking in survivors to help them find food and medicine." He pointed to the street on the left side. "It's several blocks that way. If fortune's smiling on us, there will be people there to help us."

"Well, I guess you can keep playing the leader for a while." Conrad chuckled.

Sarah eyed Tom with a smirk. Tom frowned. "What?"

"Nothing." Sarah looked away. "Nothing. It's just a bit of a surprise. You show up gun totting, and now you're like Moses leading us to the Promised Land."

Tom swallowed. "Yeah."

"I'm just curious what's changed," she said icily.

Tom's muscles in his right arm tightened. "I had a bad mistake to correct. Horrible, horrible mistake." He sighed. "The worst mistake I ever made in my life."

Sarah kept on looking ahead. She didn't add anything. So, Tom continued. "I'm sorry," he said. "Marco's men had those guns on me, and I didn't know what to do. So, I ended up taking the coward's way out."

Again, Sarah said nothing. Clenching a fist, Tom spoke up again. "I don't expect instant forgiveness. I get that. But I do care for you. And if I had to get my ass blown away out there for you, then that's how it would have gone."

Sarah's face tightened a little. "Well, maybe you should keep that in mind next time."

"Sarah, the choice wasn't staring me in the face back then. Guns were. We could have been both dead by now. Giving you up was a horrible thing to do, but you must admit it may have saved us both."

Sarah opened her mouth to protest, but Tom quickly jumped in by adding, "I'm not defending myself. Believe me, I deserve it. I deserve you being pissed at me. I just don't want you to close the door on...on us. We don't have anything else left. I don't even think my home is left. It's probably burned to the ground like so much else around here."

It was a short while before Sarah talked again. "So, what happened? You went to Conrad to rescue me?"

Tom swallowed. "Well, it's a little more complicated than that."

"He did find us," Conrad said quickly. "He told us where you were. He's the reason you're free."

Sarah frowned. "Really?" She slowed up, allowing herself to approach Conrad. "So, what'd he do? Leave Redmond to go find you? That's one hell of a journey without a car."

"We rode bikes, actually," Conrad replied, "It's become oddly popular nowadays for some reason. Maybe it's the newest fad." He stared at a stalled car on the road as he spoke. "Actually, you can thank Liam for getting the ball rolling."

"Oh God, what am I thinking? I didn't even ask about Liam!" Sarah grasped a lock of her hair in front and clutched it tightly. "What happened? Is he alright?"

"He's fine, Sarah," Conrad replied. "He came here with me, but I sent him back to my place. This was my call and Tom's. I made sure Liam and Carla would be as safe as possible."

"Carla, too." Sarah bowed her head. "My Liam," she whispered. "If anything happened to him it wouldn't matter a damn if I escaped. So, he went to you?"

Conrad nodded. "He came to me...to find you. He felt I was the only one he could turn to who could get you out of this city. But we didn't learn about Maggiano until we got here. I made sure Liam and Carla returned to my home before we went any farther."

Sarah bowed her head. "Then they're all safe. Thank you."

———

LANCE FISHED his fingers back through the straps of his backpack. He had been pushing them in and out several times during this long hike down the road. His hands still instinctively went for his pocket to pull out the smart phone that was no longer there. Before the solar event erupted, Lance alleviated his boredom by pulling out his phone and sticking his buds into it to listen to music, or texting his buddies. Even though he knew he never again would listen to streaming or electronically recorded music, he couldn't help himself. Every now and then he'd still expect his phone to be there, to work for him.

But now all he could do was walk. Sweat dribbled down the sides of his head. The day was warm, and ordinarily Lance would be miserable as hell, but Derrick's promise of food and shelter raised his spirits. He knew this trip would not be for nothing.

And judging from the generally contented looks on the other men, they seemed to believe so as well.

All of them except two were younger men. The two exceptions—Sandy and Teller—sported white hair and walked with a slower gait. None of them appeared to be overweight. Like Lance, the harsh new world had deprived them of anything but the bare essentials to survive.

Sandy's comment about ditching the party if he had a conscience still nagged at him a little. After all, if this Conrad Drake saw all of them coming, surely he'd agree to hand over his ranch in exchange for his life. It would be stupid not to do so. Hell, Lance would do it without a second thought.

He was so wrapped up in his thoughts that he didn't notice he was walking too fast—and nearly ran smack into the back of Derrick.

Gasping, Lance slowed his pace. He hoped Derrick hadn't noticed him.

"Someone's eager to get to the Promised Land, aren't they?" Derrick suddenly asked without turning his head.

Goosebumps popped all over Lance's arms. "I...I guess so."

"I know how you feel," Derrick said. "You're from around here, aren't you? Or are you from out of state?"

"No," Lance replied. "No, I was born in Lincoln."

"Gotcha. What's your name?"

"Lance Wilkins," Lance replied.

"Lance." Derrick grinned. "Solid name. A lance is actually the name of a sharp weapon. It's a kind of spear that knights used when they charged into battle. I guess that's why you're here. It's like a good luck charm."

The back of Lance's ears burned. "Thanks."

"Mister Wellinger." Kendall pointed to the horizon. A small town loomed closer.

"Yeah, I see it." Derrick looked up at the sky. The sun was approaching the horizon. "Better start setting up camp," he said. "Still got a day or two before we reach Conrad's ranch."

The whole party came to a stop. George pulled out the tent from his pack and started setting it up. Lance felt a little better about this job. A good luck charm? No one, not even his parents, ever had called him that before or paid him such a compliment. More than ever, Lance felt sure Derrick Wellinger was the man to lead them to their salvation.

CHAPTER FIFTEEN

THE ORANGE GLOW several blocks over only added to Conrad's worries. The sun finally had set. The city had awakened from its day-long slumber. The arsonists, the looters, those who wanted to wreak havoc now that they were free of the prying eyes of law enforcement, all of them were about to have another night on the town.

Conrad turned back to Tom at the head of their traveling party. "Tom, I hate to be a busybody, but this town's about ready to show its ugly side."

Tom huffed. He had been trekking onward for a while without a break, as had all of them. They just couldn't go much faster. In fact, they were slowing up as some of the women complained of callused feet and exhaustion. "I know," Tom said. Sarah was clinging to his arm to support him. "But we're almost there."

Tom then handed Sarah his gun. "Here," he said,

"just in case. If there's anybody in there, this time no one's taking you."

She nodded. "Thanks," she said.

By now the party had crossed a street and was approaching Tao's Laundromat. It was an old building with an old wooden sign over the glass doors. Every letter on the sign was likely a dark red, but now had faded to a light pink.

"This is it." Tom staggered up the concrete steps. "Last contact I know of." He approached the doors, which were covered with wooden boards. There was no way to know who was in there, if anybody at all.

"Hey!" Tom shouted in a hoarse voice. "We need help!"

Conrad raised his arm. "Okay, we can stop now!" The women were all too happy to hear that, giving out loud gasps as they halted.

Tom knocked on the door. "Hey! We have...we have women in need! We escaped Maggiano's hideout. Do you have any water, medicine?"

All of a sudden, the door opened and a bearded man popped out, gun drawn. "What the hell are you all doing out here at night. You—" The bearded man then spotted the ladies with Conrad. "Son of a bitch. You're not lying."

"Yeah. We've been traveling all day. These women need shelter. We can talk bartering, anything, but get us inside first," Tom said.

The bearded man nodded. "Alright." He pushed the door open. "In, quick."

Conrad helped the tired, bedraggled group through the laundromat doors. The interior room, which would have housed washing machines, had been cleared to make room for tables and chairs, with boxes and a few beds lining the walls.

The bearded man watched as the women took the available seats. "All these women got free of Maggiano? How the hell did you manage this?"

"Two men with more brains than that lot put together." Conrad offered his hand. "We're very grateful. I'm Conrad Drake. This man here's Tom Richards."

"I'll be damned." The man grasped Conrad's hand. "Todd Shannon. I used to be an insurance salesman. Now I'm the head of this little camp. It's a gathering point for whatever we can find. A lot of the other refuge points already have been taken out. So, we've been gathering bikes to ride out of here on. And if they're broken, we try fixing them."

"You have bikes?" Conrad asked.

"Sure do. Sadly, we got more bikes than people. Maggiano's offers for work were a lot sweeter than ours." Then he looked at the women around him. "And I guess you know he takes whatever else he wants."

"Tom, myself, and our friend Sarah, we all got a place to go to out of town. We could sure use a couple of bikes. I'm prepared to barter for them, but we've used up a lot of food and water already," Conrad said.

"Can you do a little repair job on some of our bikes? The more the merrier," Shannon said.

"I know a thing or too about fixing bikes," Tom said. "My mom was a little overprotective, but her boy never could keep his hands off his ten-speed."

Shannon led them to a back corner where a few old bikes lay propped against the wall. "Do your worst."

"What about clothes?" Conrad asked, "We're not too far from the edge of the city. I have an idea on how we can blend in."

Shannon pointed to a large box used to hold a new washing machine. Now it was overflowing with clothes. "Be my guest. But it'll cost you another repaired bike."

————

AN HOUR LATER, Shannon approached Conrad, who just had finished installing the chain on the bike's derailleur. "Got some good news. I've got some friends who are preparing a run out of the city. They've been moving bikes there for the past few days, and they're prepared to take these ladies with them."

"Where are you off to?" Conrad asked.

"Rumor has it there's a lot of farms out there that still are running. Maybe they can take some more refugees in." Shannon sighed. "I hate to say it, but maybe the cities will be safe after the crazies have killed each other off."

"With the diseases from the dead bodies and no sanitation, you'd be better off out in the countryside." Conrad climbed to his feet. He then turned the bike's front wheel. "It may be years before a city like this is reclaimed."

"Reclaimed? From who?" Jack spoke up as he suddenly marched through a side opening. The rest of his men stormed past and fanned out in the center of the room. "What's wrong with Redmond, old man? The king is here."

"Damn!" Tom raised his weapon, but he had a few rifles drawn on him. He stopped short of firing. Jacob, Ira, and Laird had rifles drawn, while one man wielded a knife and another a long baton.

"Sorry, but this party isn't going anywhere," Jack said, "I'm here to collect some lost friends."

"I saw you at the warehouse," Conrad said. "You're one of Maggiano's boys."

"I'm one of his colleagues," Jack said with a sneer. "Allies. An equal. And now I'm the guy in charge." Then he glanced at Tom. "You look familiar. I can't place you, but I feel like I bumped heads with you in the past."

"Tom Richards," Tom replied, "I helped your stores in town upgrade their network connections, back when that stuff mattered. Took a while for you to pay the invoice."

"Well, what can I say? I had my priorities. So, let's

talk about the women. You stole them from me. I want them back. If we agree, then..." Jack spread his arms. "No problems. We all live another day."

"Think again, friend," Conrad said, "These ladies aren't going back to your house of horrors. I suggest you find something a little more worthwhile to do with your time. I'm sure there are some barns out there that could use a pair of strong hands. I know some horses would appreciate it."

Jack chortled. "Who's this, Tom, your old man? Looks like a refugee from a bad Clint Eastwood film."

"Actually, he's a...a friend," Tom said. The last words seemed to surprise Tom as he spoke them.

"He's my..." Sarah stepped forward. "We were once married." She seemed both proud and ashamed at once, though Conrad didn't know exactly why. Perhaps she felt guilty over divorcing him?

Jack's face contorted in disgust. "Good God! You and that old fossil?" He then laughed. "Funny, you didn't look that old when I peeled off your outfit for Maggiano."

Tom twitched. "What?" he asked, calmly, but with an undercurrent of anger. Conrad bristled as well.

"Yeah, you don't know how we do things in Maggiano's place. He likes to check out the ladies to make sure they'll satisfy his clients when they come calling. Especially now, men just need a, a release." His eyes narrowed as he gazed at Sarah. "Of course, I do my best to help out. I'm an expert at fashioning clothes that lift all the right assets. You should have seen the pants I got for her. Lifted her ass in all the right places..."

Tom's skin turned red. He lunged forward, but the men behind Jack shoved their rifles forward. Tom stopped in his tracks.

"Easy, tough guy." Jack grinned. "Your blood will be painting your lady friend if you're not careful."

"You son of a bitch. What did you do to Sarah?" Tom asked, quivering.

"Cool it, Tom. Don't worry," Sarah said, "just pull back."

Tom did step back, just a little. Jack chuckled. "Just as I thought. Not much of a tough guy, huh?"

"You've got a small army behind you," Tom said. "Why don't you lose them and we'll see who's a tough guy?"

"Sorry, but I'm the guy in charge now," Jack said.

"You're the guy in charge?" Conrad asked. "I'm sure Maggiano might not appreciate hearing that."

"Maggiano is dead!" Jack suddenly spun around and marched up to Conrad. "He's crushed beneath a bunch of rubble. I'm in control of his whole operation now!"

The bald man frowned. "Wait, Maggiano is dead?"

Jack turned to him. "What's the matter, you hard of hearing? Yes, he's dead. When we get back to the warehouse, you can find the flies over his fat-ass corpse in the front office!"

The bald man turned to his companion. The pair nodded, then they lowered their guns and walked toward the door. A third henchman followed.

Jack's mouth dropped open. "Hey. Hey! What the hell is this?"

A fourth man shouldered his gun and followed the procession to the door. Jack ran up to the bald man and grabbed him by the shoulder. "Where the hell are you going? Come back here!"

The man simply turned and looked at him. "We do what Maggiano wants. We don't give a shit about you. If Maggiano's dead, then we're out of here."

"See ya, Jack," said the third man.

"But..." Jack trembled. "I control the food! I control the guns! Without me you don't get shit!"

The fourth man then pointed the nozzle of his rifle in Jack's face. "You mean this gun?"

Jack's eyes widened. All he could say was an "Uh..."

The man then withdrew his weapon and walked out the door with the others. Jack slowly turned around, finding himself suddenly very outnumbered. Only two men remained with him, and they weren't even holding guns. One clutched a baton, the other a large knife.

"Looks like someone just got his ass fired as king of the city," Conrad said.

Jack trembled. He was trying to put on a good face, but wasn't succeeding very well. On the other hand, Tom knew the advantage was tilting in his favor, and he walked right up to Jack.

"Hey," Jack backed up so awkwardly he nearly fell against a table. "Don't listen to those assholes. I have connections. I know people. This city is mine. It's me or nothing."

Tom raised his arm. "No, Jack, *you* are nothing."

Then he slammed Jack hard in the face with his fist, sending him spiraling down onto the hard floor.

Coughing, Jack crawled to his knees. But Tom wasn't finished with him, grabbing Jack by his shirt and hoisting him to his feet. Blood trickled down Jack's nose.

"You owe Sarah and everyone here an apology," Tom said with a low hiss.

"Go to hell," Jack said, "They're all mine."

Jack then struck back, hitting Tom in the face. But Tom wasn't felled by the blow, and was able to punch back.

Meanwhile, the man with the baton raised his weapon, but Conrad stopped him cold with a rifle butt to the head. The man dropped hard onto the floor. That just left the man with the knife, but Conrad couldn't reach him. Fortunately, Sarah was ready with a folding chair, connecting it to the man's legs. The assailant went down, his knife flying out of his hands.

The man with the baton reached for his weapon, but Conrad raised his gun at his head. "Do yourself a favor. Get lost. And don't come around here again."

The man quickly nodded and ran out the door. Conrad raised his head just in time to witness Tom deliver a nasty blow to Jack's face. Conrad swore he saw a tooth fly out of Jack's mouth. Jack stumbled and fell to the floor. Tom grabbed a chair and raised it high.

"Tom!" Sarah rushed over to him and seized his arm. "Tom, hold up."

Jack was a bleeding, wheezing mess on the floor. He wasn't making any effort to stand up. Tom set the chair back down.

Conrad turned to Shannon. "Get some of your boys and haul him outside. Let him fend for himself."

————

SARAH TOOK the gray shirt from Conrad. "Okay, I'm sorry, can you explain this to me again?"

Conrad smiled. "It's called the gray man theory. When society goes into utter chaos, one way to avoid the calamity is to go unnoticed. You don't stand out. No one even looks at you." Then he pulled out a long green shemagh scarf. "And, by choosing these dark colors, moving slowly, and sticking to the building walls, we'll be more likely to go unnoticed."

"So, we're not waiting until morning?" Tom asked.

"We're too close to the open road. We need to get home." Conrad's eyes met Sarah's. "Liam's waiting for you, Sarah."

Sarah clutched her scarf near her chest. She blinked back tears.

"What about the bikes?" Tom pointed to the two

bicycles Shannon had agreed to give them. "They'll stick out."

Conrad reached down and picked up a dull green blanket. He then set it over the bikes. "What bikes?" he asked innocently.

Tom yawned. "Great trick, Conrad." He looked around the laundromat. Much of it was still now. The women were lying on floor or in the back, sound asleep, perhaps enjoying their first real rest in weeks. The only activity came from Shannon's men, who stood guard near the door or windows.

Conrad approached Tom and Sarah. "Hey. How about you two catch some sleep? I think you've all earned it."

"You, too, Conrad," Sarah said, "You're not staying up all night."

Conrad rubbed his back. Sarah's comments seemed to give his body permission to feel tired. Perhaps, knowing that he had freed Sarah, that he was finally on his way home, he would sleep well tonight.

CHAPTER SIXTEEN

CONRAD, his fingers on the handle of his new bike, took one last look at Tao's Laundromat. Todd Shannon and a few of the women Conrad and Tom had liberated waved to him as well as Tom and Sarah beside him. Conrad raised his hand and gave a salute. "Godspeed to you all," he said under his breath.

Sarah and Tom each held the bicycle they received from Shannon. It still was nighttime, but the dawn would break in a couple of hours. After the fight with Jack and his men, the three of them enjoyed a few hours sleep. Shannon informed them that he had people to keep watch in case Jack or any of his henchmen returned, but it seemed Jack's men were content to leave them alone and go off by themselves, now that they knew Maggiano was dead. Actually, the news had encouraged Shannon to work faster. Once news got around the city that Maggiano's grip on Redmond was gone, it only would encourage the seedier elements to run even wilder.

So, Conrad, Tom and Sarah made their way out of the laundromat in their new clothing. The noises and gunshots in the distance diminished as they walked the bikes through the streets, and even though the sun had yet to rise, Redmond had fallen quiet again.

"They're probably worn out," Conrad mused. "I guess you can have too much hedonism for one night."

After about an hour of a slow, careful trek down a few streets, they approached the outskirts of Redmond. A short hike would take them toward the state road that ran toward Conrad's homestead.

Sarah stopped. She turned and looked at her city. Even though it was quiet, whiffs of smoke still rose in the distance, and a few orange glows still burned. Her heart sank. There was no telling when those fires would burn out, if they would burn out before destroying more and more of the city.

"I know it's been a mess. I know it's all ruined," Sarah said, "but it's hard to think I may never come back here."

Tom took Sarah's arm and held it. "Yeah," he added.

Conrad glanced at Tom comforting Sarah. The strangest thing about this was that Conrad's own life hadn't changed a lot. Even though his home had been deprived of working electronics, he still had conditioned himself to live off the land. Tom and Sarah, however, would need to adjust everything in their everyday routines.

But they're going to survive, Conrad thought. *That's what's important.*

A soft wind blew through Conrad's gray hair. The weather was pleasant, but they couldn't be sure how long it would stay that way. Walking his bicycle, Conrad passed the couple to walk in front of them. "We'd better get moving. Home...Liam...Carla, they're waiting for us."

Tom got on his bike. Sarah mounted it, then held on tightly behind him. "All right Conrad. Now you get to be the leader. All the way."

Conrad took them forward, out of Redmond, and finally onto the state road that would lead them home.

———

LIAM'S FACE TWITCHED. Sunlight trickled through the window blinds. He turned to his side, brushing against the back of the warm body next to him. A thin sheet lay over them. Without air conditioning, having warm blankets on top of them during sleep was an invitation for a sweating fest at night.

He wiped his forehead. His skin felt damp. Well, they did have reason to sweat last night, though not because of any hot air.

Better enjoy it while it lasts, because you won't have

many nights like that when you're waking up for three a.m. feedings, he thought.

He rolled onto his back. The comfort of this bed made him dread the thought of getting up. Not only did he have a comfortable mattress under his back, but he wasn't expecting to be ambushed or attacked by marauders or psychopaths.

I wish Dad could say the same thing. Liam rubbed his eyes. Damn. Dad still was out there. Two nights had passed since Liam and Carla had made it back home. Liam wondered if Dad finally had rescued Mom. If so, it still would be a while before they showed up here.

I wonder if I can still camp out near the road? Liam thought. *Maybe I could be on the lookout for them.* He then glanced at the head of brown hair on the nearby pillow. No, he wasn't sure he could even trek a few miles away from her. Camilla's body language unnerved him. That woman was anticipating something out there.

Carla's eyes then opened a little. Liam's worries defused for the moment. He'd rather talk to this lovely lady.

"Hey," he said.

"Morning," she said. "What time is it?"

"I have no idea," Liam replied. His watch had stopped working. His dad did have some working clocks, but none were in this room.

"Then it's whatever time we want, and I say it's four in the morning, and we should go back to sleep."

Carla then grabbed the sheet and pulled it over her head.

Liam looked at the bright light through the window and chuckled. "Yeah, I don't think we can get away with that. It's probably closer to ten a.m. by now."

"I can't hear you." Carla spoke sing-songy.

Liam grabbed the sheet and yanked it off her. He did it so suddenly that she forgot to hang onto it, which allowed Liam to expose quite a bit of her.

Liam leaned over Carla's chest. "Well, I guess those will be mine for a while longer until Liam Junior arrives."

Carla laughed. "Who says we're naming the baby after you? And it could be a girl." Then she flicked Liam's nose.

"Good point. Guess we won't know for months," Liam said.

Carla inhaled deeply. "Hey, you smell something?"

Liam sniffed the air. "Something burning?" He turned to their closed bedroom door. "No, that smells like coffee."

"Someone's trying to get us up. No fair." Carla sat up. "We're being bribed with coffee."

"Must be Camilla." Liam slid off the bed and stood up. He reached for a robe hanging off the back of the door. "I can only imagine what she's been up to. I heard some noise last night. She was doing a bit of walking around."

Carla's head sank back into the pillow. "You go

ahead. I'm going to be a little while." She coughed. "Great. I hope I'm not going to start puking."

———

DERRICK LOWERED HIS BINOCULARS. "There she is."

He backed up a few steps toward his men. The whole group was waiting just off the side of the state road. Derrick just had brought the party to a halt so he could take a look. He felt they were closing in on Conrad's homestead, and wanted to stop so he could sight the place from a safe distance.

Derrick pulled off his binoculars. Approaching Lance, he offered his sighting instrument to the younger man. "Take a look for yourself," Derrick said.

Lance obeyed. He stepped up to where Derrick had been and looked through the glasses. The homestead was a one-story structure but fairly wide. It likely could host all of Derrick's men with room to spare. Lance also was struck by how much better it looked compared to Derrick's home. While the distance was pretty far, Lance could see that the siding and bricks appeared to be in good shape. The gutters were firmly attached and weren't broken in any place Lance could see. Likewise, the roof was well-shingled. It didn't seem that any of them were missing.

Then Lance tilted his view to the crops beyond. Now he really was impressed. The rows of corn, cabbage, and squash were bigger than Derrick's.

Conrad also had orchards on his property. The apples looked incredibly tasty to Lance.

He lowered the binoculars from his eyes. "It's great," he said.

Derrick then took the binoculars from him—a bit harshly, Lance thought. "Yeah, well, it's soon going to be ours. You can be impressed then."

Lance frowned. Derrick seemed pissed all of a sudden. Did Lance say something wrong?

Kendall and Teller started hiking toward the road, but Derrick quickly spoke up. "Hey! Hold up there. We're not headed for the road." He pointed to the fields between them and the Drake property. "We're going that way. These tall grasses will give us some cover. Conrad won't even see us coming."

As Derrick started off through the fields, Lance dropped back so he could walk alongside George. "Hey," Lance asked, quietly, "did Mister Wellinger seem a little irritated to you?"

George shrugged. "Didn't think so. Why?"

"He doesn't seem to like people talking about Conrad Drake's ranch. Like how good it looks," Lance replied.

"Got me," George said. "Mister Wellinger and Drake seem to have a history. I don't know much about it. I saw someone ask Mister Wellinger about something Conrad Drake did for him. His face got red. He basically told him to screw off, but more bluntly, you know." George chuckled. "Used words you'd never say around your mama."

Lance scratched his shoulder. The promise of food and shelter had made this seem like a dream come true. But now an uneasy feeling was settling in his stomach. What was really on Derrick's mind? Was this a little more personal than Derrick had let on?

Like it matters, Lance thought. If Derrick hated this Conrad Drake person, why did Lance care, as long as Lance got what was promised for his services?

A loud shout jolted Lance back to reality. He and the other men spun to a space near Derrick. Ethan was running backward, spinning his rifle back down into the grass. Then he opened fire three times.

"Ethan! What are you shooting at?" Cal ran up to him, drawing his weapon.

"A snake! A damn copperhead! It was near my foot!" Ethan cried.

Derrick stomped through the grass to the place where Ethan had shot. He then stopped and bent over. "There's no damn copperhead. It's a small water snake. It's not poisonous at all."

Ethan panted loudly. "Really?"

Derrick glared at him. "Yeah." He then stopped so close to Ethan that Derrick's nose nearly brushed Ethan's. "So, in addition to wasting precious ammo, you might have woken up Conrad's old busted ass and alerted him that something's going on out here."

Ethan stammered. "I'm...I'm sorry. I didn't know."

"Well, here's some helpful advice," Derrick

replied, "If it doesn't kill you first, don't shoot it. Got that?"

Ethan shook. "Fine, fine."

"Good." Derrick then turned around and gazed back in the direction of Conrad Drake's property. "We're still far enough away. These tall grass blades should still cover us. We'll just move in a little slower." Then he glanced over his shoulder. "Kendall, Ricardo, keep your scopes handy. I want you to look at Conrad's property every few minutes." Derrick started walking. "If we're lucky, maybe he'll step outside. Good time to let him know he's been relieved of his property."

———

LIAM FOLLOWED the scent to the kitchen. Camilla was seated at the small table with a large smoking pot and a few cups. She was drinking heavily from one when Liam stepped through the doorway.

Camilla quickly had taken the cup off her lips. "Hey. Looks like I got your engine started. Wasn't sure if you were a coffee drinker."

"Wasn't until a year ago," Liam replied.

"Sit down," Camilla said before taking another swig. Liam obeyed. Camilla then poured some coffee into another cup. "I figured this was better than vodka. Used to enjoy that when I lived in New York, but I guess I didn't want to trade in for a new liver." She gently pushed the cup toward Liam. "I had a couple of boyfriends who may have appreciated a good drink a little too much. Guess that's why I wanted to get out to the Midwest."

Liam took the cup. "You said you were like a nomad. Did you ever want to settle down for good?"

Camilla sighed. "I thought about it. I thought about it a lot, especially lately. Maybe it's time to admit that I'm too old to run around the U.S. of A. and actually get a home to look after."

"I hope this isn't too personal, but are things good between you and my dad?" Liam asked after another sip.

"Uh? Oh, sure." Camilla poured herself more coffee. "It's like how something runs warm and hot. It'd get hot, really hot, then warm again." She smirked. "Look, he's your father. You probably don't want me giving you dirty details. Looking at you, you probably know what I mean."

Liam coughed. "Yeah. No, I was just curious why he never mentioned you. I didn't know if there was a rift."

"No, nothing like that." Camilla turned her cup around. "I guess neither one of us knows if we want to drop anchor."

Just then, Carla showed up in shorts and a T-shirt. Her hair remained a mess. She had gotten dressed hastily. "Hey, where's the fire?" she asked.

"Waiting for you." Camilla quickly poured Carla a cup of coffee.

As Carla sat down and took it, Liam eyed the

assault rifle behind Camilla, resting against the wall. This was the first time Liam hadn't seen the shotgun with Camilla. "Looks like you traded your guns up," he said, hoping he'd pull some information out of her.

Camilla nodded. "Yeah. Went from a little piker to heavy duty."

Before Carla or Liam could make a comment, they all heard a popping noise from outside. Camilla turned to the kitchen window as Carla said, "Sounds like someone shot a firework out there."

Camilla glanced out the window. Conrad's fields were visible, but the land toward the horizon was largely obscured with tall grasses and weeds. "Well, someone might have shot something out there," Camilla said. "Could be someone hunting." She turned away, her expression grimmer.

"But if you ask me, I think it's getting a little crazier out there." She folded her arms. "Look, I can't beat around the bush any longer. It's not good out there. In fact, even in the countryside there's been some skirmishes. And when I say skirmishes, I mean gunfights between groups, almost war stuff."

She then looked through the doorway to the living room. "I was doing a little busy work last night. I think it's time you lovebirds grabbed some ammo. Get dressed and I'll show you."

———

DERRICK BRUSHED the latest bundle of tall weeds out

of his face. The rest of his party followed his lead. Derrick then stopped at the edge of a barbed wire fence. "Finally," he muttered. He turned to Teller and Kendall. "Still nothing?"

The pair shook their heads. "Place has been quiet all morning," Teller said.

"Perfect." Derrick tapped the fence post with his knuckle. "Well, Conrad, it looks as though we're going to have ourselves a nice little reunion, you and me." He smiled. "Yeah, you always thought you were better than me, didn't you?"

He turned his back to the fence, facing his men. "Alright, here's how it's going to work. You're all going to spread out, two on the east side, two on the west, and two in front. When I give the word, you start unloading bullets inside that house. You stop only when I say. Since I don't expect anybody but Conrad in there, it's going to be short and sweet. But even when we see his corpse on the ground, we're not going to rest until we've given the house a big going-over. You never know if Conrad has taken in some strays."

"Strays?" Lance asked.

"Strays, you know, other survivors." Derrick passed Lance by. "Maybe a woman or two." Derrick chuckled.

"But are we going—" Lance began, but couldn't finish his question when Ethan and Teller walked by, bumping into his arm. Lance then turned to George, who passed by much more slowly.

"George, are we going to kill anyone else?" Lance asked.

George kept his eyes on Derrick. "Oh, I'm sure we're not." He chuckled, a tad nervously for Lance's tastes. "They see us coming, they'll head for the road and won't look back."

Lance swallowed. George didn't sound so sure.

Before Lance could ask anything, Cal closed in and walked evenly with him. "Hey," Cal said, "look, you might want to stow this wimp talk of yours before someone hears it. If you're not ready to spill some blood for your food, your ass is going to starve. That's the way the world works now." Cal lingered a glare on Lance before he quickened his pace.

Lance clenched his jaw tightly.

———

LIAM HAD TO ADMIT, he wasn't expecting his father's living room sofa to be loaded up with guns and clips, much less big rifles. Carla looked no less impressed. The two of them, fully dressed in fresh pants and shirts, eyed the arsenal as Camilla approached the left end of the couch. She looked up at them and smiled.

"Yeah, you're all surprised to see this, aren't you? You might call it the latest in home security," she said with a wink.

"If we're in another world war." Carla looked up. "Okay, no joke, you really think something bad's about to hit us?"

"Where'd all this come from?" Liam asked.

"Your dad's stash," Camilla replied. "He's got an arsenal in the basement. He's spent years collecting bullets, clips, magazines, guns and rifles for what was to come." Camilla now fixed on the two young adults in front of her. "Now be honest. No bullshit. What's your experience in using firearms?"

"A few shots in Redmond," Liam said while shifting his right leg back and forth.

"Had training with my adopted dad's family." Carla leaned over one of the rifles. "Can't say I've ever trained with an assault rifle."

"It's not too hard." Camilla picked up one of the rifles. "You handle it like you would a rifle. Your dominant hand, you know, if you're left-handed or right-handed, it goes on the pistol grip. That's what you use to pull the trigger. Your other hand holds the weapon and does the reloading." Camilla picked up one of the magazines.

"Now, this is your mag." She turned the gun upside down. Conspicuously, no magazine was loaded into it. "This is where you stick it in, but make sure it's secured. Oh." She then pointed to a small lever on the right side of the rifle. "This is the safety."

Carla picked up a rifle of her own and looked at the top of it. "Is this a scope?"

"You got it. Several of the assault rifles have targeting scopes, including this one." Camilla walked to their side and pointed the gun forward. She then raised the eyepiece up to Liam's face. "There you go.

Get your target between the crosshairs and squeeze the trigger. But you gotta keep in mind that your targets might not be standing still, so pay attention to how they move. If you think they're headed into the crosshairs, take the shot."

Carla looked at Liam with a wry smile. "Big league stuff, right, partner?"

Liam chuckled. "You got that right." He looked through the scope. The television set was right through the crosshairs. "Okay, I'm a little dumb when it comes to this stuff, Camilla, so tell me, can these guns fire more than one bullet at a time?"

"Total bullshit," Camilla replied. "Squeeze once, shoot once. That's the deal. You want to lay down rapid fire, you got to squeeze the trigger faster."

Liam lowered the rifle. "Have you ever had to use these?"

Camilla sighed. "Yeah." She reached for a belt of magazines on the couch. "Stories for another day. See this?" She handed it to Liam. "One for you and one for Carla." She then handed Carla her own belt. "Keep these with you. You don't want to run out of ammo in a firefight, or it's your ass."

As Carla fished the belt around her shoulders, there was a knock at the front door. Camilla spun around quickly. "Damn," she whispered.

Liam's heart quickened. Who could that be? Given what Camilla had been telling them, Liam couldn't help but think of the worst-case scenarios—a solitary killer, a band of thieves, or even a small army.

Camilla picked up a .45 ACP. "You two run to your bedroom and get out of sight." She started walking toward the front door. "I'll give the all clear if I can."

"Don't you want some backup?" Carla asked.

"Just go, sweetie. Now," Camilla said.

Liam picked up his rifle again. "Let's do it," he said. Carla grabbed her own weapon and fled with Liam into the hall.

Camilla waited until the two were gone before undoing the lock to the front door. All the while, she kept the .45 ACP behind her back. If she had to, she'd lay out a possible assailant with the first shot.

Then she opened the door, confirming one of her worst fears.

"Well, good afternoon," said Derrick, wearing a sinister smile on his face.

CHAPTER SEVENTEEN

CLUTCHING HIS STOMACH, Jack stumbled through the streets under the morning sunlight. His stomach rumbled again. The warehouse was too far away, and he was too weak to make it like this. He had been wandering the streets for a day and a night, and he desperately needed something in his stomach. He coughed. His throat was dry. And to top off his troubles, he had no men left to assist him. He was utterly alone.

Damn Tom. Damn that old codger. Damn Sarah. Damn all of them! His mind was a never-ending litany of curses toward people who he imagined had wronged him. He even threw in Marco Valentino for old time's sake, despite feeling sure Marco was long dead.

What if he was truly alone and had to fend for himself? The thought sent chills down his back. The boys at the warehouse, if there were any left, might have decided to be their own bosses and lock him out, or perhaps they'd flee with all the weapons and supplies.

My home. I still got a place in town. I had the guys barricade it. Yeah, I still can hide out there. If I can just get my ass over there.

And so, he staggered down a couple of streets, when a stream of voices stopped him cold. He glanced at the back of an old store. A lone woman was stepping outside it, pushing a bicycle. He recognized her face. She was definitely one of the women who had escaped Maggiano's warehouse.

"Tamara!" Jack hobbled over to her. "Tamara!"

She turned her head. Her eyes widened with terror.

"Hey, hey, easy!" Jack raised his arms. "Look, I got nothing. I'm not here to hurt you, or anybody, really. I'm in the same boat as everyone else, just wanting to survive. I see you got a sweet pair of wheels here. Where'd you get it from?"

Tamara hesitated. She just stood there with a slight jitter traversing her body.

"Hey, come on. I just want a bike to ride home. I'm through with Maggiano's operation. One hundred percent out. I just want to disappear. You understand what I'm saying?"

Tamara nodded once. Good, good. He was making the connection.

"You know I'm not a bad guy. I did all I could to keep the men's mitts off you. Even gave you that great skirt."

Tamara nodded again, even talking. "Yeah."

"So, we're good. Might even say we're friends." Jack laughed before taking a few steps closer to her, so close that Tamara backed off a little. "So, tell me, where'd you get the bike from?" he asked.

Tamara fidgeted in place. Jack's irritation grew. "C'mon, Tamara. Where'd you get it?"

She pointed to an open back door. This was the backside of a string of small stores in a strip mall. Jack rushed over to it. Sure enough, there were a pair of bicycles inside. Jack was only a fair bike rider, but his skills should be enough for a bike ride to his home in Redmond. He might even be sleeping in his own bed in a few days.

"Great." He smiled. "You're an angel, Tamara." He pulled the bike out, in the process knocking over a few metal pipes that lay on the side of the wall. They fell to the floor of the shop's storage room with loud clangs.

Jack walked the bike out into the alley, passing Tamara. She didn't say anything. She just stood there and watched him leave.

But then Jack stopped. He turned and approached her again. "Say, do you know where the other ladies went? The ones who broke and ran from the warehouse? I'm just wondering if they're all safe."

Tamara just nodded.

"Well, could you point me in the right direction? Just so I know they're okay."

Tamara turned away, but Jack grabbed her by the

arm. She squirmed. "C'mon," he said gently, while gripping her in a way that wasn't very gentle. "Tell me."

"Chatham Boulevard," she replied. "They went... we're going down there."

"Edge of town, huh?" Jack released her. He then turned to his bike. "So, they're skipping Redmond." He grinned. "Maybe I'll pay them a visit," he said softly.

As Jack talked to himself, Tamara reached inside the open shop and picked up a metal pipe half the length of her body.

"So, Tamara, what would you say to..." Jack began.

He didn't finish his sentence before Tamara sent the pipe swinging right into his midsection.

With a scream, Jack went down hard on his back. Wincing and wailing, Jack rolled over. Tamara hovered over him, gripping the pipe for dear life.

"Ta-mara. What the..."

Tamara's eyes were like those of an animal's. An inhuman fire blazed behind her pupils. Her cheeks twitched. Her skin was tight. She even bared her teeth like a jungle cat. Then, she let out a scream and sent the pipe smashing into Jack's stomach.

Jack shouted in agony. A third strike hit his arms. A fourth struck his chest. Jack felt horrific pain in his rib cage. A bone or two obviously was broken. When Jack shouted out again, splatters of blood hit the ground.

"Stop.... Stop.... Why?" he yelled out.

Tamara just screamed and let the pipe fly again. By now Jack's legs were broken. He couldn't move to evade the barrage. Tamara just screamed and wailed while she beat and thrashed him.

The worst part for Jack was that Tamara ran out of energy before the former clothing store magnate finally expired. She just collapsed onto the ground and sat there, heaving loudly until her breathing slowed. That left him about fifty more agonizing minutes to linger on the ground, a bloody pulp of a human being, to realize what he might have done to burn this roaring fire of revenge into this young lady.

He finally realized, unfortunately for him, not all the ladies liked and appreciated Jack Sorenson. Not at all.

———

DERRICK SMILED. "Camilla. What a pleasant surprise. Can't say I'm totally shocked to see you opening his door. Did Conrad finally stick a ring on your finger and call you Missus?" He chuckled. "Or maybe it's just plain living in sin. To be honest, I kinda like that thought better. A little bit spicier, don't you think?"

"Shove it, Derrick. What are you doing here?" Camilla asked.

Derrick looked up at the ceiling. "Funny thing, the power went out in my place and I thought I'd come over to use your phone to call the power company," Derrick replied.

Camilla's frown deepened. "You know your jokes get worse every year."

"I never did like women who couldn't appreciate a good belly laugh. Now where's Conrad?" Derrick asked.

"He's unavailable, so I'm speaking for him, and he says get the hell off his property right now," Camilla replied.

"Well, that's curious. Now, when you say he's unavailable, is he on the pot? Taking a bath? Out bartering for food?" Derrick glanced over Camilla's shoulder.

Camilla then took one step closer to block his view. "Well, someone's a little anxious tonight," Derrick said. "Did he take a long trip out of town? Well, that would be very, very convenient for me."

"I'm giving you three seconds to move your ass out of here," Camilla said.

"Oh, I'll be happy to." Derrick backed up, off the porch and onto the walkway leading up to it. "But you might want to vacate the house, and in a big hurry."

Camilla's eyes widened. "Why?"

Derrick grinned. "Ownership of this ranch has changed, to me. I've surrounded this whole house with my boys. At my command, they'll turn this little homestead into Swiss cheese. So, do yourself a favor and move your pretty little rear out of my place."

"You son of a —" Camilla raised her weapon and opened fire.

At close range, Derrick was easily struck, but her aim was off. Had she taken a few seconds to properly aim, she might have nailed Derrick in the head or someplace vital. Instead he dropped to the ground, but was very much alive.

"Now!" Derrick shouted. "Fire!"

Camilla quickly slammed the door shut and threw down the bar anchored next to the door. It fell right across the door, providing a solid brace that would make it very hard to get open from outside. "Liam! Carla! We got trouble!" she shouted.

———

GEORGE AND TELLER rushed over to Derrick as the shots rang out toward the homestead. "You alright?" Teller grabbed Derrick by the shoulders. Derrick was clutching his side.

Derrick pushed Teller aside. "Easy. You think I didn't plan on this?" Derrick quickly got up, but not without George holding onto his right arm for support. Derrick knocked on his side. "Put on a Kevlar vest." He winced. "Damn. It didn't stop the bullet the whole damn way." He hurried off toward the road while his men continued their assault.

"Sir, why'd you leave yourself so open?" Teller asked.

"I thought it was Conrad in there." Derrick loosened up his vest as he walked. "The man's too much of a good Samaritan just to gun you down in cold blood. I've seen him. He doesn't have the eyes of a killer. I thought he'd give in, let us have his home." Then he shouted in pain. By now he had pried the vest loose to reach underneath it. He pulled out a metal fragment with some blood on it. "What the hell did she shoot me with?"

"Is it bad?" George asked.

"No, the wound doesn't feel deep." Derrick tossed the bullet away. "Go tend to the house. Blow that bitch away. I'll bind this up."

George and Teller raised their weapons and dashed off, leaving Derrick behind. Getting hit with that bullet took more out of him than he thought. How the hell did he mess this up?

No, he didn't mess up. He didn't know Conrad's girl would be in there. He should have let his men take the house first.

As the gunfire continued, Derrick was content to stay out here and let it all play out. If it was just Camilla, she'd be overwhelmed in no time. And if a few of the boys got taken out in the process, it'd just be a few less mouths to feed from Conrad's land.

No, make that *his* land.

———

LIAM AND CARLA rushed toward the hall door as

soon as they heard Camilla scream, "Liam! Carla! We got trouble!" Then, a series of loud pops rang out.

"Hit the floor!" Liam cried out. He grabbed for Carla to push her down, but she was too far from his grasp. Fortunately, Carla had quick reflexes and made the dive herself.

Carla put her hands over her head. "Shit, someone's shooting at us!"

Liam drew his gun. So, Camilla was right after all. But this was even worse than he could have imagined. The pops seemed to be all around them. One shot even penetrated the window over their heads.

"Carla! Get in the closet!" Liam started crawling toward the door. "Barricade yourself!"

"Are you kidding! You need my help! It sounds like there's an army outside!" Carla retorted.

"And if there is, you got to protect yourself!" Liam crawled faster. "Now go!"

As Liam pushed the door fully open, he revealed Camilla, rushing down the hall toward to one of the back rooms, clutching her scoped rifle. Some of the windows were hastily blocked with wooden boards. Crouched down, Liam hurried into the hall and kept close on Camilla's tail. She rushed into Conrad's bedroom, smashed the rifle through the window glass, and opened fire.

"Camilla!" Liam shouted from the doorway.

"Find yourself a different window and start shooting! Derrick's got us surrounded!" Camilla shouted as she broke away from the window and raced past Liam to the next room over. "The kitchen! Go there! Don't let them into the house!"

———

CARLA PUSHED the sliding door of the closet in front of her. Her rifle was in her arms. She never had clutched something so powerful and so deadly in her life. It almost frightened her. Yet, she realized weapons like this were the key to survival, so any qualms quickly vanished.

The sound of the pops outside made her skin crawl. Liam and Camilla were out in the halls, shooting back at their unseen assailants, and what was she doing? Ducking in a bedroom closet.

What am I doing? I can't hide in here! I have to help Liam!

Her rifle then bumped her stomach. She ran her hand over her abdomen. No, no matter what she did, she wouldn't be risking merely her own neck. Her child would be in danger, and if Carla died, her baby would suffer the same fate.

Liam told me to stay out of this, she thought. But surely she could aim and fire out of the bedroom window once or twice, right? It might even frighten some of them off.

Her fingers reached for the closet door. At that moment, one of the bullets hit the wall in the bedroom, the same wall that the closet lay in. The impact sent a tremor through the wall, and as Carla's hand brushed the sliding door, she felt the quake to her fingertips.

Her heart quickening, she quickly drew back. "Damn," she whispered. What if she *had* gone out there? Just being in one wrong place at a critical moment could end her life.

"Liam..." She cringed. She could do nothing but hide in here. While a comforting inner voice told her Liam and Camilla never would think less of her for hiding in here, it hardly helped as much as she wanted.

———

LIAM, still keeping his head down, reached the kitchen, but stopped as a few loud pops cut through the air. Then, nothing. The shooting seemed to move about outside, with one room taking hits, then another next to it, and so on. Their attackers likely were changing their positions, perhaps hoping to cover as much of the house as they could with gunfire.

With their gunfire not trained on the kitchen, Liam saw his chance. He stood straight up, his back to the wall, and raised his gun. Then, he turned around to face the kitchen window. He gazed into the scope.

Through the crosshairs, he could see one of the armed men. He wore a ski mask with a skull face on it. His gun was on his legs, and he was hastily shoving a magazine into it, but his clumsiness was impeding his efforts. Clearly, he wasn't used to reloading a gun.

Liam squeezed the trigger.

The man lurched backward, releasing his gun, and falling over. He made a hit! The man lay still on the ground and did not move. Liam's shot must have been fatal, or at least so severe that the man couldn't get up without medical aid.

A part of Liam felt sick inside. For so much of his life, he never had imagined he would have to kill another human being.

You're doing it for Carla and your family, Liam reminded himself as he hurried off to find another spot to shoot from.

CHAPTER EIGHTEEN

I HATE it when I'm right, Camilla thought as she squeezed the trigger again. She knew trouble was coming. She knew she would one day take up arms to defend Conrad's home. *But damn, why'd it have to come like this?*

The number of gunshots hitting the house suggested there had to be maybe seven or eight men outside. She had no choice but to wear them down from inside the house and keep any of them from getting inside. Fortunately, Conrad had built his doors with locks and barricades that made breaking down any of them from the outside difficult. But that didn't mean that one of them wouldn't eventually give if assaulted with enough concentrated gunfire.

So, she had to shoot from different spots in the house. If she shot from any one room for too long, the men might assume another part of the house was a safe place to try breaking in. Fortunately, not every sector of Conrad's house had an entry door, but Camilla didn't know what Derrick's men might have up their sleeves. They could be carrying explosives. A well-placed explosive on one of the home's windows might blow a hole big enough for Derrick's army to enter, even blowing apart the wood they were using to block the windows.

As she aimed through another window, she laughed. *Mom, Dad, if you could see your city girl now.*

Then, she caught a break. One of the shooters was rushing toward the center of the crosshairs. She pulled the trigger. The man was struck in the arm and fell over. He tumbled across the grass, out of sight.

If that man had any sense, he'd quit the fight now. *Dammit*, she thought. *Are you assholes going to make me kill you?*

Conrad told her that people would come here in dark times. They would be desperate. Decency and civility would be driven from their spirits, to be replaced by an intense instinct to survive, no matter the cost. And if survival could be obtained by killing others and taking what they owned, so be it.

It's what separates us from the animals, Conrad once told her. *We stick with our morals and beliefs. Without them, we turn on each other in the ugliest ways.*

Camilla hurried to the next window. *Come on, give it up already*, she thought as she looked through her scope and prepared to shoot again.

LANCE DOVE for the ground as the latest shot from the homestead rang out. His whole body shook. He hadn't been able to get off a single shot in the past few minutes. Ever since gunfire started erupting from the home itself, he had been petrified. Derrick never told them Conrad would be fighting back, much less that the home had more people inside who used guns!

How long had this battle been going on? There were so many loud pops in the air from gunfire that Lance's ears stung. The sounds alone made it hard for him to make any clear shots at the house. Each time a gun was shot, he cringed and shut his eyes. More than once, he nearly was knocked over by one of his fellow shooters, who then cursed at him for not being more alert.

Lance dashed to a small hill facing the home's west side. Two more shooters were pumping in fire, but one of them just got nailed in the arm and tumbled over. Lance's skin got cold. The wounded man was Kendall.

"Dammit!" He rose to his feet and dashed away from the house as fast as he could. The other shooter retreated to the front of the house.

"Hey!" George shouted as he rushed up to him from around back. "C'mon, man, we need some more fire! We—"

George didn't finish his sentence. A gunshot from the home struck him in his right arm. Crying out, George dropped onto the dirt.

"George!" Lance ran up to him. "My God! You're hit!"

On the ground, George clutched his arm. "It hurts. Oh God, it hurts!" Blood gushed from an ugly wound on his arm. George just lay there and wept.

"What do I do? What do I do?" Lance shook. George was in even worse shape than Kendall, as he didn't even seem able to rise from the ground under his own strength. "Um, stop the bleeding. Yeah, stop the bleeding." Then he rose and shouted to the front of the property, "Hey! Somebody help us!"

Just then, Ethan came rushing in. "Keith! He's dead!" He pointed to a fallen man on the ground some feet away.

Lance and Ethan approached the fallen Keith from different sides. Their dead comrade lay on the ground, his rifle dropped into the grass next to his body. Blood trickled down his chest and across his arms. Ethan pulled off his mask. His face was still, and lifeless.

Lance clutched his mouth. He thought he might throw up at any moment. He never had been in the presence of a dead human being before. He had avoided going to any funerals, even those of his own family, so he never had seen a human being in a coffin.

Another of Derrick's men hobbled into view, clutching his left leg. Blood trickled from it.

This isn't worth it, Lance thought as he ran back toward George. There's no way there's just one old man in that house. They were being hit from multiple sides of the homestead. There had to be two, maybe three, or more people holed up in there. Did Derrick lie to them? Did he know they'd be running into more trouble here? And where was Derrick, anyway? Lance had lost track of him the moment the battle began.

"Maybe we should just bail on this and find somewhere else to go!" the man with the wounded leg cried out. "We can't take this place!"

"I hope I didn't hear what I thought I heard," Derrick said as he approached from their right. "We've got our salvation just waiting in that home and the fields beyond, and you want to cut out now?"

"But we're taking hits!" the wounded man protested.

"So are they. We've got them outnumbered." Derrick then turned to look at all the men present. "You got a choice. If you don't take this house, you'll die on the side of the road without food or water. This world's only got what you can take, and we're going to take this house." He raised his gun high over his head. "Now, regroup, reload, and get ready for a second run. They're not going anywhere. They can't run or hide. If we don't drop them to the floor, they'll run out of ammo. Either way, we win."

The men who were unwounded or still could fight nodded and hurried off. George, however, could do nothing more than sit up. Lance walked toward

George, but then Derrick stepped in and barred his path.

"Hey. You're not hit, are you?" Derrick asked.

"No," Lance replied.

"Then join the others and start shooting when they do."

Lance gazed at George. "But..."

"Leave him. He'll be fine."

"But he's bleeding badly."

"Do you have cotton in your ears, boy? We're taking this place. And if you're not helping, you're sure as hell not getting anything from here, not so much as a crumb."

Lance gulped. No, he couldn't be left out to starve again. He had come this far and knew nobody here, not in any nearby town, no one who would take pity on him in any way. He had to win this.

He rushed off to rejoin the others.

———

LIAM NOTICED the rate of gunfire was decreasing substantially. Soon the gunshots had stopped altogether.

"What the hell? Why are they stopping?" Liam asked.

"I don't know." Camilla glanced at the window she just had shot through. "They might be running low on ammunition."

Liam's mind replayed the scene of the man falling

down after Liam had shot him. Would that really have rattled them to stop their shooting?

"These guys might have been spooked after I shot that man." Liam gestured to the window. "They're not soldiers or guys who are used to gun assaults."

"Yeah, but if Derrick's leading them, he'll whip them back into a fighting frenzy soon enough." Camilla reloaded her gun with a fresh magazine. "Carla. Go check on her, now."

"Right." Liam hurried down the hall to their bedroom. His heart raced. Was she alright?

He burst into their room. "Carla?" he cried out.

The closet door slid open. "Liam!" Carla responded. Sweat dripped down her face. She looked completely unhurt.

"Thank God." Liam crouched down. "There's a break in the action," he said. "We might have spooked them. Hopefully, they'll beat it, but Camilla thinks they'll start shooting again soon if Derrick can goad them into it."

Carla nodded, her head shaking. "How are we going to know they're gone? They might just hide and wait for us to come out."

Liam swallowed. "Yeah, you're right. But we can't go outside. We have to outlast them inside. They can't have unlimited ammo."

"Neither do you!" Carla scooted out of the closet.

"Carla, what are you doing? Stay in there," Liam said.

"You need another gun," Carla raised her rifle.

"Three of us taking shots at them will be better than two."

"But you can't put yourself out here. Just hide. We can take them down."

"Forget it. I can't hide any longer. What will happen if you die? And they shoot Camilla? Then they break in here and I'm dead anyway!"

Liam raised his voice, though he hated to, especially to Carla. "Carla, it's too risky!"

"What? You think each day is nothing but a peaceful day in the countryside? No, every damn day is now risky." Carla put the gun across her chest. "Sorry, Liam, but if we want to live, we're going to have to fight for ourselves. I'm no different."

"There's movement outside, lovebirds!" Camilla called. "You better get ready for round two, because they're coming at us again!"

Carla dashed out of the room. Liam shouted, "Carla!" but he stopped short of restraining her.

He couldn't help but feel that she was right. He wanted to protect her, but they were low on options. They couldn't expect help of any kind to arrive. If Derrick's army was going to be stopped, he, Carla and Camilla would have to be the ones to do it.

Carla took up a position inside Conrad's bedroom. She peered through the scope as if it all came easily to her. Then, she pulled the trigger, shooting a round through the already shot up glass pane.

Liam quickly took a position at his bedroom

window. Camilla was right. The men outside were taking new positions and raising their guns. It was time to rejoin the fight.

———

"C'MON!" Cal shouted, "Let's waste them!"

The men started firing on the homestead, but almost instantly, gunfire from the house assaulted them. Lance was about to shoot, but the return fire made him duck again. Instead, he waited as the shots zinged from the house. Then he heard another scream, then a thud onto the ground. Conrad, and whoever was helping him, had taken out another of their force, in this case, the man who was previously shot in the leg. A quick glance told Lance the man was not so lucky this time—the shot struck him in the head. His eyes were open in frozen death.

"How the hell are they wasting us?" Ethan cried out.

"They're using scopes, you moron!" shouted Cal. "Take cover and keep moving after you shoot!"

"Take cover. Keep moving." Lance repeated it over and over as he ran, crouched down, along the house. It was simple. Very simple. He repeated it even as the gunfire made him cringe again. To his relief, it kept his head in the game.

A shot rang out from one of the windows near the rear of the home. Lance tried to think. The shots weren't coming from all the windows at once.

Whoever was inside likely was moving from room to room, not unlike how they were changing positions out here. If a shooter inside fired from one window, it was likely the window next door would be unguarded. But the shooter then would shift to that window to fire next.

Then he spotted a window next to the window where the shot had come from. Lance raised his gun. The shooter in that room could open fire from that window at any moment...

Take cover. Keep moving.

So, Lance quickly stood up and shot in the window. Then, he threw himself onto the grass and rolled away as quickly as possible.

———

LIAM SQUEEZED THE TRIGGER. *Damn*, he thought. Through his scope, he found his target moved too quickly, jumping and rolling to the right just as he took the shot. That was the second target to evade a hit. Even as well stocked as Liam, Camilla, and Carla were with ammunition, sooner or later one side would run out of bullets.

Liam picked up his rifle and rushed toward the next window. He was starting to wonder what would happen if his father arrived home in the middle of all this. Dad would have no way to know his house was under siege until he made it here, and by then several guns could be pointed at him.

Dad...and Mom, too, Liam thought with renewed dread. If his dad was successful in rescuing his mom, both of his parents could arrive right smack in the middle of a war zone.

As he approached the latest window and leveled his rifle, he hoped the next shot would take out another shooter. *Thin out their ranks. Make them see this fight is futile.* He thought this over and over again.

However, his mantra came to an abrupt end. All of a sudden, a shot popped through the glass pane and struck him in the right side, sending hot pain searing through it. The impact was like a burning pinch that threw him to the floor. With a shout of agony, he fell onto his back.

"Liam!" Carla turned and shouted to him. "Oh my God! Liam!"

She broke into a run. Liam wanted to rise to his feet, to return fire, but the pain was too intense. "Carla, get down!"

But she did not listen. Instead, she raised her weapon and fired twice through the window. Then, she dropped down next to him. "Liam, where are you hit?"

She tilted him up against the wall. Fresh blood stained his shirt on his right side. Her eyes widened. Then she turned to the hall. "Camilla!" she shouted, "Help! Liam's hit!"

Camilla raced down the hall from the kitchen. "Dammit!" She dug into her pocket. "Here, had some of this for an emergency." Then she stopped and threw a pack of gauze to Carla. "Put that on his wound and keep pressure on it. Stop his bleeding!" Then she turned back. "I've got to keep them dancing out there so they don't think they've scored a hit."

CHAPTER NINETEEN

As the gunfight raged, Derrick kept a close eye on the house through his binoculars, checking out the windows from certain spots near fence posts or a tree near the edge of Conrad's property. There was definitely movement inside. Every now and then he'd see somebody run by the glass, but as the battle progressed, more windows would be blocked off with wood or some other barrier.

Damn you! Derrick thought, *Damn you, Conrad! You think you got this all figured out? You think you can outlast me? Well, I've been preparing for this day for weeks. And once I grab your land, I'm going to have a lot of power at my fingertips. Think of all the people who will come to me begging for food. They'll make me a king if I tell them, all in exchange for the apples and corn and lettuce that your land can produce. No, my land.*

He rubbed his side. He had applied the bandage to his wound as tightly as possible to stop the bleeding before reapplying his vest, but the wound had been more intense than he had thought. Dealing with the pain had forced him out of the battle, not that he intended to get heavily involved anyway. Better to let his hired help take the risks for him.

But now he was beginning to grow antsy. The battle had gone on too long for his tastes. There had to be an opening, some way to break through Camilla and Conrad's gunfire and breach the house.

In the past minute, Derrick noticed the rate of return fire was dropping. Usually, there were two shots on opposite sides of the house, although since the second round began, there seemed to be three people shooting at them. But now they were taking fire from just around the right side of the kitchen.

Maybe we got lucky and nailed somebody. Derrick tightened his fist. *Or maybe they're reloading. Either way, it's time I got the jump on Conrad. But I won't do it alone.*

Then he spotted Teller jogging his way. "Hey!" Derrick motioned to him. "We're making a run on the front door. You're with me." Then he strolled toward the front porch. "I'm going in! Once I make it inside, cease fire until I come back out!"

Derrick motioned to Teller to go first. He obeyed, though he seemed a little hesitant about doing so. Still, he approached the front door, then opened fire on the doorknob, blasting it off. Then, he kicked the door hard. One kick jostled the door loose, but there still was a barricade holding it in place.

"Watch it!" Derrick then aimed his rifle at the

crack between the door and doorframe. He squeezed the trigger, dumping more bullets into the wooden frame, blasting off small chunks of wood. "Come on!" he shouted, "Come on you son of a bitch!"

He stopped firing. Teller took the cue and kicked the door, this time wrenching it open, exposing the living room of the Drake residence.

———

"YOU AWAKE? YOU'RE STAYING AWAKE," Carla said as she pushed hard on the gauze. "You're staying awake, right?"

Liam let out a loud breath. "Believe me, I can't fall asleep with all that racket outside." Then he placed his own hand on the gauze, while trying to ease Carla's off. "I think I can handle it. Camilla needs help." His eyes met Carla's. "You might be the last chance we have."

Carla clutched her weapon. "I...I can't..."

"You have to." Liam sat up, fighting the searing pain in his side. "This is a two--person job. You, me, we protect the house together. Remember that great Carla speech earlier about how life's different now? This is where it counts."

Carla's hand trembled. She tried not to cry. "Alright. But you..." She jabbed her finger in his chest. "You're going to have to marry me, okay? You better promise." She raised three fingers. "I want the ring, the ceremony, and the honeymoon. Not necessarily in that order, but I do want them!"

Liam laughed. "I don't know about the ring, but I think I can handle the other two." He coughed. "Now go, use that ammo. Kick some ass for the both of us."

Blinking back tears, Carla charged from the room, rifle in hand.

At that moment, the bar on the front door shattered near the lock. Camilla started running back in her direction. "They're coming through!" She aimed the rifle at the door. "Get back, now!"

Carla backed up just as the door broke open. A middle-aged man with a gun charged through. Camilla quickly aimed and fired several rounds, most catching him in the chest. But she didn't see Derrick ducking behind him in time, then spinning his own rifle around to open fire.

In the timespan of two gunshots, both Camilla and Derrick tumbled to the floor.

Carla looked down, seeing a spate of blood on Camilla's collarbone. She screamed.

————

DERRICK CAUGHT a glimpse of Camilla just before opening fire. He wasn't even sure he struck her before a gunshot hit him in his left shoulder. The sudden burst of pain knocked him down to the floor of the porch.

"Mister Wellinger!" Sandy took a few steps toward him.

Derrick grabbed onto the door and hoisted himself up. "It's nothing." Derrick patted his left shoulder. "It didn't hit anything vital." Then he picked up his rifle. "You, stand guard at the front door and act as my backup."

Sandy nodded, though as he looked down at Teller's dead body, a tremor ran over her face. "Teller," Sandy whispered.

Derrick peered back into the hall. It remained silent. Camilla must have taken cover, or was so badly hurt she couldn't return any more fire. Even so, Derrick wasn't going to step inside just yet. For one thing, who did he see with Camilla? Another woman? Derrick couldn't get a good look at her, but she seemed younger than Camilla, younger than even Derrick.

He winced. Pain shot up his side. He patted the bandage over his wound. It felt stickier. He must not have closed the wound fully. Perhaps his bulletproof vest had turned out to be a piece of garbage after all.

Two women in your house. Is that other one your daughter or something?

He stepped into the hall. Again, he encountered no resistance.

"Conrad?" he called out. "Where are you?" Derrick now crossed past an open doorway. He poked his gun's nozzle into the room. Nothing inside moved.

"C'mon, Conrad, let's be reasonable. You don't have much life left in those old bones. How about doing the world a favor and checking out early?"

Derrick returned to the hall. There was another bedroom toward the end. "So, what's the story, Conrad? How many you got in here?" Derrick called out, "I hope one of my men didn't nail your ass 'cause I got a bullet in here just for you."

CONRAD SILENCED the latest outburst from his limbs to stop and rest. He was too close to home to stop pedaling now. As much as he had wanted to cover the distance between Redmond and his home as quickly as he could, he and Sarah and Tom had to stop for one night before continuing. So far, their journey had gone off smoothly.

It almost seemed too good to be true. Just two days ago, he doubted whether he ever would step over his front door's threshold, walk through his ranch's crops, or tend to his sheep and chickens ever again. More importantly, he had thought the last time he would look upon his son's face was when he had parted from him and Carla before heading off to rescue Sarah.

It seemed like too much to hope for at the time. Perhaps the battle with Maggiano's men was meant to cap off his existence on this planet, although he would be briefly reunited with his son and ex-wife as a kind of reward. Plus, the reunion would help tie up loose ends. It seemed a fitting way for him to go out. But Conrad didn't meet his end in Redmond. So, what would happen next?

Sarah was riding on Tom's back close by. Soon, he and Sarah would meet up with Liam again. After almost thirty years, his family would be back under one roof. Would it last?

I never prepared myself for this, Conrad thought. *I thought I'd look at my home's walls all by myself for the rest of my days.* With each mile he pedaled, he recognized his life would change drastically from here on.

He gazed upon the fields across the horizon. This world seemed suddenly emptier. The carnage inflicted by the solar event was a factor. Deprived of medical services and law enforcement, millions of people across the United States died within the first few days of society's collapse. That meant the survivors had to pick up the pieces. But to truly rebuild their country as the free nation it had been before, those ideals had to be in the hearts of the people who did the rebuilding.

Conrad realized he could pass on those ideals to his son. And not just him, but his grandchild as well. Suddenly, he recognized he could do far better for his country than just waste away in an isolated ranch in the middle of the Midwest.

As he turned back to the road, he spotted the shadow of Tom's bike retreating. He slowed his pace, allowing Tom to catch up with him. Although Tom was a younger man, he was more fatigued than Conrad, with more sweat pouring off the sides of his head. They had taken a few short breaks earlier to drink water and eat, and it seemed they might need just one more before they made it to Conrad's ranch.

"Maybe we ought to pull over," Conrad said, "We're very close. A few more minutes won't hurt."

Tom seemed ready to agree, but he glanced over his shoulder. Sarah hung on his body. Then he shook his head. "If we're very close, I can keep going. Sarah wants to see her son."

"Tom, it's okay. Slow down. We'll rest," Sarah said.

Tom did slow down, but he didn't stop pedaling fully. "How about you two just go on ahead?" Tom asked. "I can just walk the rest of the way."

"Forget it. I'm not leaving anybody out here, even if you're not likely to run into trouble," Conrad replied. "Keep in mind, there may not be any robbers or bandits out here, but you never know when a wild animal can show up to make trouble. We're heading home together. That's the end of it."

Tom huffed. "I'll just keep going a little bit more." Then he stopped. "Okay, I'm stopping."

Sarah got off, then slid Tom's backpack from her shoulders and pulled out a water canteen. Tom took it. "Thanks." He drank deeply.

Conrad pulled over as well. Although he wanted to take a swig from his own canteen, Sarah continued to command his interest. Her attention remained squarely on Tom, and it seemed her anger over being sold out largely had dissipated. Either that, or she might have repressed it. Conrad hoped it wasn't the latter. In the time he had been married to her, Conrad knew Sarah to be an outspoken woman. She rarely hid her true feelings about anything. On the other hand, people can change over time. Plus, she just had been through a horrifying experience. Lord knows how that could reshape a person for the worse.

Sarah then turned and looked at him. Conrad was almost startled. "Hey," she said, "You should drink some water. You're not a spring chicken anymore."

Conrad chuckled. "Right." He took a long drink from his canteen. "First time in ages that I had to do as you said." He swallowed, wondering if that comment went over as well as he hoped.

"You always worked yourself too hard," Sarah said. "Tell me you don't still crash on the sofa without taking a shower."

Conrad didn't answer that right away. Sarah shook her head. "I should have figured."

After taking another swig, Conrad replied. "Well, I guess you could say no one complained about it. It's easy to forget those pesky habits when nobody reminds you of them."

Sarah's eyes widened a little. "So, you really don't have anybody? I mean, there's no one at your home but you?"

Conrad wiped his mouth. "Well, not always. It's a bit of a long story."

"Wait." By now, Tom's breathing had slowed. He

was recuperating well from the latest bout of riding. "There is somebody? A girlfriend?"

Conrad looked away. "A lady friend, you could say. Like I said, it's a bit of a long story."

Tom wiped more sweat off his face. "Well, I definitely want to hear about her. Is she...like you?"

Conrad frowned. "What do you mean?"

Tom thought his words over carefully. "You know, survivalist, off the grid type. Rustic."

Sarah burst out laughing. "Oh Lord!"

Tom started laughing himself. "Yeah, a female Conrad. That would be something."

Conrad, though, wasn't sharing in their merriment. Instead, he put his canteen away and turned back to the road. Sarah and Tom silenced themselves when they noticed Conrad's mood had darkened.

Sarah instead strolled up to him, her boots making crunching sounds through the grass. "Hey," she said, "Tom and I were just having fun. It's not easy to laugh nowadays."

Conrad didn't look at her. "It's not exactly easy to laugh at it. After all, once upon a time, you didn't find me such a joke to be around."

"It's not that. Oh God, I'm sorry." Sarah sighed. "With everything that's happened, I guess you're not the crazy one." She grabbed her shirt sleeve, looking away. "If you found somebody, that's wonderful. Really. I had no idea."

"You could have asked. Called. Written," Conrad said. "I'd have been happy with smoke signals."

Sarah shook her head. "This isn't going to work. I'll come with you, see Liam, and then Tom and I will find somewhere else to live."

Conrad frowned. "Sarah, where the hell are you going to go? You can't go back to Redmond. I don't know if there's a town out there that's safe at all. No, you have to stay."

"Conrad, can we really stay under one roof again, even if it's different now? Even if we're no longer at each other's throats? Even if we're just friends?"

Conrad scowled. "Well, that's a pleasant surprise. I'm glad to be back up to the friend level. We didn't exactly part on friendly terms."

Sarah folded her arms. "No. No, we didn't." She sighed.

The two just stood there, looking away from each other. The old history wouldn't stay silent, but it seemed neither of them could, or would, delve into it any further. For his part, Tom didn't want to get in the middle of this at all. Instead, he drank more water and worried about resting his tired legs.

It was Conrad who broke the stalemate. "I'm not throwing you out of my home. You're coming with me, and you're staying. Liam's there, and you should be with him, and, soon, your grandchild."

Sarah's mouth fell open. "My...grandchild?"

"Yeah." Conrad smiled crookedly. "Guess I didn't have a chance to fill you in yet, but Carla's got one cooking in the oven."

Sarah clasped her hands on her face. "Carla's

giving me a grandbaby." She turned and grabbed Tom and held him tight. "Tom! You heard that?"

"Yeah, I knew about it," Tom said under Sarah's tight squeeze.

"Well, why didn't you say anything to me?" Sarah asked.

"Because we were too busy arguing or trying to stay alive. I figured it could wait," Tom replied.

Sarah parted from him. "I wonder if it's a girl. Am I going to have a little girl to play with?"

"Hell to that. I bet it's a boy," Conrad said.

"Oh, that's just what you want. We can have another hillbilly boy running around the house!" Sarah laughed, but then quieted herself. "Sorry. That was probably stepping over a line."

Conrad drew in a long breath. "No, no, that's okay. To be honest, sometimes I miss those little jokes of yours."

Before anyone could say another word, a pop rang out through the air. "What the hell?" Tom looked up. "Someone shooting off fireworks?"

"Fireworks?" Conrad marched back to the side of the road. "That's more like someone shooting off a gun."

Conrad's comment was followed by a second shot. Then, a third. Conrad turned and looked at Tom and Sarah.

"Those are a lot of gunshots," Tom said. "I'd almost call it a shootout."

Conrad grabbed his bicycle. "Rest time's over. We got to make tracks, and fast."

———

"Do you think there's trouble at your home?" Sarah shouted as Tom and Conrad pedaled hard on their respective bikes.

"It's getting damn louder as we get closer," Conrad replied. Before he mounted his bike, he had slipped his rifle on by a belt around his shoulders. Tom and Sarah had likewise armed themselves.

"Liam, my baby." Sarah cringed. "Please let him and Carla be okay."

"Perfect. We can't even escape guntoting psychos out here in the countryside," Tom said.

"There!" Conrad pointed to the turnoff from the state road. "Dismount and get ready for action! If we got intruders, they're going to pick us off if we ride in."

Tom and Conrad quickly slid to a stop. Then, the trio got off their bikes and raised their weapons. "Keep down," Conrad said. The three of them leaned down while hurrying down the short road to the homestead. Tom, moving a little faster, got out in front.

As they approached the ground just before the porch, they found the source of the gunfire. The house was surrounded by a small group of men, all armed with rifles and shotguns. The front door already was open, with a middle-aged man standing guard by it. None of the other men were making moves to invade the Drake homestead. They were just waiting. Perhaps an advance scouting party had gone in. These men might be standing by for instructions.

Conrad's heart quickened. "Liam," he said under his breath. No, he couldn't have come home just to have his boy taken away from him, not now!

At that moment, two of the men glanced over their shoulders. Conrad, Tom and Sarah were in full view, and could not take cover if they wanted to. But then again, the intruders were in the same predicament, which is all Tom needed. Before the two men could fully turn to fire, Tom aimed and shot both of them with his rifle.

The guard at the front door turned around, but this time Conrad was ready. One shot from Conrad, and the guard was no more.

"Hey, what's going on?" shouted somebody in the distance.

"We're being shot at!" screamed another male from the east side of the homestead.

"Clear them out! Make sure they don't get inside!" His rifle in his hands, Conrad then charged for the front door. "I'm going in to find Liam!"

CHAPTER TWENTY

DERRICK TURNED the corner into Liam and Carla's bedroom. His shadow crossed those of Liam and Camilla on the floor. Both were awake, but tending to their wounds. Their guns lay on their laps.

Derrick cocked his head. "Well, seems as though you had some hired muscle." Then he raised an eyebrow at Liam. "You even kind of look like Conrad. I don't know why. I guess it's the forehead."

Meanwhile, Carla's heart quickened as she watched the scene from inside the closet. She had to stop Derrick, and quickly! As Derrick approached Carla's direct line of sight, she pulled on the rifle's trigger.

No shots. It only clicked. She pulled again. Just clicks. Her magazine was empty.

Derrick then spun around. He darted for the closet and yanked it open.

"Carla!" Liam tried to get up, but the intense pain stopped him.

Derrick looked down at Carla with a grin that was equal parts disgust and mirth. "Next time, you should keep better track of your shots." Then he raised his gun. "See ya."

"Dammit, Derrick, don't do it! She's got a child!" Camilla sputtered out in one long, anguished scream.

But Derrick was beyond the scope of human reason. His gun already was leveled to hit Carla right between the eyes.

A shot rang out.

The bang was so loud that Carla's ears rang. She cringed and fell back against the wall. The bullet. Where did it hit? Why didn't she feel the pain of a gunshot? She patted herself. No, she wasn't struck at all.

Then she looked up. Derrick was staggering backward until he slammed against the right wall. Then he tumbled over until he fell on his back.

The sound of rapidly approaching boots drew Carla's attention. As she rose to her feet, an old familiar face emerged into the room.

"Mister Drake!" Carla cried out.

Conrad carried his gun in his right hand. He quickly lowered it when Carla ran up to him. But he couldn't spare a quick hug or comforting hold. "Liam?" He turned around to discover Camilla sitting on the floor, clutching her collarbone. Liam was next to her, his eyes barely open.

"Dad?" he asked, weakly.

"Liam! My God, he's hit, isn't he?" Then Conrad knelt down beside him and Camilla. When he saw Camilla, a jolt shook him. "Cammie?"

"Yeah, it's me. Got a hole in my body and bleeding out, but I'm still glad to see you," Camilla replied.

Liam struggled to sit up. "Liam, what happened? Where are you hit?" Conrad looked him over.

"I'm, I'm not too bad. It just hurts like hell," Liam said.

Conrad then turned behind him. Derrick's breathing was shallow. His fingers moved slowly. His eyes fluttered. Conrad's shot had torn him up pretty badly. It was plain he'd die soon.

But that didn't stop Conrad from drawing his gun again and pointing it at Derrick's face. "You son of a bitch. You did this. You attacked my family!"

Derrick coughed. Blood trickled from his lips. His eyes became glassy and unfocused. "You... always...gotta...be...better...".

"Dad, don't waste the ammo," Liam said, "He's done for."

Derrick then let out a sickening gurgle, and his head turned to the side. His mouth froze open.

Still nursing fury, Conrad turned around. "Carla, help these two. I've got some housecleaning to do." Then he flashed a look to Liam. "Mom's waiting for you. Looks like she's going to be stitching you up, just like she did years ago."

Liam's eyes widened. "Wait! Mom's here?"

But Conrad didn't stick around to explain. He couldn't take pleasure in his son's joy at the news. Instead, he stormed out of the room, back into the hall, determined to flush out the bastards who dared attack his home.

He controlled his anger enough not to slam the key into the basement door keyhole. The discipline of many years took over. He understood a day like this may come, and he had practiced it multiple times. In a few seconds, the basement door was open and he was dashing down the stairs.

Adrenalin and anger were compensating for the long bike ride back here. He went right to the storage chest where he kept his supply of grenades. It appeared that Derrick's men had endured a lengthy gun battle, so more bullets or better rifles weren't the answer. He was going to rain down holy hell on their heads. If they wanted a war, they'd receive one hell of one.

He flung open the chest. Everything was there, as he had hoped.

———

TOM SLAMMED the wooden board against the window. It had come loose in the fighting, but Tom had discovered it and pushed it back into place while Sarah ducked into the living room, keeping her head down. At that moment, Conrad marched out of the hall with a grenade belt around his waist. "What's the story?"

"A few more bullets and then nothing," Sarah said, "They might be reloading or taking cover." Her eyes then widened. "You have grenades?"

Tom's eyes widened. "Holy shit, you do!"

"I'm heading out there." Conrad raced for the front door, which was closed, but the gun damage had made it impossible to lock or secure. "One or two of these babies will show them we mean business, or take care of them for good."

He pushed the door open enough for him to get outside, then slammed it shut behind him.

The front of the house lay still. The smell of smoke was pungent in the air. Plus, Conrad's property was dotted with corpses. Conrad had to step over Teller's dead form just to make it across the porch.

Derrick, you son of a bitch. This is what you wanted. To steal my land? To murder Camilla, my son, my family?

He was so furious he didn't think to check around the east side of his home when he crossed past his home's corner. But no one aimed their guns at him. Instead, he was greeted with another dead body and another man, struggling to stand up. His shirt was off and wrapped around his arm like a makeshift bandage. Clearly, he had been shot there and had ripped off his shirt to tie off the wound. At the moment, he had managed to climb onto his knees.

Conrad leveled his gun at him. The man yelped and nearly fell down again. "Wait! Please, don't shoot me! I...I can't fight any more!" he shouted. "You're Conrad, right? I'm...I'm going. I'm leaving. I won't bother you again!"

His hand still was too close to his gun. "Leave it," Conrad barked. "Now, how many of you are there?"

"Um, seven. But most of us are dead. I don't think there's anyone else," the wounded man replied.

"I'll be the judge of that. Now get going before I stop feeling generous," Conrad said.

Conrad's implied threat filled the man with enough fear to climb fully onto his feet. Then he hobbled off. Conrad didn't waste time checking to see if the intruder had beat it for good. Instead, he hurried to the west side of the house.

This time, he crouched low, creeping along the side of the house. It turned out to be a wise move, for a pair of gunshots flew his way. Conrad quickly thrust his binoculars up to his eyes. He could make out two figures several yards away, hiding in the fields next to his property. They appeared to be young men, but the wave of the tall grass made it hard to tell their features, or reveal the weapons they were using.

Conrad pulled off one of his grenades. It wouldn't matter what kind of guns they were using if they met up with one of these.

He pulled the pin, stood up, and threw it as hard as he could. Then, he dove onto the ground and held his head.

A few seconds later, the ground shook under his belly. A loud explosion kicked up a hailstorm of dirt.

Conrad raised his head. Smoke poured from a crater some yards away. He grabbed his binoculars again. The smoke made it difficult to see anything even as he tilted to the left, then to the right. Then, he finally caught sight of the two. The pair were in full retreat, vanishing toward the horizon.

He sighed. Without Derrick, and with the casualties they had taken, there should be no incentive for those two to come back and try anything.

———

LANCE CLUTCHED HIS SHOULDER. *This wasn't supposed to happen! What am I doing? I'm in a freaking war zone!*

His mind raced with the horrors of what he just had experienced. He was told this was going to be easy. This home with its crops and animals, it was going to be his! All they had to do was bump off one old homesteader.

But instead, people were being blown away all around him. It was like something out of a war movie. And now the ground just had exploded in front of him. Was that a grenade he saw coming from the house?

His head ached. The bang had produced a ringing in his ears. It wouldn't stop.

It wasn't until he reached the edge of the road that he stopped. He clutched his legs. "They're... they're not following us?" he asked.

Beside him, Cal panted. "I don't think so," he said.

Lance and Cal were the only two to retreat from the Drake homestead when those three newcomers showed up and gunned down Teller and the others. Lance cringed at the thought of what had happened to George, yet he couldn't go back to find out. They had been lucky to escape with their skins intact.

Lance wiped his face. "So, what do we do now?"

"You do whatever you want." Cal turned to the road. "Me, I'm heading to Derrick's crops and taking what I want. He's probably dead. Never coming back. And if he isn't, well, he ain't going to catch me before I get my fill."

Cal then raced toward the road.

"Hey, wait!" Lance called.

He ran after him, but tripped and fell over. No, he was too shook up to move right now. He needed to rest. But by the time he had gathered his wits, Cal would have reached Derrick's ranch, and no doubt taken all the best crops. He might even take it over and barricade Lance out. Cal didn't look like the type to share. In fact, Cal might even plug him and leave him for dead.

He stumbled toward the state road. No homes or towns were in easy sight. Lance was all alone. Now, without a bike, with no mode of transportation, and far from his hometown, he was even worse off than ever. Where would he go now?

———

CONRAD STUMBLED into the living room. Liam, seated on the couch, was being hugged tightly by Sarah. Though weak and his skin pale, Liam was very much awake and active, hugging his mother in return.

Tears flowed from Sarah's cheeks. "My baby. Oh, please tell me you'll be alright."

Liam's own eyes welled with tears. "Mom..."

Nearby, seated in an easy chair, Camilla pressed the gauze against her own wound. Tom came rushing back from the hallway. "Nothing. I think the house is clear."

Conrad stopped and leaned against the wall. Everyone's heads turned to him. "I scared the last few sons of bitches away. I'll check again, but I have to know you're alright." He turned to Liam and Camilla. "Oh Lord."

"I'll check around for you," Tom said, heading for the front door.

Conrad first knelt in front of Liam. "Hey," Liam said as Conrad checked his injury. "You made it back with Mom?"

Conrad looked up. "Yeah. We're all home again."

Liam reached out. Conrad met him halfway, and let his son embrace him. Sarah grasped the shoulders of both men.

After a short while, once Conrad had retrieved a medical kit and tended to Liam's wounds, while explaining to Sarah how to help, he hurried to

Camilla, who stood over them. Conrad offered to treat her, but she said, "Hey, I'm most of the way there. The bullet's out. It didn't penetrate deeply."

"Even so, you know the deal. Make sure it's not infected. Get yourself some antibiotics." Conrad raised a small tube. "I'd appreciate it if you stuck around, if you get my drift."

Camilla nodded. "Yeah." She took it. "So, you ran off to find your ex in a ruined city? Why the hell do you get to have all the fun?"

"Hey, I'd have invited you, but you're one slippery gal. This home isn't exactly your permanent address."

Camilla bit her lip. "Maybe it's time to change that. If you're okay with that. I mean..." She looked over Conrad's shoulder, to Sarah, Liam, and Carla on the couch. "...I'm not crowding you out, am I?"

Conrad pushed a small lock of hair out of Camilla's face. "Hell no. This house always has a spot for you." He smiled. "You did a hell of a job defending her from Derrick."

Camilla smiled slightly. "You really mean that?"

"Absolutely. You saved my boy, his girl, my grandkid. I couldn't begin to say how grateful am I, and how proud I am of you. This place always will be your home."

Camilla sucked in her lip. "Thank you." Tears started rolling her cheeks. "Thanks, Conrad." She then grabbed him and held him tightly.

———

CLANG!

Liam and Carla sprang up in their bed. Conrad was standing in the open doorway, a pot in one hand and a spoon in the other. "Up and at 'em, lovebirds," he said.

Yawning, Liam looked up at the window. The sky still was dark, though the first signs of dawn were approaching. "Dad..."

"I know you got shot, son, but that's no excuse. We got a lot of work ahead of us today. We still have to bury the last few men we took out yesterday, including Derrick." Conrad waved his spoon at the walls. "Plus, we got to figure out a replacement for a lot of the window glass. And, we got to check the house's insulation. With the holes made by the gunfire, it's going to make the home's heat leak out, and that's going to be hell come wintertime."

Liam rubbed his eyes. "I don't suppose we could wait a few more minutes. Or maybe an hour?"

"Not a chance. I leave my house in your hands for a couple of days and I find it's shot full of holes. Makes me glad I never had to lend you my car," Conrad said.

Carla laughed. "Oh, he's got you there."

"So, we've got some fixing to do." Conrad grasped the doorknob and started closing the door. "But, I'll give you a few minutes to get yourselves in gear."

Liam smiled. "Thanks, Dad."

———

Conrad approached the kitchen, where Camilla was waiting for him. "Now, are you giving those two a hard time?"

"Hey, can't let them go soft on us." Chuckling, Conrad stopped at the doorway. "Honestly, I'm not going to push them too hard. I'll let them give me a hand or two, but I'll be the one to make sure the mess from yesterday is cleaned up."

"Need a few more hands?" Camilla asked.

"Naaah. Just make sure we got some big meals ready." Conrad grasped his stomach.

"Don't push yourself too hard." Camilla strode in close to him. "We're all going to pitch in for this new life of ours." She smiled. "Maybe someday you will have to slow down and let the youngsters take over some of this."

Conrad massaged his knuckles. "I hope I don't have to anytime soon." He then looked up at the ceiling. "It's funny. I built this place pretty big for one person. Maybe in the back of my mind, I hoped someday I could share it with somebody. Now not only am I going to share it, I actually can leave it to my kids, and maybe grandkids. It makes the whole damn thing worth it."

Camilla nodded. "You bet."

———

Find out what happens in part three available now!

Made in the USA
Monee, IL
22 November 2020

2021

Imagination Station

Edited By Byron Tobolik

First published in Great Britain in 2021 by:

Young Writers
Remus House
Coltsfoot Drive
Peterborough
PE2 9BF
Telephone: 01733 890066
Website: www.youngwriters.co.uk

Printed and bound in the UK by BookPrintingUK
Website: www.bookprintinguk.com
YB0479U

★ FOREWORD ★

Welcome Reader!

Are you ready to discover weird and wonderful creatures that you'd never even dreamed of?

For Young Writers' latest competition we asked primary school pupils to create a Peculiar Pet of their own invention, and then write a poem about it! They rose to the challenge magnificently and the result is this fantastic collection full of creepy critters and amazing animals!

Here at Young Writers our aim is to encourage creativity in children and to inspire a love of the written word, so it's great to get such an amazing response, with some absolutely fantastic poems. Not only have these young authors created imaginative and inventive animals, they've also crafted wonderful poems to showcase their creations and their writing ability. These poems are brimming with inspiration. The slimiest slitherers, the creepiest crawlers and furriest friends are all brought to life in these pages – you can decide for yourself which ones you'd like as a pet!

I'd like to congratulate all the young authors in this anthology, I hope this inspires them to continue with their creative writing.

★

★ CONTENTS ★

Alfie Keen (10)	90
Bluebell Shaw (10)	92
Megan Morrison (9)	94
Lucy Moore (10)	96
Isla Sherwood (10)	98
Esme Morse-Buckle (10)	100
Isabel Underwood (9)	102
Izabella Walde (10)	104
Maria Hlebanovschi (10)	106
Reggie O'Connor (10)	108
Abbie Rose Bowdler (10)	110
Joe Chapman (10)	112
Philip Pryke (10)	114
Amélie O'Shea (9)	116
Wes Aston (10)	118
Fabian Kocinski (10)	120
Aliya Barrett (10)	122
Zenna John-Lewis (10) & Lily Owens (9)	124
Mia Visser (10)	125

Priory School, Slough

Jayden Tiwana (9)	126
Amber Badhan (9)	129
Sheza Ahmed (9)	130
Kacper Gegotek (9)	131
Nafisa Khan (9)	132
Fouzan Majeed (8)	134
Chaima Zemoule (9)	135
Asme Zemouli (9)	136
Keira Chitty (8)	137
Cora Chitty (10)	138
Rihija Eshal Ahmed (9)	139
Yasmin Zekari-Day (9)	140
Amelia Kaur Bing (8)	141
Joshua Palmer (9)	142
Evie Prescott (8)	143
Ummayma Fatima (9)	144
Hayley Foster (9)	145
Lillie-Mai Bullen (9)	146
Ella Aviss (9)	147

Queen's Hill Primary & Nursery School, Costessey

Corbin Green (9)	148
Harrison Forbes (9)	150
Zoe Chirwa (9)	152
Jack Grimmer (9)	153
Szymon Rudnicki (9)	154
Eloise Osborne (9)	156
Lucas Barker (9)	157
Lola Wright (9)	158
Skyla Rix (9)	159
Rosa Hartshorn (9)	160
Aaron Hawkins (8)	161
Lily Rust-Andrews (9)	162
Scarlett Carr (9)	163
Aimee Cusdin (9)	164
Blake Taylor (9)	165
Victoria Guziejko (8)	166
Lily Land (9)	167
Harley Bloomfield (9)	168
Sasha Smith (9)	169
Lily Fryer (9)	170
Jake Jennison (9)	171
Lennox Lown (8)	172
Isabella Cook (8)	173
Ebo Ellis (9)	174
Coco Brickley (9)	175
Oliver Cunningham (9)	176
Isla Carter (9)	177
Nina Stasiow (9)	178
Joe Rice (8)	179
Taylor Everett (9)	180
Amelia Castell (9)	181
Jenson Hurren (9)	182
Chloe Hilton (8)	183
Jack Bergin (8)	184
Louie Foster (8)	185
Mayer Hatson (9)	186
Caleb Clow (8)	187

Rice Lane Primary School, Liverpool

Nancy Lunt (7)	188
Joseph Douglas (9)	190
Emily Pierpoint (9)	192
Evie McVeigh (8)	193
Isla Burns (10)	194
Jessica Dowling (8)	195
Jack Nelson (11)	196
Lauren Millen (9)	197
Luca De Giorgi (8)	198
Axl Hook-Woolhouse (8)	199
Joseph Cornall (7)	200
Savannah Wright (9)	201
Riley Lyons (10)	202
Ashley Mcleod (8)	203
Lexi Murtagh (10)	204
Ella Bass (10)	205
Grace Wilson (9)	206
Harry Evans (9)	207
Lily-Faye Buckle (7)	208
Ava Kelly (10)	209

St Edward's RC Primary School, Westminster

Ziad Darwish (10)	210
Faustina Biniam (7)	212
Harley Dudziak (8)	213
Elisha Ntambwe (10)	214
Amira Bell (8)	215
Ariyah Abdel-Samie (7)	216
Ashton Jay Agulay (7)	217
Grace Porter (10)	218
Sienna O'Dwyer (8)	219
Amelia Zulkifli (9)	220
Mario Berishaj (8)	221
Marion Jorolan (9)	222
Kyrah Walker-Gerald (9)	223
Anaya-Rose Ntambwe (6)	224
Tristan Emmanuel Andrade (10)	225

St Joseph's Catholic Primary School, South Woodham Ferrers

Harry Thompson (10)	226
Gabriel Reid Robbins (11)	228
Lola-Alice Smith (11)	229
Jessica Nguyen (10)	230

THE POEMS

COME ON SLOW COACH

The Bear And The Motorcycle!

Hi, I'm going to tell you the story of my bear,
That looks quite cute but can give you a scare.
It all started when my bear had grown,
And she sat on her tricycle all alone.
Then to her frightening shock,
She cycled right into a great big rock.
Then after the bang,
She fell off with a clang.
Then she began to whine that she didn't want a tricycle,
But instead, a great big motorcycle.
So she walked to the shop,
And what she saw on top,
Was a great, big motorcycle!
So she threw away her tricycle,
And when she was ready, she jumped with delight,
Then she took it and rode away into the night.
So that is the story of my great, big bear,
That looks quite cute but can give you a scare.

Lara Cameron (9)
Bishop Sutton Primary School, Bishop Sutton

Alberta The Peculiar!

I have a sausage dog and her name is Alberta
Einstein,
I'm going to let you into a secret,
My dog Alberta is actually the most clever scientist
ever!
Every night, she turns into a sausage (I know,
weird!)
And she ventures out into the city.
She hides in a hot dog van.
After a long time sitting in the van,
She gets chosen.
She quickly gets eaten,
But she is okay,
So no damage (luckily!)
This is the fun part of the story!
At the same time as getting swallowed,
She looks around looking for new types of viruses
lurking about,
She also watches how the body digests food,
And sees what your organs look like,
Then of course, she has to get pooped out!
Quickly, she turns back into her former self,

By the time she gets home, it is almost morning,
And that is my peculiar pet!

Iona Purcell (9)
Bishop Sutton Primary School, Bishop Sutton

George

There was once a slimy, slippery slug,
That slipped around the streets,
But at night-time... he stalked off,
Into a cave full of slippery slugs,
And transformed into a stork,
That ate slugs.
After his slimy dinner,
He silently glided to my house,
For me to slip out of bed,
Slide onto his back,
And circle the city at dawn.
He slipped back down to my house,
I slipped off his feathery back,
And slinked back into bed.

Reuben Smith (9)
Bishop Sutton Primary School, Bishop Sutton

Dude The Teleporting Parrot

P urple plumage upon his head, framing his pitch-black sunglasses

A crobatic and awesome, he flips and flutters in the sky

R uby-red feathers and emerald green wings

R ummaging in the undergrowth for tasty little bugs

O ther creatures love to listen to his hilarious jokes

T eleporting powers make Dude the most amazing parrot around!

Ella Gray (9)

Bishop Sutton Primary School, Bishop Sutton

The Seagull Who Ate My Brother

On a beautiful, sunny day,
My brother went out to play,
He took a picnic lunch,
And sat by the water's edge,
He got out a sandwich to munch,
When a big, white seagull flew by,
My brother was about to say, "Hi!"
When the seagull opened its mouth wide,
He gobbled the sandwich as quick as a blink,
Then swallowed my brother alive!

Sophie Naylor (8)
Bishop Sutton Primary School, Bishop Sutton

The Ferocious, Terrifying, Unknown Shark

People don't need to fear,
Unless they have to go near...
The terrifying Metal Jawsdon!
It shoots lasers like spies do in London,
People say it's more fearsome than Megalodon!
As they bet it could destroy Noah's Ark,
Well, of course, it can destroy it, it's a shark!
Scientists count it as an incredibly dangerous
creature,
From ever since people have gone to the park,
Instead, humanity has found a creature...
With lots of features!
The world has never ever seen such things,
As this shark, it may be a shark king,
That does not have a crown with rings!

Jasson Maheshwaran (8)
East Tilbury Primary School, East Tilbury

The Lonely, Dangerous Stingray!

The dangerous stingray is a rare breed,
Friends in the ocean are what he needs,
Swimming around in the ocean blue,
With no one to talk to and nothing to do,
Other animals do not come close to him,
Because his stinger he can kill with,
Comes from his left fin,
Because he is purple, he is easily spotted,
He has large eyes, sharp teeth and his back is
dotted.
If other animals make any eye contact,
He will swim up towards them slowly and try to
interact,
The trouble is, he cannot control his sting,
Quickly killing everyone around him,
Then one day, a human came,
And took away all his pain,
A healing patch is all he needed,
For his life to be complete,

Now Mr Ray has all new mates,
And he can even have a girlie date.

Harper Reynolds-Burnell (8)
East Tilbury Primary School, East Tilbury

Funny Bunny

I have a cute, white rabbit,
He's my secret habit.
We call him Mr Punny,
He's very cute and funny.
When I'm sad, he cheers me up,
And makes me feel happy and glad.
He is very white and fluffy,
But sometimes he looks scruffy.
I love him very much,
Even when he's not nice to touch.

Aubreigh-Sophia Wall (8)
East Tilbury Primary School, East Tilbury

Slythering The Snake

He slithers on the floor,
He slithers every night,
If you see him in the night,
He'll give you quite a sight.
But don't make a fright,
Just wait and see,
If he catches you staring,
Then you'll become his tea!

Logan Edwards (7)
East Tilbury Primary School, East Tilbury

Daisy The Dolphin

Daisy is a goofy dolphin that's quite incredible,
She loves being sassy outside of the water,
But in the water, she is waddly, chatty and nice.
In the water, she eats loads of mangoes.
She is five years old.
She jumps out of the water,
Does a flip and goes back in.
She is very adorable but very clever.
She is unique and special in her own way.
She is very soft and loves to blow bubbles.
She is a very nice aqua blue.
She loves attention.
She is perfect.

Kerri-Leigh Yorke (9)
Johnson Fold Community Primary School, Bolton

Cutie The Koala

C ute Koala that's name is Cutie but she is a bit chubby

U nique she is

T urns into any animal

I love her so much

E xtraordinary, oh yes!

T iny as can be

H as horns

E normous yes, but so sweet

K oala, what she can be

O h, how sassy

A fluffy, puffy thing

L ives in a tree house

A dorable.

Hennessy Haywood (9)
Johnson Fold Community Primary School, Bolton

The Adventure Of My Snake

I got a new snake called pumpkin,
He was a titana boa.
In the night, he gets bigger.
One night, I climbed on his back,
We flew out the window,
And a big asteroid came crashing down.
The comet crashed into a plane,
The captain and copilot jumped out.
Pumpkin jumped up and caught them.
Then we were gone,
And went back home.
I love pumpkin,
He might be strong,
But he is my pet.

Zac Lomax (9)
Johnson Fold Community Primary School, Bolton

McNab

I went to the park,
There were loads of bugs.
The McNab ate them all.
We started to play,
But McNab got stuck in a tree.
He really likes to climb trees.
I got him down.
Then we went home.
When we got home,
He started to prank me.
He put a bucket on the door.
I opened the door,
And the water bucket fell on my head.

Joshua Flitcroft
Johnson Fold Community Primary School, Bolton

A Unicorn For An Empress!

There is an Empress,
But it isn't really human.
She is cute, fearless and rainbow coloured.
It is a unicorn, she is a secret singer,
Who wears sparkly dresses,
And even combs her hair.
She's a magical and peculiar pet,
Would you agree?

Alyssa-Luci Collier (9)
Johnson Fold Community Primary School, Bolton

Pepper The Cat

The other day, I adopted a cat,
Tiny but clever, furry and soft,
Every night, she sat at the window,
Making you want to open it,
But then,
She flew in and out of the night sky,
I hopped on her back,
Flying into the night sky.

Teegan Williams (8)
Johnson Fold Community Primary School, Bolton

Chickedy The Chick

C hick called Chickedy

H opping around the garden

I 'm playing with her

C hickedy chill

K ind Chickedy

E ggy bread

D irty chick

Y ucky, mucky Chickedy.

Sienna Bermingham (8)

Johnson Fold Community Primary School, Bolton

Jerald The Gangster Cat!

J erald the marvellous gangster cat

E ats rats and snakes

R ich in money and even owns a mansion

A nd even jumps higher than the moon

L ighter than books

D rives supercars.

Tyler Hughes (9)

Johnson Fold Community Primary School, Bolton

My Amazing Dog!

My fluffy Wooji dog,
Has fluffy Wooji hair,
He's silly and fiddly,
But he has an amazing heart,
He's strong and unique,
He's one of a kind,
My fluffy Wooji dog,
You're amazing.

Tyrone Kumire (9)
Johnson Fold Community Primary School, Bolton

Zoral The Singing Giraffe

Z   oral the singing giraffe

O   ranges are her favourite fruit

R   ich

A   dorable

L   ives in a mansion.

Emma Driver (8)

Johnson Fold Community Primary School, Bolton

Regal

R egal is the best

E xtraordinary

G uilty

A nti-flea

L oud and heavy eagle.

Damian Hughes (9)

Johnson Fold Community Primary School, Bolton

The Frog And The Fly

"Little fly, will you come and sit with me?
I have lots of questions to ask with glee."
"Oh my, oh my, you will gobble me up!
With a big buttercup."

"You must be tired and thirsty from your flight
Come and have a smoothie on my cool rock."
The frog licked his lips with a horrid smile.
"Oh my, oh my, I've heard of your smoothies that I
wish not to see!"

"Please come and have a feast in the day,
We can enjoy the sun of May."
"Thank you, kind Sir, but I am busy. I'll come
another day."
The frog saddened as she flew away.

"Magnificent fly you are beautiful in many ways.
Oh my, oh my, I have creams that will make you
gleam."
The foolish fly came nearer and *snap!*
The frog shot his tongue at the fly and ended her
vain days.

Jeremy Mazo-Wicks (9)
Meadow Vale Primary School, Bracknell

The Red Fox And The Robin

Once in a rainforest, slept a red fox who woke
hungrily,
His sharp eyes swerved and, to his pleasure, saw a
robin by a tree.
And so the sly fox said to the robin, "Little bird, will
you come to my den?
You can come and sit for dinner and we can feast
on some hen.
It shall be the tastiest food you have ever eaten,
The fruits that you eat, which are as small as a bee
to me, are surely beaten."
"Oh no, no, no, you silly fox," said the robin to the
amused fox,
"Have you ever heard of a herbivore like me eating
a hen?
And I have heard very often that whoever goes in
your den,
Will ne'er come back ever again!"

And so the cunning fox moved closer and said,
"As it is on the ground, your house surely must be
worn down,

And you surely cannot make another one in such a
pretty gown,
Go and get your lovely little chicks and come back
again here,
And we all can happily eat some delicious deer."
The robin, a little more convinced to this, replied,
"Thank you for the offer, kind sir, but no as my nest
is quite fine,
And there is more than enough for me and my
chicks to dine,
But didn't I tell you, you foolish fox, that me and
my family are herbivores?"

So the now flattering fox said,
"Oh, robin, you are as pretty as you are wise,
Surely you can't be despised,
Please do come again,
And bring your chicks into my den."
"I bid you goodbye and will come another day
now,"
Said the vain robin with a bow,
"But I shall come again,
And I'll bring my chicks into your den."

And so the foolish robin fluttered away,
But in the end, the fox, eyes glittering with glee,
finally got his way.

"Oh, where are you, pretty bird? said the sly fox
after some time alone in his den.
"When are you and your lovely chicks coming to
eat some hen?
Even though you are a herbivore,
Won't you, just for tonight, be like me: a
carnivore?"
And so the idiotic bird came with her nervous
chicks,
Only thinking of her pretty red gown, she stepped
on a rock and tripped,
Then the cunning fox took all of them,
And, along with some hen, made a tasty meal out
of them.

And thus, this is the end of the story,
Children who read, never take heed of idle words.
Always remember the moral of the red fox and the
robin.
Do not ever talk to people you do not know.
And, if you can, avoid them and lay low.

Stay like that or suffer the fate,
And please don't be like that foolish robin: bait.

Sneha Shaji (10)
Meadow Vale Primary School, Bracknell

The Leopard And The Beetle

"Would you care to step up to my main room?
It is up this long, winding stair,
It shall warm you up with a boom,"
Said the sly leopard to the beetle,
"So will you please go up there?"
"No, I shall definitely not!" exclaimed the beetle in reply,
"To ask me is incredibly rude and vain,
And I'm starting to think this is a lie,
Although, I wouldn't like to stand in the rain!"

"Dear, do you need a rest?
My nest is very warm and cosy.
I also care to give a slice of the best!"
The leopard continued, "Anything but a heap of mice!"
"No, I shall definitely not!" exclaimed the beetle in horror,
"I've seen what's inside your nest and it's not very nice,
And you seem very suspicious about the mice!"

As the curious leopard led the beetle,
He said, "Through this door, stands my awards,
One of them is for affection,
If you can't see, you may come towards,
Let me go fetch my award of election!"
The beetle replied, "No, I shall definitely not!
I am leaving with no further ado,
Although, I've seen quite a lot,
Let's do it another day when I come to see you!"

As the leopard went to his den,
He knew the beetle again would come,
He surely knew he had to do something... again,
And then his plan was done!
Then he sang, "Come beetle, come here again!
I want you to come and view my den!
Your eyes are blue and gold,
But mine are as dull as lead."
The leopard kept singing,
"And you're nice and bold,
But mine are flat and black with rot and dead!"
Soon came the beetle in such a silly hurry,
As she entered the leopard's dark and scary den,

She got slow, careful and went in a scurry,
A noise struck and then... leopard had done it again.

Now all children, read this poem,
Just learn a short and easy lesson,
Whenever you hear flattery,
You must deny and away you must rattle,
And learn a good lesson from the great poem of:
The leopard and the beetle.

Marissa Joseph (9)
Meadow Vale Primary School, Bracknell

The Jaguar And The Deer

"Will you come into my den? It is very cosy and warm," said the jaguar to the deer.
"I can't right now. Anyway, it's nearly dusk and it's dark and it's also raining," said the deer. "I fear I might lose a limb."
"Come back tomorrow if you wish."

It was the next day, the deer was on its way.
"Hello, delightful deer, would you like some food?"
"No, no, no. I've already had some food."
"But you can save some for later."

"I've made you a place to stay," said the jaguar. "Would you like to stay over?"
"I might do," said the deer.
"You look hungry. Would you like some food?"
"Yes please," replied the deer. "That was nice."
"Yes, it's getting dark. You could go to the place I told you about."

Blake Smith-Wesson (10)

Meadow Vale Primary School, Bracknell

The Ocelot And The Monkey

"Come climb into my tree, it's as pretty as can be!"
said the ocelot to the monkey.
"No, no, no!" exclaimed the monkey. "I will not
climb into your tree," continued the monkey, "or I
shall soon be food for thee!"
The monkey shook her head, staring up the tree,
"I'll never come," the monkey said, "I shall only run
and flee!"

"Why do you look so hungry? You look in a mood,
So let me give you some good food, then lose that
attitude!"
The ocelot offered, looking at the monkey who
shook her head again!
"No, no, no! You have no fruit for me! All you have
is meat and bone! From animals who lived long
ago."
The monkey looked up into the ocelot's tree.

"You're clever!" the ocelot purred.
His eyes glinted maliciously, "Your soft, brown fur!

So very silky too!" He stared at the small monkey.
"You make the still leaves stir!
Let me take you to a pond so you can behold
yourself!" The monkey thought about this.
"Oh, no, no, no! You can't fool me! The opportunity
to eat me is one you shall miss!"

The ocelot laid upon a branch, looking at the
monkey, he said, "Your eyes, so bright like
twinkling stars!"
He blinked, whiskers twitching. "They are like
diamonds that can be seen from Mars!"
"You are so small, so pretty! Come join me in this
tree!" he enticed.
Alas, alas, the monkey came; poor, foolish thing.
She climbed up the tree next to the ocelot.

"Why, oh why?" exclaimed the ocelot, "Did you
listen to me?
I only had to use a little flattery!
Animals of the forest, think carefully before you
act,
Don't be like the monkey, or death will come, that
is a fact."

Saffron Haskell (10)
Meadow Vale Primary School, Bracknell

The Jaguar And The Otter

The jaguar said to the otter, "Will you take a seat?
If you do, you can even have a sweet treat.
And if you want to stay,
We can have a bit of a play."
The jaguar spun around and grabbed a bottle
labelled: 'Poison - take care.'
The otter replied, "No way! I pity all the souls that
went into your lair."

The jaguar said to the otter, "How can I show you
how much I care?
I like you more than my friend called Tare!
I have lots of fish,
In a nice, silver dish.
Would you please take a bite,
And we can party all night."
He injected the poison into the food,
Which was very, very rude.
The otter replied, "No way! If I take a lick,
I would be very sick."

The jaguar said to the otter, "Will you wash off in the shower?
And then your beauty will truly flower."
The otter waved his head and jumped away,
"No way!" said the otter. "I think I made the right choice, the one not to stay."

The jaguar waited patiently, for he knew the otter would come back,
From his little, mouldy place along the river, his shack.
Then he sang, "Come back, otter! You're handsome, smart, silky and soft and your eyes are diamond bright. Please come back! I won't attack!"

The otter went running there,
He forgot all about the lair.
Only thought about himself,
Up jumped the jaguar,
And then he said, "Night, night!"
He picked the otter up, then held him tight,
He put the otter in his den,
I don't think you want to know what happened after then.

Now take a lesson and don't be the otter,
And stop reading silly books like Harry Potter.
Don't listen to a stranger,
Have you ever heard of danger?

Jack Dansey (10)
Meadow Vale Primary School, Bracknell

The Caiman And The Piranha

"Come into my cave," said the caiman to the piranha. "Come on, don't be a wimp."
The caiman turned and limped.
"Oh, no, no, no, I do not want to go into your beastly cave," the piranha said, then waved.
"Good day," said the piranha, "I'll be off now."
"No, what?" the caiman said. "Do you want a prize?"
"Haha, good day!" the piranha said smartly.
The caiman looked out kindly and screamed,
"Come back, come back, little piranha, look at your beautiful little eyes," said the caiman,
"When you talk, they rise."
"Got you!" screamed the caiman.
"Help, help, help!" said the piranha.
The piranha yelped.
The piranha sat there gasping.
Then the caiman bit the piranha on the back.

Cayden Pooley (10)
Meadow Vale Primary School, Bracknell

The Monkey In The Tree

"Hello, little lizard, can you step into my tree?
If you do, then I might jump up with glee,"
Lied the monkey in the tree.
"I have many magnificent things you may wish to see,
Now come upon my tree."
The monkey moved his hand aloft and pulled out a treat,
Then he stared at the lizard and threw him something neat.
"Oh no, I'm sorry, I cannot accept, I'd be too late for my meet up,
But I'm sorry, do you know where to get a cup?" said the lizard.
"I will ensure you more safety in my tree,
I might even feed you my finest tea!" said the monkey in the tree.
"I have every kind of bug,
For example, my Burmese slug."
"Oh no, oh no, no, I must not accept,
Nor must I take that boar-like bug," said the lizard.

"Would you like to see my collections,
All from ancient elections?" said the monkey in the tree.
"Oh really, may I take a look,
I am so curious from something I read in a book," said the lizard.
"Oh, wait, I am really running late,
I must come back another day, this must be fate."

"Oh, you little, little lizard, how can you leave?
I thought you would believe.
You're so colourful, I cannot compare,
I'm so horrible, I don't even have hair!
Please come back, I am so scared,
If you come back, I'm sure I'll care."

The foolish lizard came back, he climbed the tree,
And found the monkey, that was all he could see.
Oh no, a trap, realised the lizard,
Crunch! It was like a cold blizzard.
Thought the lizard.

Now to all the dear little children,
Who may read this tale,

Don't listen to enticing words,
Please listen.

Landon Bridgman (10)
Meadow Vale Primary School, Bracknell

The Snake And The Frog

"Will you jump into my hole?" said the snake to the frog.
"No, no, no, I'm happy here in this bog."
"Why not? Why not? I have tasty flies!" offered the snake,
"No, no, no, your offer is smart but fake."

"Oh, how sad," replied the snake. "Maybe my bed won't lie?"
"No, no, no, don't you possibly try!"

"Come here hungry frog! It's okay. There are no predators here!
You shouldn't be scared, you shouldn't have fear!
Your skin is clear and as beautiful as an emerald green.
While your manners and politeness are perfect and pristine."

Aidan Tbahriti (10)

Meadow Vale Primary School, Bracknell

The Harpy Eagle And The Baby Sloth

"Come in my leaf-filled den, it's cosy and warm,"
said the eagle to the sloth.
"There are cosy and warm beds and lots of
moths!" said the eagle to the sloth.
The sloth replied, "No, no, no! Kind Sir, I have heard
what happens when we dare to go in your bed."
The sloth said, "We twist and turn till we are dead!"

"Come into my fine stable home, it's luscious and
free from predators," said the sly predator trying
to hide his secrets as he ate moths.
The sloth said to the eagle, "I've heard what your
food does and I don't wish to try.

The eagle said to the sloth, "Come, come, it's safe
and homely up here,
We shall feast on leaves, why won't you come
near?"
The eagle said, "I have soft, cosy beds, why won't
you come near?"
The eagle was really trying to have the sloth for
dinner.

"Oh, no, no, no! I have heard what happens when we rest on your velvet pillows, we twist and turn, trying to escape," said the sloth to the eagle.

"Oh, your lovely eyes, so angelic and dazzling. Mine are as dull as lead," said the eagle to the sloth.
"I know you like playing with moths!"
"Oh well, dear, I will come again," said the sloth to the eagle.

The eagle was calling out to get his dinner.
The eagle said, "I am such a winner!"
The poor, little baby sloth with soft and silky skin,
Never came out again.

Dear little children who may read,
I pray you take heed,
I really hope you learn a lesson from this:
The harpy eagle and the baby sloth.

Lily Alltree (10)
Meadow Vale Primary School, Bracknell

The Ocelot And The Fish

"Will you step into my temple?" asked the ocelot to the fish,
"It's a legendary, grand place that you shouldn't miss."
The ocelot turned away, to try and hide her guilt,
As she just invited her prey to the best temple ever built.
The fish replied, "Thanks, but to ask me is in vain,
As whoever steps into your temple, will never step out again."

"Will you come into my dining room?" queried the ocelot to the fish,
"It's got all the nuts and seaweed that you could ever wish.
"Come taste my cake, it tastes so good," said the cunning ocelot wisely,
The fish replied, "Thanks again, though you treat me so nicely."

"Darling fish," said the ocelot, "your scales need lots of care,
"Come into my chamber, I have jewellery to share.

I also have a river outside my temple house,
If you step and look inside, you shall amaze
yourself."
The fish replied, "Thanks, I'll sadly say goodbye,
I'd love to come and visit you some other quiet
time."

The ocelot waited patiently and then loudly called
out,
"Come pretty, pretty fish, you make me want to
shout!
Your colour-changing scales make me jealous,
green with envy,
Your eyes are like the morning light but mine are
dull and heavy."
Hearing these wildly flattering words, the fish
nearer came,
At last, the ocelot jumped and murdered, it's her
bloody game.

To people who read this story,
Don't listen to flattering words of glory.
Take a lesson from this tale,
And don't get tricked and fail.

Nini Shi (10)
Meadow Vale Primary School, Bracknell

The Lemur And The Spider

"Will you climb into my tree house?" said the lemur
to the spider,
"You're carrying lots of stuff, perhaps I could make
it lighter."
The lemur had a glint in his eye and hid a sly, little
grin.
"No thank you," replied the spider, "I'll be pushed
off the rim."

"I have always loved you, why don't you see?" said
the lemur to the spider,
"I'll even give you some food, I swear it won't make
you wider."
The lemur ushered the spider into the dining room,
"No thank you," the spider replied, "I would rather
eat the moon!"

"You look nice today, but your lipstick's coming
off," said the lemur to the spider,
"I have some good lipstick if you want it, it's the
colour of apple cider."
The lemur held up the stick, the colour of a tomato!
"No thank you," replied the spider, "now I need to
play with play dough."

The lemur turned him back around and into his
scary, tremendous tree house,
For he knew the funny, little spider would come
back and then he would pounce!
The lemur went out and called, "Come, pretty
spider, with the golden lipstick and shiny, silver
boots!"
The spider heard these flattering words and came
running over roots.
Ah-ah! The lemur caught the little spider and sat
down at his table,
He even went into the kitchen to turn on the oven
cable.

And now, every child that does read,
Don't listen to strangers, I pray you take heed,
So take a lesson from this story,
And it won't end up gory.

Jonah Keyte (10)

Meadow Vale Primary School, Bracknell

The Tiger And The Monkey

"Oh, my lovely home!" shouted the tiger into the air.
"You can do whatever you want, I don't really care."
Then the monkey said, swinging through the trees,
His grin was getting wider but you wouldn't be able to see.
"Oh, stupid tiger, I will not be your prey,
And if you try to eat me, I'll just swing away."

The tiger's eyes narrowed, then he kindly said,
"I have fresh bananas and lots of other things for you to be fed."
The monkey started smirking, then started to laugh,
He started slapping his knees, he thought the tiger was daft.
"Just because I'm a monkey and just because I'm fat,
And just because I may seem hungry, doesn't mean I'd fall for that."

"Come into my special playroom," said the tiger to the monkey,
"You can leave whenever you want and go back to that rotten banana tree.
"He makes my home sound bad," said the monkey quietly,
"But I think that he's gone mad because this is a cave and that's a tree.
Maybe I should check to see if he's alright,
He's already gone insane, I'm sure he won't bite."

"Oh, sweet monkey," said the tiger with a purr,
"You've got such a lovely, pink face and soft, light brown fur.
You swing through the trees with such haste!
But the best part of you, I think would be your taste." *Chomp!*

So, dear reader, now that you've read this story,
If you know someone is evil, don't always feel sorry.

Samuel Browning (10)
Meadow Vale Primary School, Bracknell

The White Tiger And The Deer

"Will you come into my lair? I have many glorious things in there,"
Said the white tiger to the deer, not pausing for air.
He said this hiding a glint of evil in his eye,
"Oh dear, no!" said the deer to the tiger with a sigh,
"As I do often hear those who go in your den, never come out again."

"May you come into my kitchen, please? I have fresh food that is nice, even tea,"
Said the white tiger to the deer as his voice sunk.
"Will you come in? The kitchen is near, will you please take a chunk?" offered the white tiger.
"Oh dear, no!" said the deer,
"I do not wish to see, my friend's grandma came to tea and she didn't come back, that's what I hear."

"Come into my kitchen, it has a lovely view, I cleaned it just for you," said the white tiger.
"Oh dear, no!" replied the deer. "I heard of the blood soaking the mud and I don't want to see!"

"Come closer, lovely deer, you're faster than a cheetah, stronger than a rhino, your fur is as soft as silk. Come for there is no fee," purred the tiger who was in a stance.
The silly deer came closer to the tiger and its doom came as if it were in a trance.
Suddenly, the white tiger hurled himself at the deer, knocking her over as he bit her neck, killing her.

Now people who may read,
I pray you don't take advantage of this tale,
As the deer heard no purr,
"Poor, silly deer!" her friends would howl,
After all, it was foul.

Jaxon Lambert (10)
Meadow Vale Primary School, Bracknell

The Snake And The Frog

The snake said to the frog,
"Come into my lovely log house,
It is thatched and therefore warm,
There are no pests and not one mouse,
And it is filled with luscious corn!"
"My, oh my, no!" replied the frog,
"I do not want to come near any log!"

The sly snake said to the frog,
"Come up to my stable tree home,
It is away from predators up high,
Made into a circular dome,
And you may catch some flies."
"My, oh my, no!" replied the frog,
"Your brothers are there,
And I am definitely sure they will want to share!"

The greedy snake said to the frog,
"Come, come, little frog,
You're quick thinking and you're wise,
Come and see my timber logs,
Then I will not hear your cries!"

"My, oh my, no!" replied the frog,
I must really be going now,
Goodbye, my friend! Adios! Au revoir! Ciao!"

So knowing that the frog would come, the snake
set his table,
Ready to eat the silly, stupid, little frog this day!
"Oh, frog, you are so able,
As wonderful as May!
Your skin is smooth and in no way sharp,
But mine is as coarse as bark."
This silly frog came hopping by,
But was violently seized and held up high.

So this frog was never seen again,
The frog was lost forever,
Not once was he seen by men,
So really children, do not try to be clever!
Now basically, do not be like this creature,
And I hope you enjoyed this little adventure!

Quinn Cousins (10)
Meadow Vale Primary School, Bracknell

The Bear And The Toucan

"Will you come down from there and come into my palace filled with chocolate and some other food we can share?" said the bear.
"Oh, no, no!" said the little toucan,
"I will not dare to step into there!" whined the toucan.
"If I was you, I would go in there," said the bear.
The bear was struggling not to laugh.
"I will not come in because I don't want to be cut in half."

"If you didn't know, I have some chocolate and some other special treats just for you.
If you're hungry, this is the place to be."
"I mean, I'm a bit hungry, so I'm going to trust you."
"Trust me, I will fill your tummy."
The bear knew he would be the only one having dinner.

The toucan was looking at herself in the mirror.
This was great for the bear.
The bear was already there.

The bear said, "You look pretty and you're wise,
How wonderful are your eyes!"
"Thank you for everything,
But I really do have to go now," said the toucan.
"Okay," said the bear...

"Gotcha!" screamed the bear.
"Now you're in my hands and I could do anything,
Even eat you!" said the bear wickedly.
The toucan never came out again.
She wasn't enjoying her new den.

Learn your lesson, don't listen to flattery,
Don't talk to strangers,
Don't talk to people bigger than you,
Unless you know them.

Vinnie Mark Peter Saunders (9)

Meadow Vale Primary School, Bracknell

The Anaconda And The Capybara

"Kind capybara, would you care to come by my water bank?" hissed the evil snake.
"No, no, no!" said the capybara, letting out a shake.
"For whoever lays a foot by your water bank, shall never see the world anytime soon,
And that would be a boom!"

"I do hope you're hungry, for I have food with glee,
That will make your stomach go wee!
Why don't you come in and I will treat you," said the anaconda as kind as he could be.
"No, no, no! I shall decline your offer, for I have heard you feed people with wheat and I'm gluten-free!" replied the capybara imagining tea.

"Capybara, you are a stunning sight," hissed the anaconda trying to be right.
"Hmmm, sorry... I couldn't finish!" exclaimed the capybara, trying to be kind.
"Can you come back tomorrow?" asked the anaconda, picturing the capybara letting out a whine.

"Hello again, dear friend!" hissed the anaconda,
still thinking about the whine.
"Your eyes are as blue as the ocean and now I'm
saving time."
No, no, no! How foolish! As the capybara was
leaning in... *Boom!*
The capybara was brutally dead on the dot.
Now she lies wrapped around the snake, never to
see the light.
This must not be right!

A lesson you have learnt,
Don't let people flatter your head.
You may never get to bed...
You may be wearing red...
Don't play dead!

Hollie Smith (10)
Meadow Vale Primary School, Bracknell

The Eagle And The Monkey

"Will you come and see my favourite tree?"
Asked the eagle to the monkey.
"Oh, no, no, no!" the monkey sighed,
"It is every way too big, every way too high!"
"It's not too tall," the eagle smiled,
"Don't be so shy!"

"Please, I have a banana cake at home!" pleaded the eagle.
"Just dine alone... see ya, amigo!" The monkey walked.
"If I dine alone, I will be sad..." the eagle talked.
"Well, I must go, go with my lad..." the monkey mocked.

"Well, at least stay, I have a rose to match your pretty, little eyes," the eagle tried.
"You are so wise... Your eyes glitter in the sunlight," the eagle irritatedly sighed.
"So please stay!" the eagle lied.

The eagle started to sing and shout,
While twisting and turning all about.
"Oh, furry creature with the crystal jewel blue eyes,
Take my breath away, don't run away and cry.
Your crunchy, crunchy, crispy tail makes my mouth
water,
I smell your lovely skin when you're about to eat
your supper..."

"Actually, I want a sloth," the eagle scoffs.
"Don't be greedy!" another monkey coughs.

Don't take what people say, bad or good,
Or you may end up...
Like the monkey in the eagle's belly.
Learn from this story, children,
The eagle and the monkey.

Jemima Wedderburn (9)
Meadow Vale Primary School, Bracknell

The Jaguar And The Bird

"Will you walk into my den?" said the jaguar to the bird,
"I will be here every minute of the day, you have my word."
"Oh, no, no!" replied the bird. "I will not be your food,"
"Now do me a favour," she continued, "And stop being so rude."

"Oh, I'm so very sorry," stated the jaguar, "Come and sit at my table,
If you wish to stay awhile, my table is full of maple.
"Oh, no, no!" replied the bird. "I have heard what is in your fish."
The bird continued, "And I do not wish to be your dish."

"You are wise and witty," said the jaguar, "and your eyes are a brilliant blue,
You're colourful and beautiful, but you're also very true."
"Thank you for the compliments," said the little bird,
"Thank you, but no, don't be so absurd."

The jaguar waited patiently, then sang, "You have
diamond eyes,
It will be really sad if we have to say our
goodbyes."
But the stupid bird came near and forgot about
everything,
Soon she did know she was about to lose a wing.

"Silly, little bird, you came to me,
All I needed to use was a little flattery.
You shouldn't have come to my den, it was just
bait,
Now come closer, for you will be on my dinner
plate."

Emma Medlicott (10)

Meadow Vale Primary School, Bracknell

The Tiger And The Boar

"Come, come into my temple," said the tiger to the boar.

"There are lots of amazing, sparkly things here," said the tiger.

The tiger gave a sly cunning look to the boar.

"No, no, I couldn't go in your dwelling," refused the boar.

"Dear, little boar, would you please take a slice of this delicious boar leg pie?" questioned the tiger with a creepy glint in his eye.

"Eat my food, dine with me," invited the tiger.

"Come sit on my cosy, luxurious and soft chair," offered the tiger.

"Oh, no, no, I couldn't sit on 'your' chair!" the boar exclaimed. "My food is yummy, crummy and delicious!" snarled the tiger as he gave a deep, long stare to the poor boar.

"Come and see my shiny gems," coaxed the tiger, "you will be so jealous of them!"

The tiger secretly gave a cheeky smile.

"No, no, kind sir, I do not wish to end up in your stomach or bite," whispered the boar.

"Your fur is fluffy and silky,
Your eyes are like diamonds,
You're worth many millions," cried out the deceitful tiger.

Foolish boar came nearer,
Tiger lept and gripped the boar,
She ne'er came out again.

Children who may read this,
Never fall for flattery.

Aryian Mair (10)
Meadow Vale Primary School, Bracknell

The Leopard And The Antelope

"Will you walk into my den?" said the leopard to the antelope,
"There are many ancient treasures we will discover through my microscope."
You wouldn't dare go into his peculiar-looking den,
The antelope replied, "No, no, no, why would I fall for that again?"

"Do you want to go to my pantry?" said the leopard to the antelope,
"I have washed it down with a bar of soap,
Do you want to have a slight slice?"
"Oh, no, no, no, I do not wish to eat mice."

The leopard said to the antelope, "See my mirror on the wall,
There is absolutely no need to stall at all,
There is my lovely drinking hole,
And trust me, you will not fall."
The antelope replied, "I do not want to look into your hypnotising pool."

The leopard sang as he patiently waited,
He said to the antelope, "Your horns are so
smooth,
Your fur is fluffier than a pillow,
Your tail is so cute, I wish I had one too,
Your eyes are as shiny as diamonds, but give me
one moment,
I just need the loo,
Your ears are so cool, I wish I had some too."
Slash! The leopard cut the antelope in half.

Now children who may read,
I pray this does not lead,
Do not listen to anyone sly,
So turn around and say goodbye!

Tyne Connor (9)
Meadow Vale Primary School, Bracknell

The Snake And The Mouse

"Come here, little mouse,
Let me show you my house!"
Said the snake to the mouse.

The snake coiled tightly,
The mouse replied, "I think I'll go now,
As you snakes are quite frightening."

"Come into my living room,
And sit on my relaxing chair.
And I shall get some food that we can share!"
Said the snake to the mouse.

"Oh, I'm fine for now,
If I eat anymore, my stomach might tear."
"I have a bowl of gold upon my shelf,
It shines golden like your eyes,"
Said the snake to the mouse.

The mouse replied, "I thank you for the
compliment,
But my eyes are the colour of a blue business tie."
"I might come back at night," the mouse sighed.

The snake knew the silly mouse would be back,
And there would be no time to slack.
He went out of his door and said,
"Your smile shines!"

The mouse, hearing these words,
Came running back right on time.
The snake lunged at the mouse,
The mouse was dragged into the snake's house,
He was never seen again.

To people who may read this,
Don't talk to strangers,
As some strangers can cause danger.
And never listen to flattery,
Because they probably want something from you.

Campbell Banks (10)

Meadow Vale Primary School, Bracknell

The Panther And The Boar

"Will you walk into my cave?" said the panther to the boar,
"We can climb to the top of my cave with our paws."
The panther looked away with a smirk.
"No, no, no!" said the boar. "Because I'll never come out again and won't be able to work."

"I've got lots of food and plants for us to share," said the panther to the boar,
"Unless you think that is a bore."
The panther looked away with a bigger smile than the first time.
"No, no, no!" said the boar. "I want to go to mine."

"Oh, little boar, you're witty and handsome," said the panther to the boar,
"You have tusks that are as shiny as the sun."
The panther looked away again with a smile bigger than the other times.
"No, no, no!" said the boar. "All the other animals will hear me whine."

"But your brown, shiny fur is blinding me," said the panther to the boar,
"Your legs will touch the squeaky floor."
The panther's plan was very successful.
"Just come a little closer!" The panther's plan was stressful.

When you read this story,
Take note of the panther and the boar,
Because they will flatter you and eat you,
Like the panther did to the boar.

Joshua Burdenuik (10)
Meadow Vale Primary School, Bracknell

The Jaguar And The Tortoise

The jaguar said to the tortoise, "Will you step into my warm, beautiful home with fires on the alleyway?
Lay on my rocks that look good on display?"
The tortoise replied, "Oh, no, no, no, for your rocks are too rough,
And most probably, my shell will get scuffed."

The jaguar said to the tortoise, "I've got lots of meat behind this wall,
And if you want some, just give me a call."
The tortoise replied, "Oh, no, no, no, as you'll make me choke,
And then you'll kill me by grabbing on my throat."

The jaguar howled to the tortoise, "Come down to the vast, pretty river, you'll see yourself there,
Your shell is so charming and the colours are rare."
The tortoise replied, "Thank you for the compliments, they're very nice of you to say,
And most likely, I'll come back again Some day"

The jaguar sat far in the cave with his gloomy eyes,
For he knew the tortoise wasn't telling lies.
Scrape, scratch!
And at last, he caught the tortoise with his claws,
But when he ate him, he gave a few loud roars.

Don't listen to people that are sly,
Mostly children, please don't sigh,
Things like bad behaviour and words that flatter,
Just ignore them as they don't matter.

Taion Williams (10)
Meadow Vale Primary School, Bracknell

The Black Panther And The Monkey

"Will you step into my leafy den?" said the black
panther to the monkey,
"You could have a rest on my furniture then!" said
the black panther to the monkey with a sly smile
that was funky.
"Sorry dear, but I have to refuse, for I have heard
what happens when we step into your leafy den!"
shouted the monkey.

"Will you have dinner with me? It's fine dining,"
said the black panther to the monkey,
"The meats are fine and thin," said the black
panther to the monkey.
"Sorry dear, but I have to refuse, for I have heard
what is in your dinner and I do not want to see!"
said the monkey.

"Will you come and see my dance trophy?" said
the black panther to the monkey,
"It is the shiniest trophy you ever did spy!" said the
black panther to the monkey.
"Sorry dear, but I have to refuse, for I have seen
your trophy many times before," said the monkey.

"Your hands are feisty, sharp and long. You are clever and wise!" said the black panther to the monkey.
But of course, she fell for it.
The black panther took a bite.
"Yes, it worked," said the black panther to the dead monkey.

Now let me give you a warning,
Don't trust someone with fangs and a sly smile,
They are dangerous.

Natalie Hill (10)
Meadow Vale Primary School, Bracknell

The Jaguar And The Sloth

"Come into my den," said the jaguar to the sloth,
"If you spill anything, I will gladly give you a cloth."
"Oh, no, no, no!" replied the sloth, "I know you are going to eat me,
You're trying to trick me, you are such a big bully!"

The jaguar added, "I have many twigs, leaves and buds,
When you have finished, I would love to give you some hugs."
"Oh, no, no, no!" muttered the sloth, "I can get it myself,
I know when I do it, I can save my precious health."

The jaguar continued, "You look very cuddly, come and see my brush,
When you are done, I know you will look very lush."
Oh, no, no, no!" exclaimed the sloth, "I already look beautiful."
"Besides," added the sloth, "I don't need you, I am already wonderful."

The jaguar replied, "You look so pretty, I could give you a bubbly bath,
I have many wonders hidden behind this path."
Foolish sloth could not resist such an offer,
Slowly, it came down the tree and got closer.

For those who read this tale of the jaguar and the sloth,
Take heed, never be like a moth.
Resist, never come near a bright light,
Or you may never see another night.

Faye Tremain (9)
Meadow Vale Primary School, Bracknell

The Snake And The Rat

"Will you walk up the tree?" said the snake to the rat,
"I will be here day and night, just waiting next to a bat."
"No, no!" replied the rat, "I will not be your friend."
"Do me a favour," he continued, "And stop being so rude!"

"But there is lots of meat to be shared," explained the snake,
"And if you come up here, then I can let you have a break."
"No, no! I will not eat that, it is meat, so leave it alone,
Don't come to me because I really don't like to moan."

"Come here and look at yourself, so beautiful and eyes so green,
But sometimes, you are really, really mean."
"Oh no, I am sorry, I didn't mean to hurt you,
But I will say good morning and I'll see you in a day or two."

Now the snake sang, "Come here, hairy rat, black
fur and green eye,
And the tail, so come here, come here and don't
cry,
Because you might be mine for this night.
The foolish rat came again and now I know it is
mine."

"Oh why, oh why, did you listen to me?
I only needed to use a little bit of flattery,
Whoever is watching, don't be like the rat,
Because that is a big fact."

Lucas Gale (10)

Meadow Vale Primary School, Bracknell

The Otter And The Catfish

"Would you like to come into my house?" said the Otter.
"My house is very good because it is made of wood."
"Oh no!" exclaimed the Catfish. "People go missing on your bed of logs."
"Please, oh please, I won't come. I know your idea, I'm not walking into that, bog!"

"I have some whitebait on a table just for you,
I can add some treacle pie to the dinner table."
"It sounds very fake," mentioned the Catfish,
"although, I hope you bake."

"I have a beautiful bed to rest your wonderful head," said the Otter.
"That sounds nice, but please, I don't want to stay," said the Catfish.
"I have a bed all to myself to lie in."
"It's a very big bed just for you! Bye."

"Okay then, just this once!" exclaimed the Catfish.
"You're so wise, charming and beautiful," said the Otter.

"Look upon my mirror to see your beautiful face."
"Okay, where is your mirror?" replied the Catfish.
The Otter pounced and gobbled him up.

For anyone who is reading this,
Do not follow a stranger,
Unless you know them very well.

Oliver Vuceljic (10)
Meadow Vale Primary School, Bracknell

The Snake And The Jaguar

"Will you climb up onto my branch?" said the snake,
"I will be waiting here all day, next to this lake!"
"Oh, no, no!" replied the jaguar. "I will not be strangled!
Do me a favour and stay tightly tangled!"

"Lots of birds ready to be equally shared."
"Oh, no, no, let them go, they're most likely scared!"
"If you come up now, you can sort the portions," explained the snake.
"I forbid coming up," said the jaguar. "I have a feeling this is fake!"

"Please come and rest your fluffy fur up here," said the snake in a calm voice.
"Oh, no, no! Anyway, it's my gosh darn choice!"
"Please, please don't be scared, I won't hurt you, my dear," flattered the snake.
"I really don't trust you, you'll push me in the lake!"

"Elegance, my lovely creature, Mr Large Teeth, you have a wonderful smile, it really is quite true," He continued, "You are the most beautiful thing I ever knew."
"That was amazing singing!" shouted the jaguar.
"Thank you very, very much!" he said,
And he choked the jaguar until it was dead.

Lucas Kent (10)
Meadow Vale Primary School, Bracknell

The Jaguar And The Croc

"Will you walk on the forest floor?" said the jaguar to the croc,
"I will be here all day and night, just waiting near this rock."
"No, no, no," replied the croc, "I will not be your food!"
"Do me a favour," he continued, "And stop being so rude."

The jaguar asked, "Will you come to my tree?
There is food that you can come and share with me."
The croc replied, "No, no, no, you're a scam, I can see,
Now if you excuse me, I may flee."

Sitting on the rock, the jaguar exclaimed, "Come to my bed!"
Blinking at the croc, he continued, "You will not be dead!"
The croc replied, "No, no, no, for what goes to your bed,
Will always be dead!"

The jaguar shouted, "Your scaly skin is so bright."
He continued, "It impresses me every night."
"Oh! That's the nicest thing I've heard,
Since I met that bird."

"Why, oh why," he exclaimed, "Did you listen to me?
I only had to use a little flattery.
Animals of the forest, always think before you act,
Don't be like the croc or death will come, that is a fact."

Lucas Dale (10)
Meadow Vale Primary School, Bracknell

The Piranha And The Crustacean

"Come into my cave," said the piranha to the crustacean.

"Come on, come into my cave," said the piranha in frustration.

"Oh, no, no!" replied the crustacean, "I've heard what's in your cave."

The crustacean said, "If I go in, I will become your slave."

The piranha said to the crustacean, "Why don't you have a snack? I have a store of what you'll like!"

"Oh, no, no!" the crustacean said. "Last time, you stole my bike."

"Why don't you take a nap?" said the piranha to the crustacean. "My bed is lovely and cosy."

"Oh, no, no!" replied the crustacean, "I am not dozy!"

"Alright then, I've got to go," said the crustacean.

"Please don't go," replied the piranha, "I'm going to be an animation."

Off swam the crustacean, leaving the cave.
"Oh, crustacean, how beautiful are your pincers?
You are as red as a tomato, so beautiful," said the
piranha while dancing down his path.
Oh, poor crustacean, little did he know he soon
would die,
The piranha whispered, "I'll put you into a pie."

Stanley Johnson (9)

Meadow Vale Primary School, Bracknell

The Lynx And The Macaw

"Will you fly into my nest?" said the lynx to the macaw,
"I will be here all day and night, waiting near this floor!"
"No, no no!" replied the macaw, "I will not be your food,"
"Do me a favour," he continued, "and stop being so rude."

"Come in! Come in! For I have food,
And let's hope that it changes your mood!"
"No, no no!" said the macaw to the lynx,
"I wouldn't do it, even if I had to sit still like the Sphinx!"

"Come, come, come!" said the lynx to the macaw,
"I have a lovely bed for you to sleep in, or perhaps my lovely, smooth floor!"
"Oh, no, no no! I'm fine in my own bed,
For whoever sleeps in yours, nothing good has been said!"

"Oh, come, come, come, my pretty, little bird!
I'm very sure that from you I am heard!"

Oh, and the stupid, little macaw,
She went indeed and she ended up on the floor...

"Why, why, why? You stupid, little bird.
Animals of the rainforest, I shall be heard.
Always be careful before you act,
Because predators of the forest will make an impact!"

Lily Byrne (10)
Meadow Vale Primary School, Bracknell

The Panther And The Boar

"Will you come into my tree house?" said the
panther to the boar,
"'Tis the prettiest tree house you ever did spy."
"Oh, no, no, no," replied the boar, "I cannot climb
in your tree house up so high."

The panther leapt from his tree.
But surprisingly, the boar did not flee.
"I know what you like," said the panther to the
boar,
"It's a mudbath, am I right?"
"I shall come up," said the boar to the panther,
"But please don't give me a fright."

"You have elegant fur," said the panther,
"While mine is as black as night."
"Good day to you panther," replied the boar,
"Come again, I might."

The panther did wait and wait,
He knew he had put out the perfect bait.
"Oh, come hither, hither luscious boar, you have
sparkling eyes, while mine are as dull as coal," said
the panther to the boar.

The boar was transfixed by his words and crept
closer as if he wanted more.
The panther leapt and killed the boar with his claw.

To children who read,
Ne'er take heed,
To idle, flattering words.

Lohit Anand Rajasekaran (10)
Meadow Vale Primary School, Bracknell

The Jaguar And The Hare

"Please take a step into my wonderful tree house,"
said the jaguar to the hare,
"I have many things for the two of us to happily
share!"
The jaguar briefly smiled and showed him stunning
fangs.
"Oh, no, no, kind Sir, I've heard about your tricks
that will leave me in tons of bad pangs."

"Come into my food court," said the jaguar to the
hare,
"Please take a bite, your mind will see a wonderful
sight."
"Oh, no, no, no, kind Sir, I've seen your food and I'd
much rather pass."

The jaguar said to the hare, "Please see my
wonderful portrait of your beautiful head and
magnificent wings,
If not, I've got many other things!"
"Oh, no, no, no, kind Sir, I've watched videos and
that picture of you is not relevant, so goodbye!"

"Come here, pretty hare, so witty, wise, handsome
and beautiful, eyes like diamonds - mine are as dull
as lead!"

Dumbly, the little hare hopped over - well, he's now dead!
"Why, thank you..."
The jaguar paralysed the hare and bit his skull,
Young kids, take this as a lesson,
Don't listen to flattery.

Alfie Keen (10)

Meadow Vale Primary School, Bracknell

The Margay And The Sloth

"Come to my tree home with camouflaging leaves
as soft as a cushion," said the margay very sly,
"My home is very shady and you can relax under
the swinging vines that swing every day, I might
wave goodbye."
"No, no, no!" said the sloth. "I know what happens
there, I don't want to try."

"Come to my dinner table, have some yummy food
on the cushioned chairs as soft as hair."
"Oh no!" exclaimed the sloth. "I don't want to stare
in your lair!"

"You're fluffy, puffy, shiny and very fast,
I can barely see you when you run past.
Look in the glass and see how beautiful you are,
And see how wondrous that one is on par.
"I'll see you another day," said the sloth.

He waited patiently and sang,
"Pretty sloth with shiny and fluffy fur,
Shiny, golden eyes shimmering,

Shimmering like they are at this moment."
The foolish sloth came closer,
And the margay jumped on the sloth,
And the sloth never came out again.

Never talk to strangers,
Like the margay and the sloth,
Danger!

Bluebell Shaw (10)

Meadow Vale Primary School, Bracknell

The Jaguar And The Croc

"Oh, will you please walk onto this floor," said the jaguar,
"I am really not a liar."
"No, no, no, the place I will stay is here,
Now go somewhere else to kill," said the croc.

"Oh, but there's lots of deer to share," laughed the jaguar,
"Or maybe one hare."
"No, no, no, I will stick to my diet,"
Cried the croc, "Now you must be quiet!"

"Scaly, clean, handsome, brilliant and why so sad?
It really can't be that bad!" said the jaguar.
"The deer's bones were cleared like that,"
The croc claimed, "Say it like that, I'm going to eat with a cat."

With patience, the jaguar sang, "Of course, of course, flattery is the greatest way to find the key,
Green skin for my carpet."
The foolish croc got pinned,
The jaguar's tail skimmed.

"Why, oh why," said the jaguar, "Did you listen to me?
I only had to use a little flattery.
Animals of the forest, think before you act,
Don't be like the croc or death will come, that's a fact."

Megan Morrison (9)

Meadow Vale Primary School, Bracknell

The Ocelot And The Sloth

"Hello there, little one, would you kindly step in?"
the ocelot asked the sloth.
"No thank you, dear," he replied, "I better head
off!"

The ocelot said to the sloth, "Oh no, stay for
lunch!"
She bit into an animal with a loud crunch!
The sloth winced and then said, "I must go now!"
The ocelot screeched an angry miaow!

"Urgh, you must stay!" the ocelot called. "I can
show you my rubies and emeralds and gold!"
"No thank you, I don't want to break them for they
must be fragile and old."
The ocelot could protest no more and the sloth
turned and fled.
"I'll come tomorrow, as soon as I get out of bed."

The ocelot waited for the sloth to come back,
She knew speed was what the sloth lacked.
She waited and waited and waited some more,
It was such a bore.

Finally, the sloth came,
And the ocelot was not tame.
She ripped the sloth to shreds,
And ate all of it, even the head!

Now little children who may read this story,
Beware of the dangers,
Of talking to strangers.

Lucy Moore (10)
Meadow Vale Primary School, Bracknell

The Anaconda And The Deer

The anaconda said, "Will you come into my swamp, my lovely, little deer?
You like to eat plants and leaves, so I hear!"
"No, no, I will not be your food."
"Do me a favour," the deer stated, "and stop being so rude!"

Anaconda remarked, "Come here, my deer, I have news for you!
I have lots of food for you and me too!"
"Like I said earlier, be quiet,
Thank you, but I'll get my own diet!"

The anaconda thought and thought,
A dinner with the deer, he sought.
"Your eyes sparkle, come dine upon some food!"
The deer stated, "Maybe you're not so rude!"

The anaconda's plan worked - he waited for the silly deer to arrive,
Into the swamp, he prepared for a big dive.

"Where's your food?" the emotional deer asked.
The anaconda smirked, a shriek spread across the
vast.

The anaconda strangled the deer to death,
So, unfortunately, she took her last breath.
For everyone who may read this story,
I'm very sorry it was a bit gory.

Isla Sherwood (10)

Meadow Vale Primary School, Bracknell

The Anaconda And The Deer

"Step into my home," said the anaconda to the deer,
"Come and sit in my living room while it's clear."
The deer walked up to the anaconda and said...
"Oh, no, no, I wouldn't come in, I would flee."

"Come and sit at my table," said the anaconda to the deer,
"Sit down and I will offer you some beer."
The deer came closer to the food.
"Thank you, kind Sir, but I'm not in the mood."

"Come and see my fluffy bed,
It's better than any bed you've rested your head."
The deer drew closer but remembered where she was near,
She ran until she was clear.
She yelled, "No, I don't want to stay!
Maybe I'll call another day."

"Come, come, I've never seen a deer with fur so
brown,
Whenever I see you, you make me frown."
What a silly deer, how could she be so foolish,
The anaconda had his job done.
Bang! The giant snake had wrapped himself
around the deer,
But the deer didn't realise what was going on.

Esme Morse-Buckle (10)
Meadow Vale Primary School, Bracknell

The Ocelot And The Monkey

"Will you step into my temple?" said the ocelot with a sly grin.
The monkey said, wincing at the thought, "Kind Ma'am, this cannot be, thank you for the offer, but I do not dare go in."

The ocelot said to the monkey, "Sweet creature, you must be tired from swinging so high, will you rest in my little bed?"
The highly scared monkey replied, "Oh, no, no, no, I'm sure it must be a cosy bed, but I do not dare to go in, I would rather sleep in a shed!"

"Beautiful creature, you are as beautiful as a butterfly and as wise as an owl, what should I do to prove my affection for you?" asked the ocelot to the monkey.
"Oh, no, no, no, please, kind Ma'am, I really should go," said the monkey fearing a smile that was chunky.

The sly ocelot pounced and fiercely held her tight.
She dragged her into the dreaded temple,
But she ne'er came out again!

Now children who may read this story,
Never trust someone by their looks and words.

Isabel Underwood (9)

Meadow Vale Primary School, Bracknell

The Panther And The Parrot

"Why hello, dear parrot friend!" said the panther,
"Come up to my branch. It is very cosy here."
The panther tried hiding his nasty grin with a
friendly smile,
"Oh, no, no, I heard what happens if I go up!"
replied the parrot.

"You look tired. Why not come to my leafy bed?
said the panther to the parrot.
"Thanks for asking, but I am not tired," replied the
silly, little parrot.

"It is getting dark, I should get going," the parrot
said.
"Goodbye, kind Sir!"
"Goodbye, dear parrot friend!" replied the nasty
panther.

The panther climbed to a tall branch.
"Your colours are beautiful with majestic green
eyes.
As for mine, they are as dark as the night," the
sneaky panther sung.

The parrot flew calmly back,
As the panther pounced.

Children who read this poem,
Don't get tricked by flattering words,
And learn a lesson from the panther and the
parrot.

Izabella Walde (10)
Meadow Vale Primary School, Bracknell

The Toco Toucan And The Iguana

The predator said to the prey, "Hello, little iguana,
do come in!
"I have got a feast for your din!"
The toucan gasped. "Oh no, why the pout?"
"Oh no, no, what do you mean?" asked the iguana,
"For who goes in, never comes out."

The sly toucan grimaced and looked at a scale,
And after that, he went pale.
The lizard said, "Oh yes, I shan't be rude.
I'll feast upon your food."

The toucan sang, "Oh yes, do come by,
Up here, I have many a fly,
I surely love your blue hue,
It is unique only to you."

The iguana asked, "Dear toucan, are you sure?"
The toucan replied, "Oh yes, it is truly pure."

"Why, I heard," said the sly toucan, "that you eat
each other, what a beast!
Oh, do come in for a feast."

Poor little guy,
His time ended up high.
Oh, never do give in,
Or your bones will end up in the bin.

Maria Hlebanovschi (10)

Meadow Vale Primary School, Bracknell

The Monkey And The Lizard

The monkey said to the lizard,
"Will you step into my warm, cosy home?
If you step in, you may have a roam.
You can also have a snack for I do have lots of meat."
The lizard replied, "Oh no, I do not dare to have some of your treats."

The monkey said to the lizard,
"I have lollies, come for a lick,
I do assure you, you will not be sick."
"Oh no, I do not want to share,
That lolly bear."

The monkey said to the lizard,
"I'm handsome in my gown,
I am not an evil clown."
"Oh no, I do not dare,
To enter that lair."

The monkey said to the lizard,
"Come hither love, come in and if you don't want
to touch, then put on gloves."
Silly, little creature was put in the monkey's mouth,
Then the monkey set off south.

Don't listen to people that are sly,
Even if you're shy.
Now people that read,
Please be safe and proceed.

Reggie O'Connor (10)
Meadow Vale Primary School, Bracknell

The Jaguar And The Anteater

"Step into my den,
You can count to ten,"
Said the jaguar to the anteater.
"Behind the bushes is a prize,
You won't believe your eyes."
"Oh, no, no, no," said the anteater,
"A trick you will play on me later."

"The dinner table is full like a sea of food,
Come and lay down, you look in a mood,"
Said the jaguar to the anteater.
"Oh, no, no, no," said the anteater,
"If I come in now, I won't come out later."

"You are witty and you are wise,
You are pretty and you are prized,
Come and look at the running track."
"Okay," said the anteater.

The anteater climbed up the winding stair,
As she did, she tripped up into the air.

The anteater started running,
The jaguar scratched the anteater's leg,
Now he lays upon his feast.

The moral of the story is:
Don't listen to flattery or bribery.

Abbie Rose Bowdler (10)
Meadow Vale Primary School, Bracknell

The Piranha And The Fish

The piranha said, "Will you please jump into my river? This river is just fine..."
"Oh, no, no!" beamed the fish. "My river is perfect! Yours sends shivers down my spine!"

"Oh, lovely fish!" said the piranha. "How can I prove you mean the world to me? Come and make some fish blends!"
"Oh, no, no!" shouted the fish. "I've seen you before, you ate my friends!"

The sneaky piranha said while decorating his home,
"Oh, wise, kind fish! Just follow me deep!"
"Urgh!" replied the fish, "I'm tired, just let me get a bit of sleep!"

"Come hither, little fish!
Come home and I'll give you a dish!"
Oh no, the poor fish!
He came closer... and closer...
Until... he got caught!

And now an important lesson to all the people who dared to read,
When you are all alone in the dark, do not trust people's greed.

Joe Chapman (10)
Meadow Vale Primary School, Bracknell

The Axolotl And The Shrimp

"Come in," said the axolotl to the shrimp,
"You have been walking for ages, it looks like you
have a limp."
"Oh no, I cannot," said the prey,
"I will not come back until another day!"
"Oh, come now," said the predator, "It is getting
dark.
Stay here till you wish to embark!"

"No, I cannot." The shrimp was in a bad mood.
The axolotl said, "Why can't you accept you're
being very rude?"
As quick as a flash, the shrimp swam away before
the hunter could pounce.
Randomly, he shouted, "I will give algae and
worms."
The shrimp thought, *Hmm, we'll have to agree on
terms.*

"Little shrimp, come!" said the axolotl. "Everyone loves you.
I need you too!"
The shrimp came back not using his head,
Surely the axolotl would offer him a bed.
No one saw the shrimp again,
Ever since he entered the den.

Philip Pryke (10)
Meadow Vale Primary School, Bracknell

The Otter And The Bird

The otter said, "Will you jump into my burrow?
I know you need some rest, but why look with such
sorrow?"
The bird replied, "To ask me is in vain.
For who goes down, will ne'er come up again!"

The otter blurted out, "I have lots of food to share!
Would you like a fish or a hare?"
She moaned, "I have heard enough!
Besides, I don't wish to blush."

The otter said, "You and soft wing,
Would you like a shiny, silver thing?"
The bird did blush, "Goodbye, for now,
Stop making that sad cow plough!"

The otter sang, "Come here, you pretty thing!
Pearl necklace and soft, silky wing.
Your eyes are like a bright moon,
And mine are like a black balloon."

The otter warned, "Children who may read,
Take heed...

Don't listen to silly, flattering words!
Because the bird's now my dinner!"

Amélie O'Shea (9)

Meadow Vale Primary School, Bracknell

The Piranha And The Eel

"Will you swim into my swamp?" said the piranha,
"I will be here all day and night, just waiting near
this lily pad having dinner."
"No, no, no!" replied the eel. "I will not be your
food,
Do me a favour and stop being so rude!"

"Do you want to eat a bird?" asked the piranha,
"You like them, I've heard!"
"No, no, no!" shouted the eel. "Leave the bird,
Why are you being so absurd?"

The piranha said, "Do you want to see my pond?
You and I will have a good bond!"
The eel exclaimed, "Alright!
I will sleep, just one night."

When the eel was sleeping,
Piranha came eating,
In a flash, the eel was bleeding,
And then the eel was screaming.

If you are a listener,
Don't talk to strangers,
Or you will end up like eel, a screamer,
So take this poem away and be a learner.

Wes Aston (10)
Meadow Vale Primary School, Bracknell

The Caiman And The Turtle

"Would you walk into my green lake?
It's very spacious and there's a view of the whole
forest floor," said the caiman to the turtle.
The turtle shook his head slowly.

The caiman said to the turtle, "I have food, it's
delicious if you want to try."
The beautiful turtle shook his head and started to
cry.

"You are beautiful, wise and brilliant," said the
caiman to the turtle,
"Just look in the mirror and see."
As the turtle turned away as slowly as can be.

The caiman said to the turtle, "Dear friend, you
have diamond eyes and a silver shell that's very
beautiful."
The turtle was in shock and nodded,
Then the caiman did this...
The caiman grabbed the turtle and the caiman ate
the turtle.

Boys and girls, never go with strangers even if they say nice words.
Learn a lesson from the caiman and the turtle.

Fabian Kocinski (10)
Meadow Vale Primary School, Bracknell

The Tiger And The Monkey

"Will you come down from there?" said the tiger to the monkey in the trees.
"Oh, no, no, don't be silly, if I ever come down, I know what I will be."

"Oh, dear monkey, come down from your vines. I have all of the best food from the forest floor."
The tiger licked his lips, hoping the monkey would come down and into his jaw.
"Oh, no, no, I may never come down to become your food."

"Roam into my cave and down from your tree, I have an amazing mirror for you to see how beautiful you can be."
"Oh, why not, I am sure you mean no harm."
When the monkey came down,
The tiger started to approach the monkey.
The tiger trapped the monkey in his cave,
And thought to himself, *I am going to have a good dinner tonight.*

So this is why you never trust any stranger,
Or anyone that offers you anything.

Aliya Barrett (10)
Meadow Vale Primary School, Bracknell

The Jaguar And The Snake

"Will you slither up my tree?" said the jaguar to the snake,
"I thought together we could bake a cake."
"Oh, no, no, no," replied the snake, "I'm not a fool!"
The snake continued, "I know you're not so cool!"

"My little friend, you are looking quite small,
Come in, my little friend, and we can have a ball."
"Oh, no, no, no," replied the snake, "I will not join your dance,
I would rather be suspended on this branch."
The jaguar continued, "You are so smart and scaly,
Everybody knows you are very deadly!"

Zenna John-Lewis (10) & Lily Owens (9)
Meadow Vale Primary School, Bracknell

The Panther And The Iguana

"Will you climb into my tree house?"
Said the panther to the iguana in the banana tree.
"Oh, no, no, no!" said the iguana,
"I have heard that whoever goes in there, will never come out again."
The panther's face was smiling,
But he knew it was going to be hard.
Since the iguana was not very dumb,
But he was small and not large.

Mia Visser (10)
Meadow Vale Primary School, Bracknell

The Life Of Terin

It all began when a little baby bird
Was born in a damp, tropical rainforest
His mum and dad took care of him really well
They even taught him how to fly

When they are content
Their feathers turn blue and red
But when they are dejected
Their feathers turn green and yellow

One day, it was all calm and quiet
In the dense forest
Until someone broke the silence
People were cutting down trees
And causing deforestation

They had to leave their home
And fly somewhere safe for them
So that's what they did

Once they reached some land
They settled at their new home
Which was in a garden

A few hours later, a boy named Jayden
Took them into his house

He was quite fond of birds
And knew how to speak their language
Jayden knows that this type of bird
Eats fish, bread and cranberries
At school, he is learning about birds
That's why he has fantastic knowledge about them

When they got in his house
He called the little bird Terin
And decided it was best for the birds
To stay and eat their dinner
After that, they went to bed

Once they awakened
Jayden and the three birds had breakfast
Then they went to the park
The three birds played games with a cranberry
Whilst Jayden was walking around the park

At lunchtime, they were back home
The birds ate some juicy cranberries
And Jayden ate some mouthwatering pizza
Exhausted, they decided to get some rest
So they went back to sleep.

Jayden Tiwana (9)
Priory School, Slough

Adorable Annie

My mesmerising Annie is extremely friendly and
cute,
Oh, that fluffy tail, I especially love it when she
plays with my boat.

This sunshine cupcake is so colourful and furry,
You'll never guess that her absolute favourite food
is curry.

Oh, she is really young but she is also big,
Up to your waist in fact, of course, she was taller
than a pig.

Although she is still a child, her legs have the
power of an adult, for Annie is lightning fast,
Whoosh, would be the noise as she zoomed past.

Adorable Annie is also nimble,
A bit like a finger with a thimble.

Her cute, little nose is rose-pink and wiggly,
For that pink sniffer twitched lots, her soft, snow-
white belly was also jiggly.

Amber Badhan (9)
Priory School, Slough

My Hamster Is...

My hamster is clumsy
Once, he got stuck in a glove
And it looked like he was in a onesie
He is always hungry
He hates honey
But he still ate it
I don't blame him
For his name is Hungry Hamster
He is also known as
The Muncher or the Cruncher
He is lazy, all he does all day
Is roll about in daisies
My hamster is really fun
You can play cops and robbers using a fake gun
My hamster helps you go through time
When I say that, I mean
It's better than playing with slime
My hamster says, "Come play with me
I will spin like a bee!"
You don't want to leave my hamster alone
Because he will make himself a clone.

Sheza Ahmed (9)
Priory School, Slough

Unexpected Adventure With Meno

When I woke up,
I noticed it was going to be a boring, rainy day.
When I was thinking about what I was going to do after school,
Suddenly, my fish said, "Can you take me for a walk?"
I was shocked, but I filled up a jar with water,
Then I put Meno in the jar.
We went to a nearby pond,
Meno asked me if I could release him.
I hesitated for a while,
Then I made the decision to release Meno.
I sat on a rock thinking about Meno.
I saw Meno swimming with a group of fish,
And I quickly noticed it was Meno's family.
I was so happy.

Kacper Gegotek (9)
Priory School, Slough

Unicorns Are Cool

Unicorns are cool,
Some like to play in the pool.
Lots love sweets and yummy treats.
Some watch TV,
Some are named Evie!
A few like My Little Pony,
Some are thick and fat,
But some are small and bony.
Lots of them hate Liars,
And some go off to sleep,
With toys and teddies in a heap.
Lots are kind,
Some are fond of the bond,
They hold as they stand.
United and holding hands,
Their love is grand.
and is worth gold,
And they never get old,
And they can't be sold.
Some would sell the world,
For a friendship that is so old,

These unicorns are bold.
They aren't shy,
But help those who cry.

Nafisa Khan (9)
Priory School, Slough

I Have A Pet

I have a pet
Her name is Bet
She likes to play
That's what people say
She has a ball
So we get her more
She is a cat
Her friend is a bat
She plays with yarn
So we go to the barn
To get her some yarn
She likes turquoise yarn
When she is bored
She plays with her ball
She had a dream
Where she fell down a stream
And landed in a beam of light
When she woke up
We brought her some stuff
Some yarn, a ball and a couple more
And that is the story of my pet, Bet the cat.

Fouzan Majeed (8)
Priory School, Slough

The Mysterious Cat

In the morning time, there was a cat,
It had blue eyes like the sky,
White fur like the clouds,
A pink nose and sharp claws like a knife.
Her name was Cleara,
But the mysterious thing was,
That she was different,
To all the other cats in the country.
Everyone wanted to know where she came from.
The whole country wanted her because she was so pretty,
But she would scratch them,
Nobody knew why.
Cleara felt bored staying in the same country,
So she went to Egypt,
And saw everything in Egypt.

Chaima Zemoule (9)
Priory School, Slough

The Adventurous Cat

In the morning, a white, furry cat passed by,
It had blue eyes like the ocean,
A pink nose like a rose,
And claws as sharp as a knife.
Her name was Bella.
Bella loved travelling all around the world.
Nobody knew where this beautiful, white cat came from or where she lived.
She was a very mysterious cat because she had a secret base.
When Bella felt bored, she would go to Egypt.
She would always go to visit the interesting pyramids.
What a lovely day for her.

Asme Zemouli (9)
Priory School, Slough

My Baking Dragon

B aking Barry dragon bakes everywhere he goes
A nd wears a big white baking hat
R ed and pink colourful scales
R eally big and jolly, he loves to laugh a lot
Y ou have to try what he's creating

D elicious cupcakes and cookies
R ed velvet Victoria sponge or devil's food cake
A ll are very scrummy
G oes into his cave to prepare
O vens are not needed
N ot with his hot fire breath.

Keira Chitty (8)
Priory School, Slough

Ted The Talking Tortoise

Ted the talking tortoise talks very fast,
Unlike his speed which is more like a stroll,
He wears spotted pants on his ride to the beach,
With his star sign on his back which of course is a
Taurus
All the ladies think he is gorgeous
Ted the talking tortoise is agile and clever
He swims in the sea gliding doing backstroke
looking divine
Sometimes I let Ted hold onto my legs and we see
how fast we can go
Ted is my pet and he always will be.

Cora Chitty (10)
Priory School, Slough

The African Ant Phant

An Ant Phant is an elephant,
His body looks like an ant,
He eats tigers,
He loves spiders!
He crawls on the floor,
With a head as big as a door!
No picture ever found,
But always is around!
We say, "We won't eat him!"
Africans say, "We will always feed him!"
One thing he says is...
"I eat tigers, I love spiders!"
"I eat the bones!" his mother says.

Rihija Eshal Ahmed (9)
Priory School, Slough

The Funny Rabbit That Twitches

I have a little rabbit,
Whose ears are as soft as silk,
His eyes are as round as saucers,
And his coat is as white as milk.
My rabbit cannot talk to me,
But only twitch his nose,
I can tell when he is happy,
As twitchety-twitch it goes.
Tall ears, twinkly nose,
Tiny tail - and hop, he goes!
I feed him carrots, run, run!
As I drop carrots on the floor,
Hop, hop, he goes again!

Yasmin Zekari-Day (9)
Priory School, Slough

My Little Bird

My little bird, gentle and free
Sitting on top of a gigantic tree
When she looks down at me
I see her colourful, feathery wings
Adorable and cute, she looks during the day
But in the night, she goes away
I followed my curiosity
And Heather led me up into a wild dream
She transformed into a gigantic, dangerous beast
This is my bird, Heather
Who is magical and free.

Amelia Kaur Bing (8)
Priory School, Slough

My Weird Pet

My furry, weird dog,
Likes to sit on a log,
He has a friend,
Who likes to lend (his ball),
They play in the sun,
Until the day is done,
Chasing agile frogs,
In the wild bogs,
Roger is extraordinarily clever,
And the most adorable dog ever.
He looks so cute,
When I dress him in a suit.
Our friendship is incredible,
He is always in my bubble.

Joshua Palmer (9)
Priory School, Slough

Royal Prize-Winning Pegasus

P erfect at racing

R oyal champion

I ncredible dressage skills

Z ooming through the air

E xcellent aerial displays

W inning thousands of races

I n faraway countries

N ever giving up

N atural talent

E verlasting spirit

R adiant eyes.

Evie Prescott (8)

Priory School, Slough

Cats

Big cats, small cats and fluffy cats
Sharp cats, gentle cats and scared cats
Black cats, white cats and striped cat
The world is full of many different types of cats

But my pet cat, Oreo
Is a friendly and adorable cat

He is loyal and a gentle cat
My cat is a precious cat to me.

Ummayma Fatima (9)
Priory School, Slough

144

Corgi Shark

C ute and clever

O utstanding dog

R oyal friend of the Queen

G reat pet

I ntelligent, not mean

S hort but smart

H unting in the water

A ferocious beast

R aised by sharks

K ind, protective and cool companion.

Hayley Foster (9)

Priory School, Slough

Stary The Starfish

Under the big, blue ocean,
Floats a bright, colourful starfish,
Called Stary the starfish.
Stary lives with his family,
He floats in the ocean reef,
His big brother Beefy,
Is looking out at the big, blue sky.

Lillie-Mai Bullen (9)
Priory School, Slough

Wild Tilly

Tilly flies ever so high,
Her majestic wings beating loud,
Making friends on the way,
Over the fiery volcanoes.

Ella Aviss (9)
Priory School, Slough

Dave The Drenched Dog

A bsolutely drenched

B etter get your towels ready

C reating puddles, left, right and centre

D ave is his name

E stimate of 100 litres of water made a day

F looding house after house

G reatest tap in the world

H ouses floating away daily

I like my pet, although, he's very wet

J ack, his friend, is also wet

K nowing how he defeats criminals is a mystery

L ooping around, chasing his tail

M aking puddles, unlike hail

N o messing around, so he says, but the

O pposite is his everyday trail

P ointing criminals to the jail, if

Q uestions are asked, Dave will make you fail

R ight after, the Queen will award him in the mail

S hivering cold after he shakes his tail

T rying to get Dave dry but he goes

U p sky-high, no

V   et he goes to can get him dry and

W   et he will forever be

X   -rays show his inner self and just like a

Y   o-yo, he bounces up and down

Z   igzagging in the air and that's the poem about
Dave the superhero drenched dog.

Corbin Green (9)

Queen's Hill Primary & Nursery School, Costessey

Redge The Cat

R edge the cat had a secret base and it was very

E xtraordinary, it had his secret weapons which were glue and tea. One

D ay, he dug and dug and dug until he found a board

G ame he knew how to play, so he added it to his excellent and

E xciting collection. He had a lot of stuff such as glue and

T ea, a pillow and a bed. Sometimes, if

H e had time, he would secretly take them in his secret and

E xcellent base that all the cats loved. It was

C ool and nice. It felt like home even though it was

A secret base and everyone liked it. One of the cats had

T elekinetic powers and moved the glue. It made a

S plash! Everyone was covered in glue and it was done

B y Ronnie the black cat. He had a huge tail. He was

A clumsy cat. He said, "Sorry." Redge

S aid, "That's okay, we need to clean it up though." So Ronnie used his

E xcellent telekinesis powers and cleaned all twenty cats and they all lived happily.

Harrison Forbes (9)

Queen's Hill Primary & Nursery School, Costessey

Red Panda Corn

R eady to see Red Panda Corn - she's unbelievable

E ats like a tortoise, she never makes a mess

D on't you dare bully her, she is as clever as the trees

P lease be kind - she's tame and won't hurt you

A nd when there's someone new, she is nice and calm

N o, do not touch her horn, she will go flying like the wind

D on't try to steal her, she will zap you with her eyes

A n amazing pet to have, please be careful with them

C an you find one? They are really unique

O nly magical people can find them, be kind to them

R eally cute animals, you will cry when you see their faces

N ow you know what it's like to have a Red Panda Corn.

Zoe Chirwa (9)

Queen's Hill Primary & Nursery School, Costessey

The Levitating Viper

T his pet is magic
H e is my favourite snake
E veryone is scared of him

L evitating Viper's nice
E very day, he loves to play
V *room*, when he flies away
I t is the best pet there is
T ake care if you meet, he's precious
A fantastic snake and well patterned
T ill night, when he starts to hunt
I watch him do a sneak attack
N ight is dangerous
G asp when he is around

V iper is insane
I love to watch him shake
P otatoes are his favourite
E ating, he goes *munch, munch, munch!*
R ating is a ten out of ten.

Jack Grimmer (9)
Queen's Hill Primary & Nursery School, Costessey

The Cat Who's Like A Bat

There are dogs that jump high like frogs,
But Clever Clogs, he flies like a bat,
All while sitting on a mat.
He flies at night,
Away from the light,
And out of sight.
He likes to eat seaweed,
So he can see brightly like a yellow seed.
He likes the daily eggs,
They give him the energy he needs,
But now he wishes to meet,
Another flying cat to help him cook in the kitchen,
Just like an Egyptian.
He runs around,
Taking off from the ground,
Flying high into the sky,
Soaring with the birds,
Eating all the worms,
Clever Clogs likes unusual food,
But only when he's not in a mood.
He waits for strokes,

Until he gets poked,
Then he flies away,
To go on his way.

Szymon Rudnicki (9)

Queen's Hill Primary & Nursery School, Costessey

Baily's Walk

Baily was sitting next to his lead,
Waiting for his owner.
When his owner picked up his lead,
His tail wagged.
His owner clipped on his lead.
Baily and his owner Bella,
Were off on another adventure.

Baily and Bella were walking down to the woods,
And then they saw another dog!
Baily noticed who it was... it was Buddy!
They ran to each other and laughed.
After a while of running and playing,
Buddy had to go home.
Baily was sad, so he sniffed flowers,
Caught flies and chased the birds.
He became a bit happier,
But when he had to go home,
He knew there was a new adventure waiting for
him tomorrow.

Eloise Osborne (9)
Queen's Hill Primary & Nursery School, Costessey

Purry Pomeranian

P urry Pomeranian is a beautiful dog
U nfortunately, he is not easy
R adiant Rocket is his friend
R agged learning is his type
Y ou would love him as your pet

P urry Pomeranian picked some peppers
O nomatopoeia is his favourite word
M r Menton is his head teacher
E ats peppermints and tuna with BBQ sauce
R adiant Rocket ruins all his spectacular shows
A ngry anteaters are his foes
N o one has a Purry Pomeranian like me
I ssue with old people, he has
A ngry anteaters will get revenge
N o one has a Pomeranian like me.

Lucas Barker (9)

Queen's Hill Primary & Nursery School, Costessey

Daisy's Crazy Day

Daisy is very crazy,
She dances all day long,
No one can stop her,
As she is not slow,
When you first meet her,
You think she's all cute,
But when you get to know her,
Her mischievous actions,
Will really give you the hint,
Although she acts naughty,
She is really lovely,
Everyone loves her,
Even the teddies,
No one can deny,
She is kinda greedy,
But who can blame her?
She is really lovely,
Even though she's a pain,
She's the best doggy in the world,
So no one can say she's annoying at all.

Lola Wright (9)
Queen's Hill Primary & Nursery School, Costessey

Super Snowflake And Me

S uper Snowflake is so fluffy and cuddly

N o one has a flying bunny like mine

O n June the 7th, it is Snowflake's birthday

W e go on adventures together and it's so much fun

F licker, her best friend, and her play together all the time

L ake Furious is Snowflake's favourite place to go

A mazement is in Snowflake's shimmering eyes

K icking a ball, me and Snowflake like playing together

E ven before I got Snowflake, I had no one to play with, but now I do.

Skyla Rix (9)

Queen's Hill Primary & Nursery School, Costessey

Adventurous G

Girald is a great influence,
He's amazing and lives in a tree.
You'll find him in the deep parts of the old Amazon
tree.
His looks will give you a prize,
You'll maybe even cry.
His sassy attitude will give you a laugh,
And he'll call you a beeping car.
His spots and marks are only ancient,
Maybe even painted with old black and brown
mud and yellow-painted skin.
You could go on a journey with friends from all
around,
But really adventurous G is the one to go to town.

Rosa Hartshorn (9)
Queen's Hill Primary & Nursery School, Costessey

Jeremy's Worst Day

J eremy is a dragon

E ats everything

R uins the whole lot

E ats so much, he is as fat as Shrek

M ate, he's only good around me

Y ou ought to stay away

T en years old

H e will attack

E at you all up

D angerous as can be

R egret having a pet like this

A te at least 100 humans

G o, go, go, go!

O n your feet, come on!

N oooo, oh, you're gone!

Aaron Hawkins (8)

Queen's Hill Primary & Nursery School, Costessey

Tahliah The Independent Tiger

T remendous wings take off into the sky

A stonishing stripes, different to everyone else

H appily encouraging everyone to just be themselves

L aughing together, making jokes and being themselves

I magining a world where everyone is being themselves and never letting anyone get them down

A mazement of everyone staring at her balancing books on her head

H ugging everyone, making friends. You're amazing just the way you are!

Lily Rust-Andrews (9)

Queen's Hill Primary & Nursery School, Costessey

The New Dog

L ena is a very good pet, she follows my

E xtraordinary cat. She met my cat called Rex

N icky is the person who looks after the pets

A nd Rex is a kitten.

T he dog is a puppy and it looks after my cat

H e is the best cat ever and so is the dog.

E xcellent dogs go over hoops and my dog can do it.

D ogs are good pets.

O lly, my best friend, looks after pets. He

G ives pets treats.

Scarlett Carr (9)

Queen's Hill Primary & Nursery School, Costessey

Firework

F irework is the fire in the sky

I f you cross her, make no mistake

R un while you still can

E ating upon the fear she now brings upon the villains

W atch out for her sidekick Spyro, he will call her down

O ut of the sky, she will put you down behind the bars where you will stay

R un while you still can, her fear will put you down

K ill your life, Firework will get you in an hour with her power.

Aimee Cusdin (9)

Queen's Hill Primary & Nursery School, Costessey

Percy The Pirate Parrot

Percy the pirate parrot,
Lives on a ship on the sea,
He is a small, marvellous bird,
Who enjoys eating the occasional pea.

A champion sword fighter,
A swashbuckling thief,
He stole Blackbeard's treasure,
Smiling with his set of golden teeth.

Sailing the seas is his goal,
Beating the mighty, indestructible Kraken,
That rules the seas,
Percy the pirate parrot says, "Just smack 'em!"

Blake Taylor (9)
Queen's Hill Primary & Nursery School, Costessey

Bubbly Bubbles

A day that Bubbles is going to love,
It is birthday time today,
She can't wait for everything,
She bounces and bounces around,
And makes me giggle all the time.
So you better watch out!
She will jump on you,
And make you be nice.
But then I realise...
She has gone missing.
The day I wouldn't want it to happen to her,
On her birthday.
Oh, it was just a dream.
How obvious, now I see.

Victoria Guziejko (8)
Queen's Hill Primary & Nursery School, Costessey

Danger The Dragon

D angerous in his sleep
A ngrily eating his veg
N ever excited to eat his treats
G agging on BBQ ashes
E nchanted pet
R ustling in my roommate's bed

D rowning in lava and fire indoors
R oaring! All night long
A rranging the charcoal
G iggling at my messy hair
O n and on, flapping its wings
N ot a respectful pet.

Lily Land (9)
Queen's Hill Primary & Nursery School, Costessey

Cataroo

C ataroo has great powers like a superkick

A nd most normal cats don't like swimming, but Cataroo is a super swimmer

T akes enemies down to his prison

A nd can camouflage itself so he can catch fish

R unning is his favourite power so he can catch fish

O ne of his least favourite foods is chicken

O ne of his favourite foods is fish.

Harley Bloomfield (9)

Queen's Hill Primary & Nursery School, Costessey

The Powers Of Pankaroo

P owerful Pankaroos

A dorable, little, tiny face can hypnotise

N earby people

K now how she does it?

A s she lives in the wild, she's so

R eady for anything. She bounces

O ver houses to the science study dome and takes

O nboard awful chemicals that make her hypnotise and shapeshift herself into anything.

Sasha Smith (9)

Queen's Hill Primary & Nursery School, Costessey

Miss Glitter

M ight be able to get home,
I t's enjoying the sunshine.
S o glittery,
S o big and fluffy.

G oes on holiday in August,
L ikes people,
I t likes to play,
T alks Spanish,
T oo friendly,
E yes are rainbow-coloured and
R ides roller coasters.

Lily Fryer (9)
Queen's Hill Primary & Nursery School, Costessey

Rocky Drark

R ocking

O utside

C alling dragons

K icking their footballs to everyone

Y ou will love him

D rark will fly with you

R ocky will play with you

A nd surf with you

R acing like a shark

K aw-cawing around the neighbourhood, waiting for someone to play.

Jake Jennison (9)

Queen's Hill Primary & Nursery School, Costessey

The Story Of Fury Slice

F ury Slice is special
U nlike some other pets
R eluctantly, it is fast
Y ellow and green is its style

S urprisingly, it can fly slowly
L ikes to race unsurprisingly fast
I t can fly fast
C an also jump
E verything is unknown to him or me.

Lennox Lown (8)

Queen's Hill Primary & Nursery School, Costessey

My Weird Lil' Puppy

C ute, furry ball of cheekiness

H as tiny toes but a big personality

E pic powers to fly

S unny days are his favourite days to play

N uts he eats, then falls asleep

U nique wings that help him fly high

T alent is being so cute and the best at snuggling.

Isabella Cook (8)

Queen's Hill Primary & Nursery School, Costessey

Snorecorn The Snake

S norecorn the snake is better than Superdog

N ever will you ever see him cry!

O r die - he is immortal

R eady to fly and lie

E normous as a dino

C ool like a dragon

O n it like a dog

R ude like a frog

N ever kill his army.

Ebo Ellis (9)

Queen's Hill Primary & Nursery School, Costessey

174

My Dragon

D izzy is lovely and kind but gigantic
R eally happy, playful and messy
A cute and lazy dragon
G rows into a good, little dragon
O nto rooftops, she goes and parties all night
N o one can stop her, so if you hear a crunch on your roof, it might be Dizzy.

Coco Brickley (9)

Queen's Hill Primary & Nursery School, Costessey

Batdog

B atdog is the best dog

A nd Batdog can fly through the air

T here he was, flying through the air like a bat

D igging and digging, Batdog was digging

O ver the horizon, Batdog was flying

G reat, big Batdog was digging into the ground.

Oliver Cunningham (9)

Queen's Hill Primary & Nursery School, Costessey

Frogoroo

F orever special and unique

R ockets flying over him

O n the hop, out every day

G etting ready to bounce away

O n the moon, he lands ready

R evving up his hopping machine

O ff he goes

O n and on.

Isla Carter (9)
Queen's Hill Primary & Nursery School, Costessey

Camo Dog

C amo is a hidden dog
A nd it takes me hours to find him
M y pet is so special
O h, I really love my pet

D igging around in the dirt
O h, how naughty he is
G oing around and hiding around the house.

Nina Stasiow (9)
Queen's Hill Primary & Nursery School, Costessey

Speedy

S peeding through the hall, his

P ower strikes again, no one can stop him. For

E ver he will speed. Have you

E ver seen such a fast tortoise?

D o you know how fast he can go? I will tell

Y ou... 200 miles per second!

Joe Rice (8)
Queen's Hill Primary & Nursery School, Costessey

Spiny The Peculiar Dinosaur

S piny the spinosaurus loves
P ies and he never dies, he hates
I ndominus rexes because they stomp on his toes
N ever does he give up, he races forever
Y early, he goes to the amazing arena and fights for his family.

Taylor Everett (9)

Queen's Hill Primary & Nursery School, Costessey

Cateep

C ateep is the best pet ever

A gile and adorable

T his pet wants to be my pillow

E veryone loves my pet

E xcept it is very tiny. My

P et is the best ever. See, my pet is also like a cloud.

Amelia Castell (9)

Queen's Hill Primary & Nursery School, Costessey

The Weird Man

Will went to school,
Then he went to go and play with a ball,
He heard a cluck,
And it was a terrifying duck,
Then there was a Viking,
And a person who was biking,
Then there was a biker,
With a tiger.

Jenson Hurren (9)
Queen's Hill Primary & Nursery School, Costessey

All About Meleny

M eleny is adorable and furry and
E xtraordinary like a vicious tiger
L ike a lazy sloth
E ntertains other unicorns
N ice as a gentle puppy
Y ellow is her favourite colour.

Chloe Hilton (8)

Queen's Hill Primary & Nursery School, Costessey

Hybrid

Hybrid the shape-shifting tortoise,
That can tweet like a bird,
And lays in something moist,
He is not a nerd,
Then here is something really wild,
He likes all his food very, very mild.

Jack Bergin (8)
Queen's Hill Primary & Nursery School, Costessey

Roke Wo

R are and cute

O bviously stupid

K ind and nice

E veryone enjoys him

W here is he?

O range and tall.

Louie Foster (8)

Queen's Hill Primary & Nursery School, Costessey

Detective Dave

Detective Dave looks for suspicious people,
Who are stealing stuff from people or the bank,
He has eyes everywhere,
You can't stop him.

Mayer Hatson (9)

Queen's Hill Primary & Nursery School, Costessey

Niro

N iro the speedy dog

I ncredible and awesome dog

R esponsible, caring, cute dog

O n walks, he is quick.

Caleb Clow (8)

Queen's Hill Primary & Nursery School, Costessey

The Peculiar Zoo

Today I wrote a poem,
I wrote it just for you,
About a special place,
Called the peculiar zoo.

Some funny looking animals,
Are sure to make you laugh,
The first one's great, he is my mate,
It's Jerry the giraffe.

Now Jerry has a big, long neck,
It really is so big,
He has the most amazing eyes,
But he has the snout of a pig.

The second one's an elephant,
She has the cute name of Mini,
Now elephants are usually fat,
But this one's really skinny!

Number three lives in a tree,
And he is very funky,

He has a lovely singing voice,
It's Max the singing monkey.

The last, well, she is a blast,
She's really not a bore,
It's Lesley the lion and I'm not lyin',
She hasn't got a roar!

It really is peculiar,
But believe me when I speak,
She doesn't have a lion's roar,
She has a mouse's squeak!

Now that's the end,
Of my very own poem,
That I wrote just for you,
Now you can go and tell your friends,
About the amazing, peculiar zoo!

Nancy Lunt (7)
Rice Lane Primary School, Liverpool

The King Of The Dinosaurs

With taloned feet and razor claws,
Leathery scales and monstrous jaws.
The king of all dinosaurs...
Tyrannosaurus rex.

With sabre-like teeth no one ignores.
It rants and raves and royally roars...
The king of all dinosaurs...
Tyrannosaurus rex.

The largest of all the carnivores,
It stomps and chomps on city roads,
Arriving at my doorstep with a loud *roooarr!*

The Tyrannosaurus rex,
Charges through my steps,
Destroying everything in sight.
Large footsteps all in the city,
Nothing in sight,
Just the footsteps of Tyrannosaurus rex.

All the city was horrified and scared,
With more Tyrannosauruses coming.
They were all friendly and became my pets,
And that's how I have dinosaurs for pets.

Here's a little joke Jeff told me:
What do you call a dinosaur with a good
vocabulary?
A Thesaurus.

Joseph Douglas (9)
Rice Lane Primary School, Liverpool

The Plastic Sea

My friend was strangled by something strange -
Is it plastic?
Well, whatever it is, it's not fantastic.
There seems to be a whole lot more,
Not only is it bad, it's an eyesore.

Their round and square and sometimes flat,
And it's not very pleasant, I'll tell you that.
How long has this lasted? It seems like years,
Sometimes it's so bad, it breaks out tears.

The humans on Earth laugh and have fun,
While me and my friends are on the run.
Who am I? You may ask,
Well, to figure it out, that's your task.
To give you a hint, my name is Myrtle,
To help you even more, I am a turtle.

Emily Pierpoint (9)
Rice Lane Primary School, Liverpool

My Two-Headed Horse

So my mum asked me to choose a new pet,
I looked and looked but didn't know what to get.
I decided on a horse but this one was cool,
It was no ordinary horse, it looked like a fool.
It had two heads and a great big mane,
I thought this horse would bring me some fame.
My two-headed horse lives in a shed,
He has a big bale of hay that he uses for his bed.
He takes me for a ride,
As he walks with pride,
And he greets me at the gate,
And he's my best mate.

Evie McVeigh (8)

Rice Lane Primary School, Liverpool

Twixy The Sausage Dog

I love to rhyme, I do it all the time.
Now, this is a poem about my dream pet,
You will want to meet her now, I bet:
This is Twixy,
Her best mate is Dixie.
She loves toys,
She plays with the other boys.
Twixy loves to play fetch.
She is amazing at catching.
She's cute and gentle,
If you're afraid or scared.
She's strong enough to round up a herd,
And those are the things I love about Twixy!

Isla Burns (10)
Rice Lane Primary School, Liverpool

Tiny Hamster

T iny hamster, she is very small
I n her cage, she is mischievous
N icely gnaws on her toys
Y awns very loud when she sleeps

H azelnut likes to eat cucumber
A nd loves to play on her wheel
M unches a lot on different vegetables
S he is brown and fluffy
T eeth are very sharp
E ats cheese as it's her favourite food
R uns very fast.

Jessica Dowling (8)
Rice Lane Primary School, Liverpool

My Cat

This poem is inspired by my fat, cheeky cat Tabatha

My cat is abnormally fat,
My cat occasionally wants to hit me with a gigantic bat,
My cat always wants more food than she'll ever get,
My cat makes me question: "Does she realise that she's a pet?"
My cat from afar looks like a lump,
My cat acts like a plump chump,
My cat loves to steal my chair,
She sits there preening her hair,
But I love my cat,
Even if she hits me with a giant bat.

Jack Nelson (11)
Rice Lane Primary School, Liverpool

Our Neighbour's Cat

Dodgey is our neighbour's cat,
We often find her on our doormat.
Fast asleep, she snores all day,
But when it rains, she runs away.
On her food, she likes to nibble,
Although when she purrs,
She sometimes dribbles.
When she walks, her legs bend in,
Sometimes she ends up sleeping behind a bin.
Dodgey is our neighbour's cat,
This is a bit about her and that is that.

Lauren Millen (9)
Rice Lane Primary School, Liverpool

Shrinking Shrew

Deep down in a hedgerow,
There could be a shrew.
Or a garden and grassland,
It could be there too.

A diet of worms,
Slugs, snails and insects.
It'll eat every few hours,
And can sniff out their scent.

Dark brown and fluffy,
To keep safe and warm.
The shrew can shrink its body parts,
To protect it from harm.

Luca De Giorgi (8)
Rice Lane Primary School, Liverpool

My Delightful Diplodocus

My delightful, dancing diplodocus,
Swimming swiftly,
Through the fun, flashing fish,
In the wishy-washy water,
Sneakily swallowing the fish,
In one big, guzzling gulp!
Together, we love to play,
Running and racing,
Catching and chasing,
Until it's time for bed.
Curled up, tucked up tight,
Sweet dreams... Goodnight.

Axl Hook-Woolhouse (8)
Rice Lane Primary School, Liverpool

The Elepanthercoon

The Elepanthercoon has lots and lots to eat,
The Elepanthercoon eats slimy meat.
His teeth are tiny but are as sharp as blades,
Its growl is very loud and doesn't fade,
And when it is in the sun, it wears cool shades.
Now you've learnt about this awesome beast,
If you meet him, be careful he doesn't eat you for
his midnight feast.

Joseph Cornall (7)
Rice Lane Primary School, Liverpool

My Dog

My dog, my dog, so perfect and sweet,
Always wants something to eat.
Your fur is soft like my blanket,
It's as dark as the midnight sky.
Your fur on your chest is like the stars,
So white and as clean as ever.
I love you dog, don't ever change,
You're perfect, so stay that way.

Savannah Wright (9)
Rice Lane Primary School, Liverpool

Gilly

My dog is called Gilly,
As in Billy, but with a 'G'.
She likes to chew her chewy toys,
She loves to do a wee.
She licks us when she's happy,
And sits upon my knee.
And if more people were like Gilly dogs,
A nicer place the world would be...

Riley Lyons (10)
Rice Lane Primary School, Liverpool

My Playful Chocolate Labrador

I love my chocolate Labrador,
He loves to play with me,
He chases me around the house,
And eats up all my tea.

He always sneaks up into my room,
I chase him down the stairs,
He turns around and looks at me,
And chases me back up the stairs.

Ashley Mcleod (8)
Rice Lane Primary School, Liverpool

My Dog Roy

Roy the dog,
He will be your friend to the end,
So stick around and be his friend.
He is your boy, your partner,
He will fill your heart with joy.
Our boy named Roy,
Our boy Roy is a naughty boy,
Food: that's all Roy thinks about.

Lexi Murtagh (10)
Rice Lane Primary School, Liverpool

My Two Rabbits

As white as snow,
As grey as a cloud when it is having a bad day.
They have the touch of silk,
And the eyes of an ocean,
And the kindness of a puppy.
As shy as a newborn kitty.
Soon to be a beautiful flower,
Just waiting to bloom.

Ella Bass (10)
Rice Lane Primary School, Liverpool

Pumpkin Pie

There once was a bear that loved to fly,
He loved to fly with a pumpkin pie.
He loved to run with a shoulder bump.

There once was a bear that loved to fly,
He loved to fly with a pumpkin pie,
He loved to fly with a pumpkin pie, yeah!

Grace Wilson (9)
Rice Lane Primary School, Liverpool

Paradise

I like to prance around in a stealthy state.
I like to sleep in a nice, warm place.
I may be small,
I may eat mice,
But my heavenly purr is paradise.
What am I?

Answer: *Moonlight, my peculiar pet.*

Harry Evans (9)
Rice Lane Primary School, Liverpool

Chat

A Chat has pointy ears.
A Chat has a grumpy face.
A Chat has clawed feet.
A Chat has a long, slim body.
A Chat is colourful and gentle.
A Chat is very lazy.
But most of all, a Chat is...
Very chatty!

Lily-Faye Buckle (7)
Rice Lane Primary School, Liverpool

Bunnies

Bunnies go hop.
They do not chomp, chomp, chomp!
They like to pomp.
They munch, munch, munch!
On their lunch, lunch, lunch.
They like to dress up,
After the tub!

Ava Kelly (10)
Rice Lane Primary School, Liverpool

Behind The Innocent Face

It feeds on your nightmares,
It feeds on things such as crows,
It feeds on your shadows,
It feeds on your woes,
Don't ask who,
Because it'll try to catch you.

Behind the innocent face,
It fulfils your dismay,
Its darkest desires,
Are like flowing, inordinate wires,
But I'm sad to say,
I have bad news for you,
The curtain of pleasant lives rings down on the
stage.

It has no paws,
Yet it has murder claws,
The pet will seal your doom,
And you'll already be in your tomb,
Once the clock begins to chime,
He will drink the blood that drips from you.

The pet will keep you running,
As long as you're thumping,
It'll tell you all its lies,
It'll turn your mind from fine,
You'll think you're really insane,
But he won't let you leave,
He'll never let you step into the light,
When you're happy with glee.
More importantly, he'll never let you be.
Just run!

P.S. Beware of his auto-suggestion.

Ziad Darwish (10)
St Edward's RC Primary School, Westminster

The Charmy Kitty And The Town Mall

It all started when Charmy Kitty woke up to get ready,
She tied up her robe and put her coat on ready,
She headed out the door and rode a bright pink car,
My kitty, kitty, kitty, my little Charmy Kitty.
She went to the mall and bought a pink baggy,
My little kitty cat, kitty, kitty, kitty.
She liked to buy treats and plenty of meats,
She always liked being ready, ready, ready,
She bought some Milkies and plenty of mince too,
She also liked to cuddle, my little kitty,
My little kitty cat, my little kitty, kitty,
She went home and dined on mince, treats, meats and Milkies, to make it lovely,
I love my little kitty cat, my kitty, kitty.

Faustina Biniam (7)
St Edward's RC Primary School, Westminster

Herbie The Birtoise

My pet is very peculiar, you will see!
Sometimes he crawls along,
Or sometimes he sits in a tree!
He is a cross between a tortoise and a bird,
I know you will say, "That sounds absurd!"
He lives in his hard shell,
But he is very fluffy as well.
I never know where he is,
It gets me into a real tizz!
He thinks it's funny that he can fly and climb,
Especially when it is feeding time.
He is incredibly clever,
I wish he was as light as a feather.
He's my special, extraordinary pet,
His name is Herbie,
He's a creature you won't forget!

Harley Dudziak (8)
St Edward's RC Primary School, Westminster

My Little Parrot

As the little parrot sings and flaps his wings,
They show that the bright day begins,
They have soft feathers and a long beak,
Just because it's small doesn't mean it's weak.

Normally it has colours pleasant for the eyes,
They have wings and are birds that can fly,
They choose quite small food to eat,
They stand upright and have two feet.

I have two red parrots back at home,
But how old they are is unknown,
I love them both very, very much,
But they bit my uncle's hand, what a klutz!

Elisha Ntambwe (10)
St Edward's RC Primary School, Westminster

Uni Jess

There was a unicorn called Jess,
Who liked to play with her friend Tess.
They went for ice cream every day,
And always had a laugh, hey, hey!
They went for rides and had some fun,
And this is when the fun began.

There was a boy whose name was Jim,
His friends were always good to him.
He went to ride on Uni Jess,
Then was so rude and rode on Tess.
Soon, he forgot about Tess,
And always looked at all the rest.
When he realised what he'd done,
This was the day the fun began.

Amira Bell (8)
St Edward's RC Primary School, Westminster

Mango's Banana

Mango the monkey loved bananas,
But they were stolen by those cheeky koalas!

He swung on trees all through the leaves,
Avoiding all those buzzy bees.
"Mummy, Mummy, help me please!"

Mango's mummy swung up to help,
When she heard his big loud yelp!

Mummy monkey gave him a cuddle,
As he sat on her knee,
"Look Mango you made it,
You're on the banana tree!"
And they happily ate bananas.
Yippee!!

Ariyah Abdel-Samie (7)
St Edward's RC Primary School, Westminster

Armadillo Girdled Lizard

Little, sticky fingers are trying to touch me,
Green and grey in colour, very peculiar to see.
Their tongues stretch out when getting their prey,
Because in such manner their tummies will be jolly.
A tiny looking dragon, that's what they say,
And looking at you is even nicer during the day.
An animal like you is very hard to find,
Well, that's the armadillo girdled lizard,
That we'll only see once in a lifetime.

Ashton Jay Agulay (7)
St Edward's RC Primary School, Westminster

A Zebra With Half Of His Stripes Gone

I'm a depressed zebra,
Half of my stripes are gone,
Am I a zebra or a zeebra?

The rain, day by day,
Washes half of my stripes away,
Am I real or not?

Black stripes or coloured,
Red, blue, pink,
Or stripes depending on my mood.

Trees screech,
As I turn peach,
And everything is sweet.

Oh no!
Rain today!
My peach will turn to mush!

Grace Porter (10)

St Edward's RC Primary School, Westminster

My Adorable Pet

My adorable pet named Izzy,
Has no time because she is very busy.

My pet likes to fly in the sky,
But she always goes way too high.

She always ends up falling down, down, down,
Amongst the people in the town.

Then she goes swimming in the sea,
And then she always feels free.

My pet is very cute,
And also likes to play the flute.

Sienna O'Dwyer (8)
St Edward's RC Primary School, Westminster

Rat In Hawaii

Rat is a little mouse,
He's a little businessman,
Rat has a mansion for a house,
Anything you say he can't do, he can!

Rat got tired and laid in the sun,
Up above on the floor in Hawaii!
If you ask for his papers for work, he'll have none,
He laid down and listened to the sea.

Amelia Zulkifli (9)
St Edward's RC Primary School, Westminster

Roxy The Dog

There is a dog next door called Roxy,
Roxy is always chasing Foxy the fox,
When Foxy visits the garden at night,
Roxy the dog barks at the fox and tries to bite,
The fox is quickly running away,
Roxy is letting him know that it's not safe to stay.

Mario Berishaj (8)
St Edward's RC Primary School, Westminster

Aslan's Roar

The lion's roar is deafening,
The tiger's roar is proud,
The lion that roars is Aslan,
Aslan, the king of animals.

How is your roar so fierce?
Is it what you eat?
Is it when you sleep?
Or is it the animals you hunt?

Marion Jorolan (9)
St Edward's RC Primary School, Westminster

My Dog Called Charlie

I once had a dog named Charlie,
He had brown hair that felt like barley.
He chased and chased his tail,
And caught it every time without fail.
He jumped so high,
It was so sad when I had to say bye,
To my best dog friend Charlie.

Kyrah Walker-Gerald (9)
St Edward's RC Primary School, Westminster

The Koala In The Tree

Miss Koala liked climbing up the trees,
She lived in the jungle, so there weren't many bees.
She ate lots of leaves and liked to sleep,
She heard lots of secrets that she would keep.

Anaya-Rose Ntambwe (6)

St Edward's RC Primary School, Westminster

The Cat

There was a cat,
Who sat on a mat,
Which was fat,
Because it ate a rat.

The cat was scary,
Not hairy,
The cat was kind,
You never knew what was on its mind.

Tristan Emmanuel Andrade (10)
St Edward's RC Primary School, Westminster

Dean The Chameleon

Welcome to my colourful pet Chameleon whose name is Dean,
Normally, my marvellous Dean is a very bright luminous green.
He is, however, very clever as he can change colour in an instant,
To fit in with his surroundings and keep his dangerous enemies distant.
His cute eyes are unusual as they can be individually focused and rotated,
This enables him to have a 360° view so that his prey can be easily located.
Dean has a fast-firing tongue to catch the small insects that he likes to eat,
Sometimes, he also catches a tasty cricket or two as an extra special treat.
Dean lives in a wooded landscape within a specially created glass vivarium,
This is kept in my bedroom even though space there is at a premium.

During the day, he likes to laze on a log, relaxing
under a warming sun lamp,
With food, water and warmth to hand, he must
dream he is at a holiday camp!

Harry Thompson (10)

St Joseph's Catholic Primary School, South Woodham
Ferrers

The Gorgeous Gorilla

Rampaging through the city,
A figure came out of the zoo on a transfer,
It was let loose,
And it was being hunted down by the police,
But luckily for the gorilla,
It was very gorgeous and funny,
So people would stop in their tracks,
Turn around and walk away.
Leaving the gorilla by himself,
The city turned into a lovely place,
Where there were no riots or fights,
Or starving or homeless people,
It was a wonderful place to be.

Gabriel Reid Robbins (11)

St Joseph's Catholic Primary School, South Woodham
Ferrers

Opie The Sausage Dog

There is a dog,
Longer than a log.
He darts around in joy,
As he plays with his shiny toy.
He leaps around like a frog
To the catchy sounds in the air.
He munches on his crunchy kibble food,
When he's in the right mood.
Opie is a very dopey dog.
He loves to throw people's socks in the air with delight,
And cuddles you with care.
I love my dear dog Opie,
Even though he's a bit dopey.

Lola-Alice Smith (11)

St Joseph's Catholic Primary School, South Woodham Ferrers

The Silly Snake

The silly snake,
Was always awake,
But he always ate cake,
He liked to play with hay,
Even though he didn't like the day,
The silly snake was very lazy,
And he had a friend called Daisy,
He laid some babies,
And they were all ladies.

Jessica Nguyen (10)
St Joseph's Catholic Primary School, South Woodham Ferrers

YOUNG WRITERS INFORMATION

We hope you have enjoyed reading this book – and that you will continue to in the coming years.

If you're a young writer who enjoys reading and creative writing, or the parent of an enthusiastic poet or story writer, visit our website **www.youngwriters.co.uk/subscribe** to join the World of Young Writers and receive news, competitions, writing challenges, tips, articles and giveaways! There is lots to keep budding writers motivated to write!

If you would like to order further copies of this book, or any of our other titles, then please give us a call or order via your online account.

Young Writers
Remus House
Coltsfoot Drive
Peterborough
PE2 9BF
(01733) 890066
info@youngwriters.co.uk

Join in the conversation!
Tips, news, giveaways and much more!

 **YoungWritersUK**    **YoungWritersCW**   youngwriterscw